ALEX WEBSTER
AND THE GODS

ALEX WEBSTER
AND THE GODS

A Novel

DAVID DENT

iUniverse, Inc.

New York Lincoln Shanghai

Alex Webster and the Gods

Copyright © 2007 by David Dent

iUniverse, Inc.

iUniverse books may be ordered through booksellers or by contacting:

iUniverse
2021 Pine Lake Road, Suite 100
Lincoln, NE 68512
www.iuniverse.com
1-800-Authors (1-800-288-4677)

This is a work of fiction. All of the characters, names, incidents, organizations, and dialogue in this novel are either the products of the author's imagination or are used fictitiously.

ISBN-13: 978-0-595-42316-3 (pbk)
ISBN-13: 978-0-595-86655-7 (ebk)
ISBN-10: 0-595-42316-7 (pbk)
ISBN-10: 0-595-86655-7 (ebk)

Printed in the United States of America

To the memory of John Dent,
a natural-born storyteller

ACKNOWLEDGMENTS

For all their help with this book, I owe my deepest gratitude to Gisella Sherman, Edith Smith, Sandy Lloyd, Linda Parker, Barb Rebelo, Robert Osborne, Lise Levesque, Alexandra Waller, Jennifer Paul, Brian Henry, Jim Smith, Burke Richards, Susan Swan, and Marylou Miner. Special thanks to everyone at iUniverse for all their help and support.

PROLOGUE

▼

God is alive. Magic is afoot. God is afoot. Magic is alive.
Alive is afoot. Magic never died.

—Leonard Cohen

Had he waited too long? For him the dark side of immortality was boredom, because boredom begat procrastination. Easing back in his lounge chair, he looked out over the horizon. This was his home beyond the great white sheen of the Milky Way, beyond the space and time of the known universe, beyond the chill and chaos of the unknown void. For him it had once been a place of dreamy perfection, a land of everlasting spring. Both virgin and fertile, it still was a land of perfumed rivers and blossomed trees. Cloudless skies were of softest blue, lush gardens of richest green. Flowers paraded their unsown bloom. Neither hot nor cold, it was the place of the creators. But for Jupiter, it was no longer enough.

This opening in an old oak grove had once been his favorite garden. Roofed columns bordered it, providing shade. His eyes lingered on the white-silver disks that hung between the columns, dancing and flashing like tiny mirrors, as they caught the sun. Fountains played in marble basins, their light spray watering nearby trees and the ground beneath them. Other fountains had bowls surrounded by tiny jets of water. Jupiter listened to their soft whispers, but no longer felt peace here, just a relentless unease of missed opportunities. Something caught his eye at the base of the fountains—*mildew*; it was everywhere. Damnation. Not only had boredom inserted itself into his inner core, but also there was the creeping anxiety of unwanted chores.

An oval table of white marble dominated the center of the garden. Around the table sat a group of gods and goddesses, all in flowing, white robes, except for Jupiter. He wore a three-piece black pin-striped Brooks Brothers suit, a blue shirt, and a black tie emblazoned with a lightning bolt. He appeared taller than the others, with a full beard and a tanned, ruddy complexion. His hair was dark brown with a few streaks of gray.

As demigods, fauns, and satyrs served ambrosia and nectar, Jupiter stood and cleared his throat.

"Listen to me, immortals, every one of you. I want to make my mood and purpose clear." He started slowly, trying his best to sound godly. Making eye contact with each being around the table, he continued.

"The time has come to reclaim the soul of humankind, to regain our former glory."

"Oh no, Jupiter," interrupted Juno. "I thought all that silliness was behind us. We have eternity to enjoy without the headaches and humiliations from humans. And, of course, the fountains need cleaning."

He hated when she interrupted him, especially in front of the others. She did not understand him; she had never understood his need to redeem his name. And now she was suggesting that he, the former king of the gods, Mr. Optimus Maximus, must stoop to clean the tiles. This loss of esteem by his wife was yet another reminder of the cost of his procrastination. As if feeling his discomfort, the skies darkened and lightning flashed in the distance.

The group grew tense; some even trembled, fearing the fury of fighting that these two could exhibit. They hadn't had a scuffle about making a comeback for almost a thousand years, not since the Muslims and Christians were slaying each other during the Crusades. At the time, Jupiter had wanted to offer himself as a compromise between Allah and Yahweh. Juno had won that battle, but only after all the lesser gods were rebuked by one or both of them. Everyone knew that if you sided with one, the other chastised you, and if you stayed neutral, you suffered the wrath of both. After that, peace had prevailed ... until now.

"You promised to help me if the time was right. Well, it's time."

"But I fear the dangers are great."

"You could at least listen to my plan."

"Go ahead, expound, my husband most noble."

"Then don't harass me with your questions."

"No harassment, just nurturing words of caution to the love of my life."

Eyes afire, Jupiter stared at her for a long moment and then said, "If we leave Earth for good, then it must be on our terms, not because of the skulduggery of that sneaky Yahweh."

After some hesitation, Juno asked, "Why now? Why not later?"

He knew she would not understand the *whys*—she never understood his *whys*—so he kept it simple.

"Mortals have entered a new millennium, a new world order. They have a sense of expectation."

"So?"

"So we will meet those expectations, fulfill their dreams. Besides, all the old religions are fighting each other, especially the Christians and the Muslims. We can come up the middle and be everybody's second choice."

"Dreams, dreams. My husband glories in being second choice."

"Do you have a better idea? Spending eternity cleaning mildew around the fountains is not exactly good for anyone's self-esteem."

At this point, Mercury jumped into the clash.

"Dear parents, what a miserable day for us all if you two continue to raise your voices about those shameless mortal creatures. More than enough already. Must you cloud this great feast with your noisy bickering?"

Jupiter and Juno paused for a moment, then Juno, holding her hand out to Mercury, said, "Of course, son; we must think of all of you." Turning to Jupiter, the queen of heaven continued in a softer voice, "Why not just create a new universe with mortals who are more like us and who would be forever grateful?"

"That's how I ended the Silver Age, and look what that did to us. But I'll think about it. Mercury's right; let's not debate."

Juno nodded in agreement, and a collective sigh of relief issued from the group. Jupiter knew he did not have her support, but at least he had her silence for now.

"I am convinced Yahweh is right where we want him."

"And where's that, most wise father of mine?" asked Minerva.

"Exactly where he had us two thousand years ago, dear daughter."

The assembled gods and goddesses smiled at Jupiter's cleverness, but he knew they wondered what he meant. He wanted to tell them that mortals had reached a historic inflection point; the tides of great change were forcing Yahweh's hand. However, they had been out of touch with Earth since the fall of Rome.

"What does the great Pan feel about this?" inquired Juno, turning to the old master.

Knowing Pan's support carried more weight than anything he could say, Jupiter decided to show off the new leadership skills he had picked up at Harvard Business School and stayed silent. Anticipating something like this might happen, he had briefed his old friend of many millennia before the banquet.

Pan was well known among the gods for his trips back to Earth to create trouble for humans. Jupiter knew his friend's story well. It had all started when some Christian zealot started a rumor that the great Pan was dead. Since then, Pan had inserted himself in human affairs no longer as the god of goats, sheep, and shepherds, but as the god of fear and disruption.

He had found his way into the languages of mortals, and that pleased him. He felt good every time someone said the word *panic*. It was almost as good as people praying to him. It didn't matter whether they *said* panic or *felt* panic; both made him feel good. So whenever panic surfaced in the hearts of mortals, you could be sure that Pan was nearby. After messing up affairs in some corner of Earth, he scanned the newspapers, checked the media, or Googled the key word—"People fled in *panic* as the revolutionaries took over"; "Investors were in a *panic* over the latest Wall Street rumors." At these times, he felt a rush of pleasure. Like a freshly struck match, his glee was short-lived, but it was enough to keep him going till the next bit of mischief. Some mortals called him the god of revolutions, which pleased his flute-playing heart even more.

Pan, the oldest god at the table and enjoying a special reverence and affection among them all, stood to speak. With his elegant silver-gray hair and goatee, he looked even more distinguished than he had in his impish youth. "Jupiter is right—the time is ideal."

"I have a plan, and I need your help," started Jupiter again. "I have been on Earth in the guise of a man, looking into the best way for our return." He saw their looks of curiosity. He heard their whispers. Cupid, with a lustful upward shift of his eyebrows, said, "I look forward to toga parties and beautiful young maidens."

"Dress has changed," interrupted Jupiter. "What I wear here today is what men of influence now wear."

He opened his suit coat and turned around to display his new sartorial splendor. The group sat silent, skeptical that anyone would voluntarily wear such confining clothing, especially the strangling noose around the neck. Jupiter sensed their uneasiness and wondered if he should have worn his lighter, summer-weight, seersucker suit.

"What is our great Rome like?" asked Apollo.

Pan jumped in. "The Roman Empire is long gone. Much has changed, though mortals still aspire to be gods."

"There is a great deal for all of you to learn and prepare for," added Jupiter.

Like scolded dogs, their eyes drooped, and their mouths sagged. They folded their arms across their chests as if led by an offstage choreographer. Disgruntled murmuring erupted among the gods. Jupiter picked up on their chatter and allowed them to vent.

"We're gods after all. We've nothing to learn, at least about humans," said one.

"It's always the other way around. Any god knows that," said another.

"Maybe Juno's right. Why allow humans to humiliate us any more than they already have?" asked yet another.

After several minutes Jupiter resumed. "That's the bad news. The good news is that mortals still live for just three goals: sex, money, and power. They still cheat and lie and kill to get them."

As if sensing that Jupiter still needed help, Pan piped in, "Indeed, there's a whole generation called 'boomers,' millions and millions of them, so eager to indulge their greed that they study the stars to time their parents' deaths. Honor and love are servants to expediency and lust."

"So it'll be just like the old days. To use an old expression, 'once you learn to ride a chariot you never forget.'"

The group brightened again at the thought of dealing with mortals living by plunder. This they understood. Jupiter decided to go for the hook.

"At first I need a few of you to join me, but only those who want to. Some who have volunteered already."

This caution struck a tangible chord, as almost all the Roman gods and goddesses turned to look at the alien, arresting beauty sitting to the right of Jupiter. Blond with eyes of ice blue, she was as tall as Jupiter. With her head held high, her pose was one of subtle grace and self-assurance; her silken robes draped her as if in respect for her soft skin.

"I should introduce to you our special guest, who will join me in the first group," he said as he turned to her and held out his hand to introduce her. "Morrigan, the Celtic goddess. Welcome."

As he had expected, introducing a new goddess caused an immediate stir. Contracting-out to alien gods would produce a clear wake-up call to this partying flock. They couldn't take their positions for granted—another tip he had picked up in business school. The three Furies were aflutter; the three Graces were aghast, tittering nervously. Juno cast a jealous glance at Morrigan and then at Jupiter.

"I have heard of you," she said with polite and distant reserve. "But someone told me you were a crone."

No sooner had Juno uttered the word *crone* than Morrigan, the blond beauty, transformed to an old, stooped woman. She wore soiled and worn rags of black and brown, which gave off a bitter, musty stench. Warts of differing shapes and sizes covered her leathery, wrinkled skin.

"Is this more true to form and legend?" asked Morrigan as she smiled, revealing a mouth full of rotting, jagged teeth punctuated by striking gaps. The odor that came from her mouth was fouler than her appearance. The junior gods and goddesses drew back in disgust. And then, without warning, the old crone transformed into a huge crow, which flew at Juno. Just as it seemed to descend on her, the beautiful blond Morrigan stood again before her, proud and defiant. "Now you know me in all my glory. I look forward to joining you and Jupiter."

"I'm sure you do," said Juno, turning her hot glare to Jupiter as she continued. "I'm sure the three of us will make a great team."

The others delighted in this captivating display of their new ally and Juno's commitment to the venture. They applauded and whistled at length. This turn of events appeared to build their confidence and convince them that joining with Jupiter was the best path forward.

"What country shall we rule?" asked several gods.

"The world is in turmoil and transition. No country is safe. So for now we will use something even better than a country. It is something that will allow us to move around the world, to amass great wealth, and to buy and influence rulers of nations. We will have thousands and thousands of servants who will act on our every word without question. Most of all, it is a place where we can bide our time and prepare for our comeback."

"Indeed, what can surpass the grandeur of a country?" came the response from the group, almost in unison.

"Something well suited to our needs—humans call it a *global corporation*. These organizations are headed by CEOs, people who think and act like gods. So it will be a natural for us."

Many more "oohs" and "aahs" emerged as the assembly tried to imagine how a global corporation could possibly be so wonderful.

"The first stage will not be easy. Each of us will need to work hard. Frustrating times await us," added Jupiter, who then paused and turned to his wife before continuing. "As my dear Juno says, there is no guarantee of success."

How rapt the attention of his audience was now, thought Jupiter. He could almost tangibly feel their excitement at his proposal. This result pleased Jupiter, and he guessed that he would have more volunteers than he needed.

"Once we're settled, I'll be back for others to join us. So don't despair if you are not chosen this time."

Cupid interrupted again. "Oracles, prophets, do they announce our imminent and glorious return?"

"Not yet, not yet," said Jupiter. In fact, he thought, not ever. He didn't need some mystical prophet or doped-up oracle; he was finished with them. No, his immediate priority was to hire a management consultant. This group needed some training to bring them up to speed with modern times. For one, their speech was hopelessly out of date. They would need to crawl before they walked in this new world. Only then could he be confident in his takeover plans. But this was not the time to tell his suddenly eager gods that they would need to go back to school. And also, he needed help to design a religion suitable to modern humans. Raising his goblet of nectar to the group, he continued, "But enough of this serious talk. It's time to celebrate! A toast to the team and our successful return."

The god raised their glasses too, and without hesitation, started to drinking. Jupiter appraised the group before him, of gods and goddesses merrily partaking of their nectar, and realized his unease had lifted. No more dawdling, no more delay, he said to himself, as he felt the magic of first steps. Suiting the mood of a would-be ascendant god, he sat down to take pleasure in his ambrosia and nectar.

PART ONE

THE MAKING OF A DIVINE CONSULTANT

ONE

The very substance of the ambitious is merely the shadow of a dream.

—William Shakespeare

"Adjust your Webcam so I can see you and not that damn cat."

Alex looked at Max, his silver tabby, who yawned, as if in reaction to the derisive comment. Stifling a yawn himself, Alex glanced at his bedside clock. Seven o'clock. What an ungodly hour for a conference call with parents. Dad was in New York, Mom was in Boston, and Alex was ensconced in the family townhouse on Hilton Head Island, off the coast of South Carolina. Many families have Sunday dinner together as a ritual of reinforcement, for catching up on the week's events, for sharing, and for giving thanks. Disdaining the routines of the many, Randolph Webster had founded a Monday morning power breakfast with his wife and son.

"Dad, I just woke up," said Alex, adjusting the camera until it showed his own unshaven face and rumpled hair.

"It's OK. This isn't a beauty contest," chimed his father, who was fully attired in a dark blue business suit. "Never allow a lost moment. Start the week with clear goals. Big plans will keep you on the highway of hope. And, as always, I'm here to help you."

"Oh, Randolph," rejoined his mother in mock disdain. She then paused. Alex smiled as he admired the elegance of his mother, attired in a camel blazer over a white blouse. She continued, "You sound just like Robert Preston in *The Music Man.*" Then, with a lowered voice, she mimicked the actor's gusto. "Friends, the idle brain is the devil's playground."

Alex listened, amazed they had continued this practice for over twenty years, though the session around the breakfast table had long since given way to telephone conference calls, such as today.

"So Alex, now that I can see you, when are you going to return to McKinsey and start making an honest living again?"

"Dad, you know I can't give it up at this stage."

"Alex is right, Randolph. You sound like a broken record, Monday after Monday," said Augusta Webster. "He needs our support, not our advice."

"Life is not a dress rehearsal, Augusta. Alex could be a superstar at McKinsey, if he wanted to be. Setting up a Web site portal for spiritual seekers, some cyber commune for latter-day hippies, doesn't seem like a path to earthly success as I know it."

"Randolph Webster! What's your problem? McKinsey already loves him. He's published two books on religion. He's been on *Larry King Live.* And for your information, I plan to join his cyber commune myself when it's ready."

Alex turned his head from the camera and rolled his eyes. This dialogue was part of the routine as well, Mom as cheerleader, Dad as army sergeant.

"You need to use a service that plays matchmaker and conciliator between gods and men?" said Randolph Webster, his voice edging toward sarcasm.

"Randolph, you embarrass me. It's *men and women.*"

"How about gods for women and goddesses for men?"

"You're a chauvinist bigot, Randolph. Alex, ignore your father. I'm sure all will work out for you, according to your own plans."

"Listen to your mother, Alex. She's always right."

Alex marveled at this Monday morning mix of debate, teasing, and advice from his parents. His father was a successful investment banker on Wall Street, while his mother, located in Boston, was a principal of one of the country's leading advertising agencies. Augusta Webster was a model of elegance and refinement, whereas Randolph reveled in his self-designed caricature of the predatory capitalist. Despite these differences, despite careers that consumed their time like greedy lovers, and despite the challenges of geographic separation, they were fiercely committed to each other and to their son.

"It'll be OK, Dad," said Alex, in a reassuring tone that belied his own reservations. Hoping to bring the call to closure on an upbeat note, he added, "Hey, I'm meeting tonight with an angel investor."

"Anyone I know?" asked his father, curiosity replacing the edge in his voice.

"I don't think so, Dad, but he's insisted I keep our discussions confidential at this stage." Alex wanted to finish the conversation as soon as he could.

"Good luck," said his father in grudging response. "And call me if you need any, shall we say, support."

Relieved that his father didn't probe, Alex reclined on his bed, smiling at the camera.

"That's wonderful, dear," said Augusta in quick succession. "Now tell me before we go, how's Victoria? Do you two keep in touch?"

Alex scrunched his eyes and pretended to yawn. His insides cringed. Each parent had a separate agenda. His mother had visions of being a young grandmother. She liked the idea. Now smiling again, he sighed, "Fine, Mom."

"That's not a real smile, darling. I can tell you are cringing inside. Your voice gives you away," said his mother, in the same way she had when she found him sneaking cookies and milk after school as a young boy. "Do you still see her?"

How did she know about his feelings? He threw off the sheet and sat up on the edge of the bed. He smiled. Victoria had once told him that a smile on your face puts a smile in your voice. "We're having lunch together today."

"Lovely, lovely. You two should never have broken up."

"We didn't break up. We simply agreed to spend some time apart," said Alex, sounding more contemplative than he wished. Augusta Webster had never liked any of Alex's girlfriends until Victoria. Her beauty and her energy reminded his mother of her older sister, Abigail, who had died in a plane crash in her late twenties, on the verge of a promising career in publishing. When she had first met Victoria, she had felt an immediate bond, a substitute for her lost sister.

"If you know what's good for you, you'll get down on your knees and beg her to marry you."

"Mom," protested Alex. Ironically, the reason they had decided to take a break was that Victoria shared the same view as his father. He recalled the argument that had led to their breakup. Hands on her hips, standing before him, he could imagine her saying, "You can be more successful than 99 percent of your classmates by staying with McKinsey, so why fool around with this risky scheme of yours?" The word *scheme* had offended him; her lack of support had hurt him. So they had agreed to disagree and, in so doing, had agreed that it might be best to spend a little time apart while he played out his dreams.

"Meddle, meddle. Give him a break, Augusta," piped in his father, much to Alex's relief. "Well, son, sounds like you have a busy day. If you were an optimist like your mother, you could be engaged by lunch and on your way to financial success by evening."

Alex smiled. He knew that if he paused long enough, one parent would take him off the hook from the questions of the other. "Thanks, Dad."

"And if not, we can talk next week about you joining me in New York."

"Sure, we'll touch base then," said Alex. He ducked the bait of becoming a partner with his father, even on a trial basis. Taking a deep breath to produce his best cheerful voice, he finished, "You two have a good week. Love you both." And then he hung up, got up from his bed, walked across the room, and opened the French doors. Six feet tall, sandy colored hair, big toothy smile, athletic, and tanned, at thirty-three he looked more like a surfer than a graduate of Columbia and Harvard.

Raising his arms in a wake-up stretch, he stepped out onto the balcony of his parents' oceanfront townhouse. Alex loved this semitropical paradise of manicured landscapes and premeditated palm trees. When people asked why he called them premeditated, he would invite them to travel to any of the unplanned islands nearby, even the relatively developed Tybee Island, down the coast by Savannah. Yes, there were the magnolias and the live oaks, but nature did not come close to the developers of Hilton Head Island in either the number of palm trees or their artistic placement on golf courses, shorelines, and entrances to plantations. This area was not marked by the same spontaneity and sparseness of the palm population on Tybee Island. No, the palm population of Hilton Head Island was studied, well thought out, and premeditated.

He loved the summer heat and humidity that surrounded him like a womb, June through September. He loved to sit crosslegged, on the balcony and meditate facing the sky and the ocean. His goal in meditation was to let the scene dissolve into an everlasting moment of bliss, although right now twenty minutes of eternity was all he could afford. By 8:45 AM, he was back inside.

While preparing breakfast, he reviewed his plans for the day. Victoria Malik, his erstwhile inamorata, his ladylove on hold, who played Dulcinea to his Don Quixote, was on the island for a business conference, and he would meet her for lunch. His mother was right. He missed their closeness. With any luck, he hoped to mend the tear in their relationship. His other hope was for a successful dinner with J. J. Jones, his angel investor. For that meeting, he needed to review his pitch. Max brushed against his leg with a sense of urgency, reminding him of his immediate duty. Alex reached for the bag of cat treats, always ready on the counter.

"Well, buddy, this could be our big day." Max simply looked at Alex with no comment, so Alex continued. "We've been waiting a long time for this, remember?"

Still no reply from Max. His eyes had not strayed from the hand in which Alex held his treats. Alex knew he was taking advantage of Max's expectations, but there were only two times a day the American shorthair greeted him at once—at 8:00 AM for morning treats and at 6:00 PM for evening treats. The rest of the day Max did everything on his own terms. Alex felt too good to press his patience any further. After all, Max had been his unwavering partner of the past four years. Everyone else in his life during that time had been either arriving or leaving—the unavoidable fallout of the transition from grad school to some semblance of making a living.

Alex flipped the first treat into the air. Max followed its arc and pounced on it as it hit the floor. Such was their ritual of the treats—seven pieces in the morning and seven more in the evening.

Alex then sat down at his dining room table to a breakfast of granola, yogurt, and an orange. To balance the goodness of it all, he sipped a cup of coffee. Single coffee bags were surely one of the great modern inventions, essential for those times of the day when he couldn't get to a Starbucks and didn't want the bother or the volume of a full pot of freshly brewed at home. With the coffee bag he got what he wanted, or close enough anyway, within two minutes from the microwave. What he lost in taste, he gained in convenience. His mind momentarily wandered to analogies, then pulled back to upcoming events of the day.

TWO

"How can we be sure?" asked Gerry in his deep, stentorian voice. The morning sun beamed through the wall-sized windows of his executive conference room on the forty-fourth floor of the Ernst and Young Tower in Toronto's financial district.

"Sorry, sir?" said Ted Allaby, a junior analyst from Pharmaglobe's Treasury Department. He avoided Gerry's eyes, as Gerry knew he would. As if signaling for help, Ted glanced at the other three attendees, all executive vice presidents: Larry Kirkpatrick, finance; Ann Horowitz, legal and general affairs; and James Waite, security and information technology. They said nothing.

Gerry Schilling, chairman and CEO of Pharmaglobe, learned forward, head bowed as he supported his elbows on the armrests of his chair, hands raised and joined as if in prayer. His chin rested on the tips of his fingers. He wanted to appear deep in thought, as he had seen done in a men's fashion magazine. It showed his Zegna three-button suit to advantage: the fine, soft wool woven in navy with a subtle light blue plaid overprint and the Tate English silk tie, with its bright geometric design, a controlled work of art. His pose also displayed his Sea Island shirt's French cuffs and monogrammed silver cuff links—*GS*. He liked that. He wanted Allaby to see the perks and polish of power. He knew that when

Allaby got back to his office, he would get those certain questions from his friends and associates, "What's he like? How'd he look?"

He let the silence of the group give the floor to the fleeting keyboard runs of Brahms's Piano Concerto No. 1 playing in the background. Music could soothe the soul, and one of Gerry's tasks each day was selecting the playlist for his office suite. The music filled the room from speakers hidden behind five-foot-high plants with fernlike finger leaves. Like captives from prehistoric times who were now imprisoned in tapered square planters, they were silent witnesses to the inner secrets of Pharmaglobe. Standing in the corner, a banana tree that was almost ten feet tall leaned toward the two walls of window as if more interested in what was happening outside. A huge plasma screen dominated one of the interior walls. The display on the screen was the source of Gerry's question. It was the closing overhead from Allaby's presentation—"PHARMAGLOBE—TAKEOVER TARGET?"

"Look, anyone who reads the *Wall Street Journal* could come up with that." Gerry nodded at the screen and then leaned back to mimic the report of a few days earlier. "Let's see. How did it go—'The stock of Pharmaglobe—longtime favorite on Wall Street—is suddenly looking sick. Pharmaglobe executives spin lame excuses as its share price drops again this week following almost five years of blazing growth. Further declines could make it an attractive takeover target.'"

Gerry leaned forward, "So, tell me something new. What evidence do we have? How can we be sure a takeover is under way?"

"Unusual trade activity in Pharmaglobe shares is our main evidence. Let me show you." Ted hit a button on his computer, and the plasma screen on the wall showed a graph full of colorful lines and arrows. Gerry had a long-standing rule for presentations, the KISS rule—keep it simple stupid. Ted had failed, but it wasn't bad for a junior analyst, and Gerry tried to be gentle.

"Looks like Pickup Sticks with all those colors."

Ted showed no signs of distress and carried on

"Each time Pharmaglobe's stock dips, let's say from a rumor of a bad ruling by the Food and Drug Administration, people start dumping it. The worse the rumor, the greater the volume," said Ted, using his laser pointer to highlight these events on the screen. "But then blocks of buying come in to pick up the dumped stock. Someone is getting our shares at a discount, while keeping our share price in a stable trading range."

"How long's this been going on?" asked James Waite, speaking for the first time. At six feet four inches, Waite towered over the other employees. He was the highest-ranking African American in the company and Gerry's most trusted employee. Gerry liked Waite's silent, reserved manner. It reinforced Waite's image as the man who saw all and knew all. And he answered only to Gerry.

"About two months ago based on my data."

"Do we know who the buyer is?" Waite narrowed his unblinking, reptilian eyes on the young analyst. Larry Kirkpatrick, Ted's boss and mentor, jumped in.

"Not yet. This is just a macro view. Ted has a special tracking program that analyzes trades in Pharmaglobe stock. Our next step is to identify who it is."

"So what are you telling me?" asked Gerry softly, not wanting to intimidate Allaby. He wanted the junior analyst to leave this meeting enthusiastic, so he would tell his colleagues and friends what it was like to be in the inner sanctum of the CEO's conference room. In relative terms, Allaby was doing a superb job, running on pure adrenalin.

Still, the possibility of a takeover unsettled Gerry. It wasn't supposed to be this way. Pharmaglobe was one of the largest drug and pharmaceutical companies in the world and one of the fastest growing. Analysts expected it to break into the big ranks with Pfizer and Glaxo within the next few years. If there were takeovers in the future, his plan called for Pharmaglobe doing the taking. Gerry had worked too long and dedicated too much of his life to creating and building this company to have it snatched away from him.

Who were they? What was their agenda? What deal could he make? Gerry couldn't afford a high-profile battle with probing questions; other issues were at stake.

"Well, it's an early warning indicator. Worst-case scenario, it could be the beginning of a stealth takeover," said Ted.

"Thanks, Ted, excellent work. I want you to keep me personally informed of anything new on this." Gerry wanted Ted out of the room as quickly as possible, while his temper was still under control; he wanted no witnesses to any sign of concern, beyond his inner circle. "And please, speak to no one except James, Larry, Ann, or me about it."

Ted took his cue and left the room, head bowed before the four senior executives, his mouth locked in a bland expression of the dutiful servant.

"Two months. And we still don't know who the buyer is. Why are we here?" said Schilling tapping his Cross pen on the table before he went on. "You should have seen this coming. Why did you have to wait for some bright kid to spot the obvious?"

He issued his words in a seething monotone; his lips receded and his eyes glowered at each of them in turn. And then he bit off a final, uncharacteristic "Jesus Christ." He surprised even himself by his outburst.

For the next few minutes, Larry and Ann kept their heads down and studied the table in front of them as if waiting for some secret signal that might help them respond. James Waite stared out the window. It was Waite who broke the silence.

"*Jesus Christ?* This must be a two-alarm issue for you, Gerry. Up from a simple *Jesus* or a lonely *Christ*."

Schilling smiled. He trusted Waite and took his comment as a signal that his venting had crossed the line. Gerry was an orderly man, even in anger. He reserved epithets for a small group of people, those who reported directly to him, plus consultants and advisers, all of whose financial well-being and lifestyle depended on him. One of the tacit conditions of exchange was that they got to see the man behind the mask, the simmering cauldron behind the cool facade, and it was rarely a pleasant sight and often an unpleasant experience. For all their boasted titles, their stock options, their club memberships, their rights to the corporate jet, all these perks obligated them to him. They owed him, and Gerry knew it. But as Waite often reminded him, even slaves rebel. Gerry couldn't risk a whistle-blower, a deep throat, or worse caused by one of his temper tantrums.

"OK! Where are we really at?"

"We're working on it," piped in Larry. "We should be able to pinpoint the buyer soon."

"We wanted to alert you, get your thoughts on an early response," added Ann.

"What are you proposing?" said Gerry, while looking out the window over Lake Ontario. The blue skies and calm waters were a counterpoint to the storm of emotions that raged within him. He should have seen this coming.

"We need to confirm if it's true, and if so, then who. At the same time, we need to get a counterstrategy in place." It was always Ann who managed to get Gerry back on the issue. She changed the subject with the skill of a surgeon, focusing on the problem and staying away from anything that would add to Gerry's inner rage. He admired that. He was thankful. But he never told her. Ann continued, "We're in a good position to fight a takeover."

"No. Too defensive." Gerry was quick to respond. A takeover fight could lead to much media coverage. And media coverage could lead to the wrong people digging into the details of the company. And that could be costly to Gerry Schilling, the man and the legend. "Here are the priorities. First, identify our secret buyers and what they might want; second, do everything possible to improve our next quarterly earnings report. Larry, freeze all discretionary spending—and see if there is something we can do about our accounting policies." Larry nodded and scribbled as Gerry spoke. "We can't wait like sitting ducks. We've got to take control of our agenda."

"All we need is a few weeks of stable trading, and we'll be on top of this," said Ann.

"We'd better be, or we're all toast," said Gerry, his emphasis on the *we*, his tone ominous, his eyes full of anger. He stood and said, "For now, I'm going to lunch."

THREE

All of us are guinea pigs in the laboratory of God.
Humanity is just a work in progress.

—Tennessee Williams

Putting on his designer sunglasses, Alex headed out of his condo for the fifteen-minute walk along the beach to the Hyatt oceanfront bar. He found the flat, packed sand of the beach perfect for walking, jogging, and even bicycling. Today, however, he walked slowly along the sand, allowing the sun to wrap him in its radiant heat. The smell of salt in the air filled his lungs. Three black-legged sandpipers charged between him and the surf's edge, scampering like nervous servants as they probed the soggy sand for prey.

The rhythm of the waves sent his thoughts into the pathways of his past, while his body moved on autopilot along the sand. After university, Alex had joined McKinsey and Company, an elite management consulting firm. McKinsey was just breaking into the business of global religion, which had become big business. Numbers alone made it one of the largest global industries. His baptismal project was helping the Vatican avoid the collapse of its billion-dollar financial empire. His second challenge was promoting transparency in communication between the Vatican and its flock. Like many organizations, the Vatican had trouble letting go of outmoded tactics to cover up its clergy's nasty habits. And why not? Saint Peter was the original denier, the patron saint of organizational spin. For just three denials, Jesus had rewarded him the position of founder of the church. "You're the man, Peter, my rock."

"If it worked once, it would work again" had been the mind-set for two thousand years. Denial, not confession, had produced over a billion followers.

The work fascinated Alex; he speculated about the nature of God and his relation to the created order. In his spare time, he took as many graduate courses in religion as he could.

When the Pope made his visit to the American West, the Vatican and McKinsey set up a joint venture, New Papal Frontiers, to manage the multimillion-dollar event. Alex had been appointed to head the venture. It turned out to be a hugely successful event with the partners making a handsome return on their investment. Alex introduced many innovations, including a profitable deal with Disney and General Motors to develop a fleet of white popemobiles, based on the one the pope used, available for lease or rental. They turned out to be an unexpected hit with young Catholic couples getting married and looking for something different to celebrate the holy sacrament. The bubble of the popemobile became a mobile chapel of love, where couples made their vows to each other.

Profits soared. As a reward, McKinsey approved a two-year sabbatical for Alex to complete his PhD in religion. Being a natural cross-pollinator, he combined his experience in management consulting with religion for his thesis topic. He had kicked around these questions during his first assignment for the Vatican. What was Yahweh's management style? Was he consistent, or had he changed over time? If he had changed, was it for the better? That is, did Yahweh behave rationally? Did he learn from mistakes? After all, if subordinates are messing up, a good boss needs to ask these kinds of questions.

Dr. Martina Luther, professor emeritus of philosophy of religion at Columbia, was his thesis adviser. A woman of shapely figure, although past the age considered tasteful to display such a shape, she acted as part mentor, part skeptic for Alex. "What a wonderful metaphor, Mr. Webster. You may open our eyes to an unusual understanding of Yahweh. But perhaps we need a business adviser as well for your thesis."

Acting on her suggestion, he arranged for Kenneth Laydback, professor of corporate governance in columbia's business school, to critique his thesis as well. Whereas Martina wore tailored suits of dark navy that would have positioned her well for either the boardroom or the clergy, Kenneth Laydback preferred a style that could be called monochromatic dishevelment. His favorite outfit consisted of tan pants, matching tan suspenders, tan shirt, and sandals with no socks. This unconventional style covered a six-foot-three frame that was losing the battle of time. His muscle tone was in full retreat, free radicals scavenged his skin, and his hair had deserted him thirty years ago, save for the outposts of his craggy eyebrows and salt-and-pepper beard. But his mind was the diamond in the rough called Laydback. *Fortune* 500 companies appointed him to their boards. Like people who buy books but don't read them, thinking the act of purchase alone will give knowledge of their contents, so too did these companies buy the services of Laydback. He was their trophy academic, and they hoped shareholders and investors would infer that their governance practices somehow reflected the benefit of his expertise. "I don't know much about God, Alex," he'd said. "In fact, I don't even believe in him, at least a priori. No logic, no facts, that's the literal definition of nonsense, wouldn't you say? But I've got an open mind."

For six months, Alex had reviewed Yahweh's actions using a standard business model. He studied the Bible closely. Did Yahweh plan his works? Did he have a vision? Did he set out a goal with strategies, policies, and procedures? Did he delegate authority? How was he at day-to-day actions like recruiting people, providing rewards and punishments? Did he follow through, checking performance against targets, auditing compliance, redirecting people as necessary? Did he learn from experience? Did he adapt his ways in response to changing circumstances?

Every Tuesday morning during those months, Alex took a cab to the Columbia campus on Morningside Heights on Manhattan's Upper West Side, the heart of a residential neighborhood full of bookstores, restaurants, shops, and coffee bars. His destination was Dr. Martina Luther's office in the Center for the Study of Science and Religion. Her office was appointed in the style of a midtwentieth-century academic, which meant modest and conservative, a balance of oak and Arborite. Alex would sit on an aging leather divan, whose closeness to the hardwood floor meant he had to look up, as a supplicant might, to his two advisers. In turn, they sat across from him in wing chairs, like two heads of state competing with each other for his mind.

The critical session occurred when Alex had placed his full argument before them. He liked to replay that afternoon whenever he was pondering major decisions or preparing for big presentations.

"The argument of my thesis is that Yahweh's management style evolves from an entrepreneurial, hands-on deity to a maturing manager who introduces more sophisticated control processes to help achieve his goals. The cause for this evolution is arguably due to his learning from experience. His evolution is similar to that of many entrepreneurs who create new ventures and navigate them to a sustainable organizations."

His presentation, including questions, took almost three hours. Completing his presentation, Alex sat down, remaining calm on the outside, but felt his adrenalin ebbing. Silence followed while his advisers looked at their notes, then at him, then at each other, then back at him. Finally Laydback spoke. "So," he said, leaning back in his chair with regal authority, signaling a judgment. Alex had held his breath, expecting the volley, knowing he needed to receive and return to secure his victory. "Today, as we speak, Yahweh is like a chairperson of the board."

"That's right," replied Alex, feeling confident that his argument was secure. He paused a few seconds, then added, "Just like Henry Ford or Bill Gates, he's evolved from a temperamental, even eccentric, entrepreneur to the distant senior executive."

"Well, I'm from Missouri," said Laydback, "but if I were Yahweh, I would have moved on to bigger challenges in the universe by now. Earth's a bit player in my universe, an outpost subsidiary. He clearly delegated day-to-day operations long ago to subordinates. My guess is he has no idea what's going on here right now."

Martina Luther, teacup in one hand, saucer in the other, displayed a smile that showed the delight and pride of someone who has mastered a new skill. "Well, if that were the case, Professor Laydback, then the situation would be ripe for a takeover on Earth, wouldn't it?"

Her words produced a wince, a grudging nod, but no ready reply from Laydback. Alex breathed a sigh of relief. Yahweh was in his heaven, and all was right with his thesis.

FOUR

The lunatic is the man who lives in a small world but thinks it is a large one; he is the man who lives in a tenth of the truth, and thinks it is the whole. The madman cannot conceive any cosmos outside a certain tale or conspiracy or vision.

—G. K. Chesterton

His reverie faded as Alex sidestepped a sea nettle lodged in the sand. Deposited by the receding tide, the jellyfish looked like an incomplete biology experiment, a simple floating mouth and intestine housed in a see-through muscle-skeleton smeared liberally in the sand. Yahweh's cosmic efforts cast as abstract expressionism.

The boardwalk to the Hyatt emerged. Alex jogged up from the beach to the outdoor bar, where he was meeting Victoria. Taking a seat at the bar, he ordered a Perrier and lazily watched *CNN Headline News* on the bar's television.

"Is this seat taken?" asked a familiar voice behind him, bringing his mind back to the bar.

His eyes lit up as he smiled and replied, "It's reserved for someone special."

He turned on his bar chair to welcome his former classmate and regular date from Columbia University. In fact, most friends had considered them an item, and many thought they would marry after grad school. Victoria Malik was thirty-one years old, five feet ten inches tall, slim, and fit, wearing a discreet, white, two-piece bathing suit that offset her smooth, caramel skin. She had a model's face with high cheekbones and slanting eyes; her sunglasses rested atop her head on her shining, straight black hair. She had a gorgeous smile and graceful manner that drew people to her, especially men, and now, Alex.

She sat down on the bar chair beside Alex, "Well, I'll keep it warm until they get here."

Alex waved to the bartender to get his attention, and then turned to her, "How's life as a high-priced Washington consultant?"

"Good enough, thanks, Alex," said Victoria, and touching his hand with hers, she continued. "Human resource specialists like me are in demand these days. I'm well regarded. My speech to the conference was a great success. So I'm going to take a long weekend here for some hard-earned R & R."

The bartender arrived, and Victoria ordered a Diet Coke.

"Still living on Diet Cokes, I see."

"I try to limit myself to five a day, except in emergencies and high stress. By the way, I hope you're going to be a good host and tour guide."

"Still shy as ever, aren't you?" said Alex. Her proximity tempted him. He wondered if he should cancel his meeting with the financier but decided that at least he should meet the guy and play it by ear from there. To win Victoria back, he needed success. Besides, he was brightened by the thought that Victoria planned to stay for a few days anyway. He hoped it was to spend time with him.

"Sure, it'll be fun," he said finally. "I've got some business tonight, but then I'm all yours."

"And you're still as chivalrous as ever," said Victoria, now touching him lightly on the arm. Victoria was a toucher, and not just to make a point; it was one of her ways of keeping you within her world while she was with you. "How's life in the leisure class?"

Alex smiled. Life with Victoria, taunt, challenge, and tease. "It works Victoria."

This was play for Alex, a distraction to help him settle his nerves and pass the time before his big meeting this evening. After that, he was looking forward to the next few days of fun.

Victoria brought him out of his reverie. "So tell me, what's the big business meeting about tonight?"

"I'm meeting with an investor for my new company," said Alex in an assured tone that gave him a sense of momentum more imagined than real.

Victoria perked right up. "New company? What company does a specialist in religion and business set up? Alex, what have you been hiding from me? And who's your investor?"

"It's a long story," said Alex, recognizing that he had not kept her up to date on his activities of the past year. He checked his watch for the time. "Why don't we order lunch? You could put it on your business expense. After all, I'm a potential client."

Victoria laughed, "Everything has a price, but I guess this story is worth at least a lunch."

FIVE

Entrepreneurs are simply those who understand that there is little difference between obstacle and opportunity and are able to turn both to their advantage.

—Machiavelli

They studied the hotel menu. Alex opted for the Hyatt cheeseburger and fries, while Victoria went with the grilled yellowfin tuna melt with another Diet Coke.

Orders placed, Alex started his pitch. "The idea is to provide consulting services to organized religions, at least the mainline Christian ones in North America and Europe for starters. You know, the ones with declining members and revenues. You might say a consultant to the shepherds of the flock, offering them better ways to manage the herd, make it grow, make it give more wool."

"Novel idea. How would it work?" asked Victoria, with genuine interest.

"Proprietary statistical models tailored to the needs of any flock, combined with modern management. For example, some religious groups are using sophisticated methods of organization to achieve success, you know, setting objectives, using mass media and most of all, getting people involved."

Alex continued outlining his dreams until their server arrived with their orders, placing their respective dishes before them. Silence ensued, as they examined their choices through a well-established hierarchy of senses, the sight of a freshly grilled hamburger on a whole wheat bun, the sensuality of the melting cheese on the tuna, savoring their blending aromas. Touch and taste followed as they each took an introductory bite. Their eyes closed in the same pleasure that might declare the kiss of a lover. Victoria volunteered, "I'm hungrier than I thought. I'm glad you're doing the talking. Tell me more about how your business will work."

"To do any of this within a reasonable time frame on the scale necessary to build credibility with the big organizations, I need serious start-up funding to hire people, conduct surveys, set up database platforms, and develop and run my models."

"Right. As the old saying goes, 'All you need are time and money.'"

"True, but the more money I can arrange the less time it will take to launch full tilt—about a two-year time frame. The guy I'm meeting tonight could unlock the door to getting my dreams off the ground."

"Exciting," said Victoria, now listening like an eager child, leaning over, blocking out other sounds. "So, who is this angel investor?"

"His name is J. J. Jones, chairman and CEO of Imagen, the biotech darling of Wall Street."

"I've read about him," said Victoria. "He cultivates a low profile. It seems as if he goes out of his way to avoid media coverage, not much beyond the blurbs in Imagen's annual reports and various filings with the SEC. Something about research into life extension. I forget the details."

"Yeah, there's that too. They're right at the forefront in so many areas of bioengineering. And life extension is the sexiest, I suppose."

"Yes, and supposedly he has an almost magical way of blending science and commerce. Everything he touches turns to gold," added Victoria with growing enthusiasm. Finally, Alex thought, she was coming around to see the charm in his proposal.

"So knock on wood that I'm next on his list of successes."

"I don't mean to rain on your parade, but why is he interested in investing in a company like yours? His ideas and yours don't seem remotely related," said Victoria, her tone now half serious, half mocking.

Alex took the comment in stride. "Good question. One that I've asked myself."

Laughing, Victoria jumped in again before he could go on. "I gather you've come up with a good enough answer that you think it's worthwhile meeting with him. Or are you just after a free meal?"

"Hardly. I feel good about it. And besides, in a few hours I will have the answer," said Alex joined in her laughter. He did not want to reveal how much of this was simply to win her heart back.

SIX

And Yahweh said, "Thou canst not see my face; for there shall no man see me and live."

—Exodus 33:20

"Call me J. J.," said the man, extending his hand to Alex. He was larger than Alex had expected, particularly his head. Not that there were any rules on head-to-body proportions, but if there were, then J. J.'s head was over the line. His long combed-back hair complemented a well-trimmed beard, giving him a lionlike air. Dressed in an open-necked white shirt, blue blazer, taupe dress pants, and sandals, his outfit was casual, like his manner.

"OK, J. J.," said Alex, shaking his would-be investor's hand with exaggerated firmness. He regretted wearing the tie, but decided to keep it on.

"Did you know, Alex, that I've read not only your business plan, but also your PhD thesis and everything else you have published? You're a genius, my friend." Like the cologne J. J. was wearing, Alex found the man a little overpowering.

"Well, I don't know about that," demurred Alex. And he wasn't sure yet they were friends. He was always a little skeptical of people who befriended him quickly. How did they know what he was like? Victoria would say it was vibes and body language. But he felt uncomfortable with judgments based on gut feeling.

"Don't be bashful. From the moment I read your stuff, I knew you were the guy I needed for my next project." Jones was passionate in his praise. He spoke quickly. "Using the marketplace to figure out what made Yahweh thrive. Entrepreneur of a backwater start-up to CEO of the biggest religion in the world. I don't know how I missed it. Didn't see it coming."

Alex blushed. Such lavish praise made him feel uncomfortable. What was this guy talking about? What had J. J. Jones missed about Yahweh? Why did he even care? He felt distinctly uncomfortable, worse than if Jones had put his hand on his thigh and winked. Filling the emerging gap of silence, Alex said, "I just built on the work of others."

Jones raised his arms and held his hands out to reinforce his point, as if speaking to a much larger audience. "Einstein built on the work of others—but he changed the building. You're like him, a man ahead of your time, and I want to help finance your project."

Although the flattery took his breath away, this was the moment Alex had been waiting for. Should he jump in if he was right about why Jones wanted to invest in his venture? What if he was wrong? Or should he let Jones continue just to make sure they were on the same wavelength? He chose a middle ground.

"I'm glad you like my ideas, and I thank you for the vote of financial confidence. But just how do you plan to capitalize on my work?" Alex stopped. This was far enough. He would let Jones spell out the detail, and then he would tailor his pitch based on those needs. He hoped he was on the right track.

"To make over some old gods and help me with a corporate takeover, obviously."

"Sorry?" started Alex. This was not the expected response. Make over old gods? He had no idea where J. J. was going.

"No need for sorry. You are the man with the answers I need. I want my family back into the god game, and I've decided to start by taking over a big corporation," J. J. kept right on going.

Alex started to feel a light-headed. The Carolina Café of the Hilton Head Westin Resort, where they were dining, had taken on an otherworldly glow as if the maître d' had somehow imbued the air with flecks of gold. The room's windows captured the retreating sunbeams of the day and employed them as special servers to raise the Low Country Carolina decor, complimenting the blond woods and off-white linens. The restaurant had just the mood that Alex had wanted for this meeting—elegant but casual, open, but quiet enough to give them privacy. And the café's bountiful seafood extravaganza buffet ensured ease of choice in eating. He was pleased with the success of the meeting. The eccentric, bombastic J. J. Jones was going to invest in him. And in keeping with Victoria's advice to go with the fuzzy gut feel, he felt an increasing rapport with his new partner, even if he was a little brassier, maybe even a little cheesier, than Alex expected. It probably came with age; he could live with it. Alex felt so good, he had allowed the ever-discrete server to top up his wineglass throughout dinner, and he now felt the agreeable flush that helped mellow the emotional turmoil of the day. Now the conversation was taking an offbeat turn—makeover of gods, takeover of a company. What did J. J. want? Alex felt he had not done enough homework. Or maybe he was just out of his league. On the plus side, their styles complemented each other. It would be nice to have such a dynamic partner, if he could just tone it down a bit.

"As you know, I hire only the best experts for my businesses—McKinsey and Company quality in all fields. Hire the best, develop trust, define the need, and give them free rein. That's my philosophy."

"Yes?"

"Well I see you as superior in your field, Alex, the man to help me with my comeback."

"Comeback? I thought you were pretty well established." Alex had lost control of the agenda. He could only listen and look for an opportunity to get back in.

"I have a proposal for you," said J. J. Jones. Then he paused. Alex felt relief, the man was finally moving toward details. They were now going to get beyond the sales pitch and into the substance. He straightened in his chair as Jones leaned forward, "I want you to help me restore a god; a guy who has been sitting on the bench for a while, has learned a thing or two, and now would like to make a comeback."

Alex's stomach sank. So much for substance. Was J. J. Jones an aspiring cult-ist? Was he related to Jim Jones? He wasn't sure he wanted to hear more. He regretted the extra wine. He tried to sound glib as he replied, "Which god is that? There have been so many."

"I'll give you hint." J. J. reached into the inside pocket of his blazer, pulled out a photograph, and handed it to Alex. "Take a look at this."

Alex studied the photograph. He saw J. J. in a black three-piece suit surrounded by a group of men and women who looked as if they were on their way to a high-class toga party. Except for J. J., they all looked into the camera with puzzled expressions. Did the photographer do something unusual, he wondered? He searched for a suitable response. "A great group shot. Was it taken at a special fund-raiser? The costumes are fantastic, very realistic."

J. J. leaned forward even closer, as if he was about to disclose a great secret. "Alex, take a deep breath. I must explain something to you."

＊   ＊   ＊   ＊

When J. J. had finished his story, Alex was sipping cognac, at J. J.'s insistence. He was unsure if he were dreaming or simply drunk. What he discounted was any semblance of reality connected to what he had just heard in the last half hour. J. J. Jones had claimed he was Jupiter, the supreme Roman god. He was getting things in order so he could make a comeback by taking over a major pharmaceutical company. His family of gods, the toga party people in the picture, needed to be made over into modern times.

Was Jones deluded or just playing an elaborate hoax, testing Alex's gullibility level? And how should he respond? He desperately wanted J. J.'s dollars, but did that mean taking on a full-time nutcase? And what would that do to his credibility if it got out that he was funded by a religious screwball?

"Do you follow sports, Alex?"

"Yes, some. Big events, play-offs."

"You know names like Muhammad Ali and Michael Jordan?"

"Yes."

"The greatest in their fields?"

"Yes." Alex felt like a windup doll, nodding back and forth to punctuate J. J.'s monologue.

"You know how tough it was for them to retire. They kept making comebacks. Right?"

"Yes."

"They had to be able to go out on their terms. Remember?"

"Yes." Alex sensed that no other answer was acceptable. He vaguely recalled the details of both men. He felt both had stayed a little too long for their own well-being.

"Well, that's what it's been like for me for two thousand years, only worse. I want a rematch. One more shot. But I'm going to have to fight to get the starting position back." Alex wondered if Michael Jordan knew he had an immortal soul mate.

"I've done elaborate training and preparation, years, indeed centuries. But it wasn't until I read your thesis that I understood how Yahweh had done it. He evolved and grew, entrepreneur to sophisticated chairman of the board, while I just screwed around, taking my supremacy for granted. He was like Bill Gates. I was like a rock star who shines brightly for a while, but burns out." It sounded like a divine Rocky script.

"Now, nobody has any idea of who I am," said J. J., and Alex's dismay deepened. It must have showed, because J. J. touched his shoulder with a fatherly gesture and continued. "Don't look so glum, Alex. I understand your sympathy. But it's OK, really. Things are going well. I think I understand this game of business, so it's a good entry point for me. But now I want more of my team here with me. So your job, Alex, if you accept, is to help make over this crew in the picture so they can fit in as well as I do and then help us with our corporate takeover."

Alex decided to play along for the time being; he wanted to preserve the multimillion-dollar cash injection promised by the financier. Deep down he had a growing curiosity about how far this charade could go. And besides, it was one thing for J. J. to be an off-center eccentric, but who were the people in the picture? "How long would I have?"

"Oh, I want a good job. Time is not critical for me. But sooner is better, say a few months."

"A few months?" Alex was incredulous. The guy waits two thousand years and then wants everything to happen in a hurry? The approach of a typical CEO, even to run this as a hoax, would take a few months just to find out who they were, run baseline tests, find out what would work best, and get a plan in place.

"You're right, it might not take that long, they are gods after all," replied J. J., and Alex stifled a laugh. The man was a borderline personality as far as he could tell. "You see, while you are doing that, I will be expanding my business interests."

"And what about the corporate takeover?"

"That too, as soon as you complete the makeovers. There's so much to do."

"Tell me about it," said Alex, then pausing for a long moment, unsure of what to say next. He thought of the money. He thought of his lack of knowledge on how to deal with troubled people. "Well, I could do with some time to think about everything you have told me."

Alex needed more than time. He needed sobriety. He remembered reading about John Nash, the MIT mathematician, who had won a Nobel Prize, but had suffered from schizophrenia, the one they had made a movie about. At one point Nash had thought he was being contacted by supernatural beings from outer space to save the world. When a friend asked how a talented mathematician such as he could believe such an absurd thing, Nash had replied that they seemed believable because they came to him in the same way the mathematical ideas did. Alex wondered if J. J. Jones was mad in the same way. And then he realized if he told anyone this story they might think he was mad as well. He would need to test it with Victoria. He could trust her. How would he start? "An old god who wants to make a comeback has contacted me. Can you help me? The money is great."

J. J. smiled at him for a long moment, then said, "Of course you do. Take all the time you need and then get back to me with a proposal. This will be a contract separate from my investment in your company. Give me a plan, billing rates, you know, the whole nine yards. You're the expert, give me a PowerPoint presentation. Or, better yet, create a Web site for me," said J. J., laughing at his own wit. Alex displayed a reticent smile. This was a game to Jones, he thought. As well, Alex hated PowerPoint presentations. They were the modern business equivalent of a snake-oil pitch—dripping with the words du jour, the jargon of choice, style over substance. He would be different. For him, a well-chosen word was worth a thousand PowerPoints. But was this a contract he wanted?

"And what if I said no?"

"No hard feelings," said J. J. "I make only one request. If you do say no, then you will be obliged to give me the names of everyone you tell about this conversation."

"Why?" said Alex, wondering if he would survive a refusal.

"So I can purge your memory and theirs of Jupiter and our discussion," said J. J. without rancor. "It's a harmless procedure. It will make tonight seem no more than a distant dream, wisps of memory, good grounds for poetry, but nothing else. It would, to put it more gently, free you of your responsibilities on this matter. And of course, I would still honor my commitment to invest in your venture."

"Seems reasonable," said Alex smoothly, as if he got offers like this every day. He was, in fact, horrified. What did purging mean? Surely the man could have used another word. He thought again about John Nash. He had often wondered if Nash's voices could have been real. Had he simply failed in his mission because conventional definitions of normal behavior rejected him out of hand? There were risks in being too far ahead of your time. J. J. had made it clear that he shared his delusion with only true believers. But what did he do with those who declined his invitation?

Alex heard a low beeping sound from J. J.'s cell phone that was sitting in front of him on their table. Jones paused. "Excuse me for a moment," he said, and reached for it.

While Jones looked at the screen of his phone, Alex wondered what he was checking. He didn't want to judge Jones prematurely—there could be a reason. Still, he found it odd that the man was singing his praises one minute and preoccupied with other business the next.

"Just checking my e-mails and phone calls, I'm expecting some important data," winked Jones. "Now where were we? Seems reasonable, you say? Oh, it's more than reasonable, but let's not focus on negatives. I know you'll come on board." J. J. stopped briefly while he checked his watch. "Now enough of business. Let's take a walk on the beach; I want to show you something."

J. J. stood, signaling the end of their discussion.

$$* \qquad * \qquad * \qquad *$$

The sun had set by the time Alex and J. J. walked through the French doors of the restaurant to the multilevel, multipool complex. At this time of evening there was no one outside. They wound their way over the endless decks until they at last crossed the hotel's boardwalk over the sand dunes and stepped down onto the beach. J. J. suggested they walk away from the hotel and the buildings.

Alex marveled at how dark the beach grew at night, the lights of the hotel fading as they walked. Soon he could barely make out J. J. beside him, and indeed his form appeared more ghostlike than real. They walked in silence, and Alex listened to the voice of the ocean speaking a language that had remained unchanged for millions of years. After twenty minutes of walking, emboldened by fear at getting too far from the hotel, he asked, "You said you had something to show me. What is it?"

In that instant the forces of nature overwhelmed Alex's senses. Out of the darkness burst a blinding bolt of lightning, as if hurled by an unseen assailant. The night skies exploded with peals of thunder that rumbled and roared with deafening effect. The earth shook as if mortally pierced by the resplendent streak of light that hit the water just beyond them, giving Alex a spectacular photoflash of the skies, the ocean, the dunes, and the fields of sea oats. Alex looked at J. J. The appearance of Jones's face had changed; his eyes were like burning torches, and his clothes were a radiant white. And then, all was quiet, still, and unfathomably dark. Alex could not think; his head was spinning. He could only feel, and what he felt was awe. At that point he fell to his knees and threw up.

SEVEN

It is a myth, not a mandate, a fable not a logic, and a symbol rather than a reason by which men are moved.

—Irwin Edman

Alex lurched from a troubled sleep into a hazy consciousness. Aches streamed like spawning eels through every limb of his body. Twinges of undefined anxiety lurked like muggers in the dark corners of his mind. He felt as if neurons had misfired like the blinks of a flickering neon light. Still, he was grateful to have returned home intact. He wished he could get some real sleep now that he had escaped, but his body would not cooperate. It had a separate agenda, one that preferred the guilt, the self-loathing of voluntary excess.

Not wanting to get up right away, he closed his eyes and replayed the previous day from the top. How much was real? How much was fake? Conjured imagery shimmied on his consciousness, painted by the elves of too much booze and too little sleep. The day had started with such promise. In some respects, it had delivered everything he had hoped for, but it had been delivered shrink-wrapped in a strange new world.

He grabbed the remote from his bedside stand and switched on the TV. According to *CNN Headline News*, the world was still intact. He turned his concentration to his meeting with J. J. Jones. This was his personal nightmare. Or was it a daymare? Scattered images flashed before him: J. J.'s story, the lightning, throwing up. Then J. J. helping him home and telling him to call if he had any questions. Alex had enough experience in hangovers to hope that some of his memories could be faulty, that it may not be half as bad as he felt right now.

Finally getting up, he dragged himself to the bathroom for a hot shower. As he toweled himself, Max looked look at him, as if in disgust, as he waited by the bathroom door. Alex grabbed his watch on the bathroom counter and checked the time. He had slept in, at least as far as Max's schedule was concerned. Quickly he found the Max's treats and flipped a few to him while he thought about breakfast. His stomach groaned, and he settled for several glasses of water with orange juice.

Feeling serviceable, he sat down at his computer to search the Internet for new gods and gurus. Googling with different search angles yielded an incredible churning of soothsayers and seekers. However, nothing connected to J. J. Jones.

Lunch with Victoria was his next hope.

∗   ∗   ∗   ∗

"So you were drunk, and he's a storyteller," said Victoria, laughing.

Alex had feared this response and waited a moment to collect his thoughts. At length he said, "How about the lightning?"

"Could be anything. Could be as simple as real lightning hitting your drunken imagination, sheer coincidence, no more, no less. You did get sick, didn't you? Can't hold your liquor?" teased Victoria, with a hint of judgment.

Alex regretted having added that detail, but he thought it better to get all the facts on the table, as many as he could remember. A second set of ears might give perspective that he was missing.

"But, could he really be, you know, Jupiter?" Alex was aware of the plaintive tone in his voice, but he couldn't help it. He had counted on Victoria being a more sympathetic listener.

"I can't believe you're asking the question. Jupiter is a myth, as in a story, as in not real. Mr. J. J. Jones is, as they say in Texas, all hat and no cattle."

"But can't myths have a historic base?"

"Well, then we call them legends, some little fact that generations of people build into something monumental. You know, the flea that becomes the size of King Kong."

"But aren't there exceptions?"

"None that I know of. Well, hold on, maybe the closest would be Schlieman's discovery of Troy, which gave some truth to the story of Helen of Troy."

"And?"

"That's an example of a flea that's been discovered. Still no pictures of the face that launched a thousand ships, though."

"Are there any other examples?"

"Who knows? Who cares? Alex, what has gotten into you? You're like a little boy testing for Santa Claus. Where's the cold, objective Alex, the detached voice of reason? How much exactly did you drink last night?"

Alex ignored the jibe. "I did a net search this morning, checked all my regular sources, no hints."

"Are you surprised?

"Well, not really, but what did interest me was the number of new movements leveraging off the idea of a new cosmic cycle, the Age of Aquarius."

"A hippie dream from the 1960s. You were born fifty years too late for that ride."

"Well what about J. J.'s offer? Let's go back to the offer, the makeover of his team to bring them into the twenty-first century. Then the corporate takeover. And assume I got it mostly right about what he told me."

"I agree that's pretty wild, maybe even disturbing. I mean, many CEOs think they are god, so it's a cute twist for a god to think like a CEO. I think the guy read your thesis and thought he would have some fun with you. Do you have the photograph he showed you?"

"No, I gave it back."

"Consider the choices. It could be an elaborate hoax. He's rich and creative and could have a really weird sense of humor."

"Why?"

"Because you are so earnest and naïve. And he's trying to bond with you, seal your partnership with a practical joke. It's a male thing."

"Next."

"He could be a cultist. Again, he is rich, creative, and, therefore, eccentric, almost by definition."

"Any other possibilities?"

"He could simply be crazy, a borderline personality. And this alternative is not inconsistent with the cultist theory."

"Any others?"

"No, Alex, I'm not going to consider the possibility that he really is who he says he is."

Alex was disappointed that Victoria wouldn't even consider the alternative, that J. J. was Jupiter or perhaps an emissary. Deep down inside, he had hoped that she would tell him of a secret passageway, a 1-800 number, perhaps, that would connect him to the numinous side of reality.

This conversation was more revealing than Alex had planned. Victoria was a Gemini; she had a playful side and a serious side. It was the playful side of her that had attracted him initially. The serious side didn't show until she graduated and moved into her career with single-minded resolve.

"What about the people in the photograph?" asked Alex.

"Hard to say. I haven't seen it. But that perhaps is evidence that it's a joke."

"And the purging?"

"Well, that's intriguing, especially because I'm now officially on the purgee list."

"What next then?"

"You could just walk away, refuse the contract, the investment. After all, whoever he is, he has an ability to mess seriously with your mind."

Alex slumped in his chair as he considered the possibility. "I could, but it would be like throwing the last three years away." Then he sat up, revived at the thought of the money. "His investment is key. It's not like I have several suitors."

"You could play along, at least for a few more meetings, and hope that he says 'Gotcha' real soon."

Alex smiled; he would like something like that to happen. He would have liked it even better if he had heard "Gotcha" last night and didn't have this dilemma.

"Yeah," he took a deep breath before making his final pitch, "but I could use your help. I'd like you to meet him, if you don't mind. I'd like to get your first-hand impressions. Besides, you're the first person who came to mind to help me do the makeover on his crew."

She paused and looked at him for a long minute, then spoke at last. Alex thought his heart would stop.

"Well, if it helps calm your mind, OK, why not? Maybe I can get some business from him, too." Alex felt a small victory for the first time since his meeting with J. J. Jones. Victoria smiled and leaned closer to him, then said with a wink, "I thought you'd never ask."

EIGHT

What do we tell our children? ... "Haste makes waste. Look before you leap. Stop and think. Don't judge a book by its cover."
We believe that we are always better off gathering as much information as possible and spending as much time as possible in deliberation.

—Malcom Gladwell

J. J. Jones agreed to meet with them the next day. It may as well have been a year. For Alex life had become an abyss of horror. He had no appetite. He couldn't sleep for longer than two hours at a stretch. When he did sleep, he had nightmares. No, he just had one nightmare, over and over. He would be walking along a path that became narrower and narrower. Buildings disappeared; trees disappeared. In fact, everything disappeared, and he was simply suspended in space. In the undefined grayness, he would sense something, which he then identified as a dot. But the dot grew at an exponential rate, larger and larger, until it became a dark and foreboding monolith. Either that, or he became smaller and smaller, until he became the dot, and the original dot became all powerful. At this point he usually woke up screaming, with a deep sense of foreboding, his heart beating rapidly, his breath short, and his body sweating profusely.

When he felt fully awake, he considered the offer of J. J. Jones. He did not like to be rushed in making a major decision, preferring reflection and deliberation before action. How had he arrived at this strange point? There was no logic, no rational explanation for what was happening. Science denied all this.

Not that he doubted religion's importance in people's lives. He just hadn't taken the divine stuff too seriously. He knew religion from an academic's point of view. He understood it as literature. Still, he considered himself neither religious nor spiritual, neither atheist nor agnostic. He simply was ignorant, literally ignorant of religious feeling, spiritual awe. His mother was a Catholic, his father a Baptist, not that it mattered, because to Alex's knowledge they neither attended regular church services nor followed any other observable practice. They belonged to that larger group known as lapsed Christians. It didn't matter which denomination—lapsed Catholic, lapsed Baptist, lapsed Lutheran—because one feature of being lapsed was ignorance of your origins. Thus, most lapsees had far more in common with one another than with devotees of their original churches.

Indeed, lapsed Christians were the largest and most rapidly growing denomination in North America. The lapsees had simple beliefs, according to multiple surveys and studies. They believed in God and the devil. Many were waiting for Armageddon, the final war of good and evil. They believed in an afterlife, maybe even reincarnation. Who knew? They recognized evil in the world but did not believe in hell. Too risky given their lifestyle. Their connection with all this religious stuff was an ambiguously defined feeling that was uniquely personal, warm, and fuzzy. Churches and mainstream clergy continued to serve for important rites of passage, mostly weddings and funerals.

Ironically, Alex had converted his skepticism into his first book, *Lost in Lapse-Land: America's Spiritual Crossroads.* It was moderately successful, and he had gained some national media exposure, including a ten-minute appearance on *Larry King Live.* He had appeared with Pat Robertson for the Christian Coalition of America and the "star" of the evening, Tanya Harding. Ms. Harding had announced that she had taken a hard look at her past, found Jesus, and was now volunteering weekly at a soup kitchen for the homeless in downtown Portland, Oregon.

Now Alex had to deal with J. J. Jones. If J. J. Jones was Jupiter, then what of all the other gods. What of Yahweh? Alex usually felt nausea when he got to this point. He felt like Jeremiah, the reluctant prophet. When Yahweh had called on him, Jeremiah had demurred, pleading, "I am only a boy." But Yahweh told him his fate was sealed before he was born, to get off his butt and on to do what he was told. Yahweh said he'd protect him.

Alex couldn't recall J. J. promising protection. On the other hand, he was only being asked to be a consultant. That didn't seem as committed as a prophet. But what were the risks? What if God intervened and found out about J. J.? Would helping J. J. be held against him? On the other hand, if J. J. was right, then perhaps there were other gods who needed help. The thought made Alex both giddy and apprehensive. This could be the start of something much bigger. Big rewards. Big risks. Life could never be the same. Perhaps he should just forget J. J.'s unusual offer and restore normalcy. The purging alternative could not be discounted. His life was not that bad. But still, time was running out on his dream.

Did he really have a choice? His life, in some respects, was over. His choice frightened him. If he accepted J. J.'s offer, then he entered a world of awe, where humans were at the beck and call of competing gods. And if J. J. were any indication, very needy gods. If he declined, then J. J. would zap his memory of all this, and he could return to normal. But Alex realized it would be a spiritual lobotomy, leading to a half-life as a cartoon human.

PART TWO
DEALMAKERS
DEALING

NINE

Eyes are more accurate witnesses than ears.

—Heraclitus of Ephesus

J. J. had suggested that they meet at his villa on the ocean, on a secluded part of the island. Partly hidden behind tall pines and great old oak trees draped with Spanish moss, the home sat well back from the road. The circular drive defined a garden of colorful begonias and grape holly, and in its center was a fountain with a sculpture of a spouting dolphin. As Alex and Victoria turned into the complex, a great blue heron gracefully took flight from the lawn, signaling its visit was over.

J. J. greeted them at the door and led them to the multilevel back deck with its heated pool, Jacuzzi, and change rooms. Surrounding the deck were gardens rich with magnolias, oleanders in full pink bloom, colorful impatiens, yarrow, and Mexican sage. Iridescent butterflies fluttered and danced from flower to flower. Palmettos bordered the property of the back complex, except for the ocean exposure that was open to the gentle dunes and sea oats waving in the breeze. Alex whistled softly to himself. Forget the house; he could settle for living on this deck.

They seated themselves in a raised gazebo on the far side of the deck, away from the house and looking over the ocean. When J. J. offered them drinks, Alex followed Victoria's lead, who allowed herself her usual Diet Coke. Alex admired Victoria's moxie; she took charge from the start, asking J. J. to consider her consulting firm for future work with Imagen. Remarkably, J. J. told her the timing was perfect. They would have a real need for someone with her talents soon. Something about Imagen taking over or merging with some big global drug company.

For the next half hour, she grilled him on every feature of Roman life and myth, many of which were new to Alex. It was clear from her rapt attention and admiring eyes that J. J. had intrigued her with his knowledge.

Finally, J. J. paused, smiled at Victoria, and then asked, "How am I doing so far?"

"Very well. I'm impressed. You're a walking encyclopedia of Roman myth," said Victoria, sincere in her praise.

"Glad to meet your standards of excellence. But what if they were more than myth?" said J. J. as he leaned toward her, jabbing his forefinger at her.

Victoria leaned toward him in turn, jabbing with her own forefinger, as if accepting the challenge to a duel. She said, "Myths are stories, fictions to help people understand the world. There is no factual basis to them."

"Oh really," said J. J. with a confident grin. "Then how do you think I know so much about the personalities of Jupiter and his Olympians?"

"Archetypes. Jung taught us the gods are just cookie-cutter models in the collective unconscious." Victoria was as assured and smooth as if she was giving one of her presentations. "They stand for different sides of personality, or they can deal with circumstances that we must deal with, such as birth, love, death. You know the drill."

"I had difficulty with Jung. He would never listen to me," interjected J. J.

Victoria's mouth dropped open, then she laughed and said, "He's been dead for over forty years. How could you have known him?"

"I met him face-to-face almost a hundred years ago. I posed as a pupil of Greek and Roman myth. He was a stubborn, egotistical young man, full of himself. We debated endlessly when he was just getting started in his career and developing his ideas."

Alex saw that J. J. clearly enjoyed telling this story by the way his head tilted to the side, as he traveled back through the memory.

"When he wouldn't listen, I infused his dreams with truth and insight. Unfortunately, he took them for his own dreams and his own insights. That is how he came up with archetypes. At times I think he thought he was god," mused J. J.

"And I suppose you knew Freud as well?" said Victoria in a mocking tone.

"Freud was hopeless, everything had to start and end with sex. I had nothing to do with that."

Victoria laughed again. "You are a fantastic storyteller, Mr. Jones."

"The trouble with people today is they can longer accept the idea of god. No, that's not it. They can no longer understand what it is like to be in the presence of a god," said J. J. in a tone of regret.

"J. J., they are all stories, and you know that," said Victoria as she raised her right arm with her fist clenched and forefinger extended like a gun barrel pointed at J. J., as if correcting a naughty student. "But I concede that they appeal powerfully to the imagination. Just ask Alex."

Three brown pelicans distracted Alex. With their wings extended, they looked like B-52 bombers cruising over the incoming tidewaters. Without warning, one of them dove with its bill open and hit the water with a great splash. Within seconds the hunter surfaced, beak pouch full, and climbed skyward to rejoin the flying formation. Alex felt empathy for the fish that, mere seconds ago, had been swimming free.

What could he add to this conversation? Smiling a weak smile, he shrugged. "Obviously."

"A silly question, and the poor boy answered under duress," said J. J. indignantly.

Victoria laughed and stood. "Nice try, but I still don't know who you are. But before we go further I need to use a washroom. Directions please?"

"Why don't you try one in the house? Closest one is your first left turn down the hallway off the kitchen," said J. J., standing and pointing the way as he spoke. "Argie, my security guy, is inside if you need help. Introduce yourself. He knows the two of you were coming. He can give you a quick tour if you like."

Victoria got up and made her way around the pool to the house.

J. J. turned to Alex and said, "Well, Alex what do you think of this place?"

"Simply magnificent. You own it?"

"Just renting for now. And the houses on either side as well. I'm using them as an executive retreat for my senior team from Imagen. Planning strategy. They are in workshops this afternoon."

"Boy, great way to get creative."

"Well, they work hard, and I wanted to check out the place for my other team, the one you will help build. They could stay here for their makeover training," said J. J., picking up from where he had left off the other night. Clearly J. J. had arranged all of this long before their first meeting. On the one hand, Alex felt good that J. J. confirmed the previous night's offer, because it meant he had not been as drunk as he thought he might have been. On the other hand, he felt uneasy because he still had to come to grips with the real identity of this charismatic charmer and whether he would accept his offer. He was glad Victoria was along.

J. J. went on, "It's quiet, out of the way, and convenient for you. And by the way, I think Victoria would be a terrific partner for you on the project."

Alex ignored the comment as he sniffed the air and said, "By the way, I've wanted to ask the whole time we've been sitting out here, do I smell chocolate?"

"Yes, but you'll never guess why."

"So I won't try. Tell me."

"The mulch in the gardens. It's made of cocoa beans, and that creates a unique chocolate aroma. Pleasant, isn't it?"

At that moment a scream pierced their conversation. It was Victoria. Alex jumped up and looked at J. J., who quickly got up as well.

"Sounds like she met Argie," said J. J. as a smile of delight and mischief overtook his face.

Puzzled, Alex jumped up and ran to the French door of the house off the deck. J. J. followed close behind. They reached it as Victoria emerged from the other side. She grabbed onto Alex's arm with her both hands.

"Who? What on earth is that? That freak!" she said as she pointed behind her at the person who was inside. Alex could not see because of a combination of the bright sun on the deck and the smoky, sheer drapes. He moved closer to the door and saw a man, in casual wear, about six feet tall with a large head. Taking one more step for a closer look, his eyes popped open and his heart jumped. The large head was a mass of eyes, front, back, top, there seemed no end to them. He could make out a nose and what he assumed was a mouth that showed a friendly smile. No facial hair to speak of. There wasn't room.

"Hi, J. J. How do you do, Alex," said the creature, holding out its hand to shake. "I'm Argus. I didn't mean to upset Victoria."

"It's OK, Argie," said J. J., continuing in a tone of mocking irony. "It's my fault. I apologize, Victoria, only I thought you would recognize him right away."

"I thought Argus was killed," said Victoria, trying to cover. Even Alex recalled the story of Argus, a creature in classical mythology who had a hundred eyes. Juno set him to watch over Io, a girl who had been seduced by Jupiter and then turned into a cow. With Argus on guard, Jupiter could not come to rescue Io, for only some of Argus's eyes would be closed in sleep at any one time. Mercury, working on Jupiter's behalf, played music that put all the eyes to sleep and then killed Argus. Juno, in a gesture of respect, put his eyes in the tail of her bird, a peacock.

"You're right, he was. This is his android successor, developed in one of my labs," said J. J., and showing the same enthusiasm Alex had seen at their first meeting, he went on. "And, he's far better than the original. For starters, he will never fall asleep on the job. And all his senses are superior to humans. Besides 360-degree vision, his sense of smell is greater than a dog's, and his hearing more sophisticated than a bat's."

"I never envisaged anything so alien. Why'd you make him?" said Victoria.

"A gift for Juno. She still blames me for the death of the original. My scientists loved the assignment."

"How did he know who I was?"

"His artificial intelligence is at least twenty years ahead of anything available commercially. He's connected to the World Wide Web. I told him you were coming."

"I just looked you up on the Internet, Victoria," Argus jumped in. "Your picture is on your company's Web site, and I read all your articles that are posted there as well. By the way, call me Argie, everybody else does."

Argie's appearance disconcerted Alex. Not wanting to stare, he tried some form of eye contact, searching the android's head for eyes that might be focused on him alone. Argie carried on. "I have many talents and I'm still under development. J. J. is testing me as a security agent."

"Victoria, please complete your trip to the washroom, while Alex and I return to our chairs," said J. J. as he started toward to the deck. "Argie, please bring us fresh drinks and some appetizers. The caterers left everything in the kitchen."

TEN

A man must dream a long time in order to act with grandeur, and dreaming is nursed in darkness.

—Jean Genet

"Well J. J., you know what they say about a boy and his toys. You are a complex man," said Victoria as she returned and sat down. Although her words lacked her usual edge, she quickly found it again as she narrowed on the issue that had brought her and Alex to this meeting. "And I don't believe for a minute you're the Roman god Jupiter—although you admittedly have a passion for him."

Ignoring her assertion, J. J. said, "I hope you'll join Alex on the makeover project. You'll be perfect." If he was offended, he showed no sign of it.

"Alex tells me you have a picture of your crew that needs the makeover," replied Victoria, picking up this new thread. She had talked with Alex about the picture for the last two days, the way a lawyer might talk about a key piece of evidence.

J. J. perked up, as if he had been waiting all afternoon for the question. Reaching into his shirt pocket with great flourish, he took out the picture and handed it to Victoria.

She studied it with care. "Charming group, J. J. Great costumes. If they are who you say they are, then the makeover you are asking for is a big job." Victoria paused to consider the photograph further, then continued. "You know, it would make more sense to start with just a few of these characters. Then, once we work out the wrinkles, we could move on to the others."

"Seems reasonable. Does that mean you're on board?" said J. J. enthusiastically.

"Slow down. I'm just thinking out loud, not committing to anything just yet. I'd like to discuss the project with Alex after we're finished here. Besides, I prefer that we give you a well-thought-out proposal. However, I do have two more questions before we go."

Alex released his breath. The conversation had moved faster than he was comfortable with. They had agreed that they would not decide on J. J.'s offer for twenty-four hours, regardless of what happened. "Always best to sleep on it," she had said.

"Fire away," said J. J.

"First, why now? Why is it important to make a comeback now?"

"Well, for a long while, hundreds of years in your time, I was depressed. You have no idea what it is like to be the number one divinity of the greatest nation on earth and then poof, nothing. Emperor Constantine's decision to go with the Christians came totally out of left field for me. I didn't see it coming."

"An accident of history?" said Victoria with genuine sympathy.

"Perhaps. That's how I felt for a long time, until it dawned on me that I had simply grown out of touch with humans ... and my competition."

"Well, that's positive," said Alex.

"It was an important step. And as you will find out, I have been working on this a long time, waiting for the right moment. I'm sure that now the timing is right. People are in need. They've reached the zenith of spiritual entropy," said J. J., in a more thoughtful tone than he had displayed so far.

He paused, and Alex noticed a glazed look in Victoria's eyes as she shrugged and said, "Keep going, in plain English if possible, please."

"Breakup of the spiritual fabric that has governed for a millennium. It's like a sand castle crumbling under the tide and washing out to sea or like a snowman melting away in a winter thaw."

"Meaning?"

"The malaise has set in. Yahweh's center cannot hold, cannot be put back together, like Humpty Dumpty after his great fall."

"Meaning?"

"Meaning time for a new sand castle. Yahweh's rule has hit a wall, something like mine did. The time is ripe for a new agenda for the sacred and divine, a new spiritual infusion, if you like, what the New Agers call The Age."

"Of Aquarius," Alex jumped in. This was his "gotcha" moment for Victoria. She just rolled her eyes and threw her hands in the air.

"Exactly, Alex, right on. It's a giant recasting of the heavenly pecking order— that leads the way to Jupiter. *Moi*. But I don't take anything for granted any-more, so I want to start slowly, by taking over a global corporation. It will serve as a base while my gods get reestablished."

Before J. J. could say more, Argie appeared, "Here we go gang. Victoria, another Diet Coke for you, with a slice of lemon."

Alex did a double take. Covered in a silver reflecting sphere, Argie's head looked like a tenpin bowling ball.

J. J. laughed and volunteered, "Argie's got his sunglasses on. Cool, aren't they?"

"Now he does look like a space alien. Why does he need them if he's an android?" Alex marveled at how lifelike Argie was, even if his head appeared bizarre.

"He doesn't. His artificial intelligence is so advanced that he's picked up van-ity." J. J. laughed again and then added, "Victoria, you still have one more ques-tion."

"But why should people choose you over some other god, say, Yahweh? What is your philosophy?"

Jupiter looked perplexed by the question. "Alex will work it out. That's part of his next contract, after the makeover and takeover are complete. He's the expert. I'm flexible—whatever works."

Alex jumped at this turn. Was this a detail from last night that he had missed or forgotten? Although he was glad that J. J. had refreshed his memory so dis-creetly, the demand scared him. Would he create a Frankenstein god? Would he become the Mother Mary, Mary Shelley that is, of a new age on earth?

"But he doesn't know what gods think." Victoria spoke rapidly as if Alex wasn't there, as if his body was just a stage prop. Alex had never seen her so intense.

"I know what gods think. I need help with how humans think," replied J. J. glibly.

"Why not just declare that you and your family are back and open for busi-ness," said Victoria.

"Would that I could. But you know as well as I do that humans aren't that easy. For now, I'll settle for being the head of a global corporation, enjoy some glory, and plot my next steps. What I need from Alex right now, and you, is help with the makeover and takeover. You know, walk before you run."

ELEVEN

Setting a goal is not the main thing. It is deciding how you will go about achieving it and staying with that plan.

—Tom Landry

Argie interrupted again, announcing, "Angela Cooper is here for her 3 o'clock meeting, J. J."

Alex looked up and saw a businesswoman, lean in an athletic way, gray hair, but otherwise youthful, standing in the doorway. She wore a formal gray lightweight suit, white blouse buttoned to the top, and gray flats. Her look was conservative, with practical concessions to the climate.

"Angela is my president and chief operating officer at Imagen. She keeps Imagen humming like a hive of busy bees so I can have meetings like this one," said J. J. with a wink. He waved her over and did the introductions.

"These are the two people I told you about. They will be able to help us with our merger plans once we go public. But they are a tough sell."

"Why don't you two join our meeting?" said Angela extending her hand to Victoria's. "The more you see, the more you will want to get on board."

"Great idea," boomed J. J., who got up to pull out a chair for her. "Here, sit down, and tell us how our takeover plan is coming along."

Alex wondered how much Angela Cooper knew of J. J.'s life as a god. He prayed that Victoria would not start asking questions.

"Progress every hour," said Angela, running her hand through her short salt-and-pepper hair. "We're proposing that you name the new company Imagen-Pharmaglobe. Imagine the world with Imagen-Pharmaglobe is the angle to the shareholders."

Alex listened carefully, pleased that J. J. would take him and Victoria into his confidence on the takeover target. Pharmaglobe was an emerging major player in pharmaceuticals. Imagen-Pharmaglobe could be huge.

"Imagine it with J. J. Jones as chairman. How are we doing with our purchase of Pharmaglobe shares?"

"We've reached our target by using various front organizations. It's time to go public. I don't like this stealth stuff."

"Have our friends at Pharmaglobe figured out what's happening yet?"

"They're close. They've had much help from the business press."

"Let's give them a few weeks and a few more hints. Ideally I want them to make the first overture."

"Why J. J.? We could take them over so easily." Angela preferred to go by the straightest, fastest path to the goal line.

"Because our profile of Mr. Gerry Schilling suggests that he likes to be in control, he will be much easier to work with if he thinks he is in the driver's seat."

"In his dreams," said Angela, with a nervous laugh. She then added, in a more serious tone, "But promise me, J. J., that I never have to report to him. The man creeps me out." Angela's candidness with J. J. provided some comfort to Alex that the man—god was at least easy to approach.

J. J. laughed and then said, "Don't worry Angela. He'll never be a threat to you."

Always positive, always the salesman, Alex thought, wondering what was going through J. J.'s mind. But he also noticed that J. J. hadn't answered her directly.

Angela, if she noticed, chose to ignore it and went on with her briefing. "We can plan on a fight for control. Schilling has one of the top corporate espionage teams in the world. James Waite, a former military commander, heads it, and its effectiveness is well known. So we can plan on him snooping for anything that he can use against us, including personal stuff."

"Are we prepared for that?"

"I've checked out everything with our security people, but …," said Angela. Alex could see a smile of mischief in Victoria's eyes at these words.

"Sounds like your usual comprehensive job, why the *but*?"

"OK, J. J., I'll tell you why. The tiger teams declared you clean. But just to make sure, please assure me that there are no skeletons that could come out to haunt us." Angela paused. Alex thought she was uncomfortably close to, if not over, the line of acceptable questions by a subordinate of a superior. Angela turned to him and Victoria and continued, "You two need to watch this charmer. He's like a reflecting surface; you only see facets of yourself, but nothing behind the mirror. I'm always a little worried that this charismatic Wizard of Oz may have a little gnome behind him."

"Now don't scare our new friends, Angela, I assure you I'm skeleton free," said J. J., laughing heartily at his second-in-command, as he threw his hands in the air to show he had nothing to hide, adding, "want to frisk me?"

Angela sat back in her chair, shaking her head by way of declining his offer, and J. J. dropped his hands, saying, "Enough of the serious stuff. This planning session was supposed to have some fun as well. Are we set for tonight? Argie's been looking forward to it all day."

"You're right, you win, we're set. And our work's done," said Angela to her boss. Then she stood. "You know I'm not a fan of these retreats at posh resorts, but I agree it's time to relax, at least for a few hours. I'm going to get out of here and change into something more fun. Tonight, I'm going to stump Argie. Nice meeting you, Alex and Victoria." Alex stood to shake her hand, as did Victoria, and then she headed off toward the house.

J. J. glowed with the confidence of a winning quarterback. A lull in conversation followed Angela's departure. Alex averted his eyes by watching the ebb and flow of the waves. Then Victoria spoke; the mischief was back in her eyes and her voice.

"So tell us, J. J., are there any skeletons in your closet? Or better yet, do gods have skeletons?"

J. J. just looked at her. His expression gave no information, neither cold nor warm. Inscrutability is an art form that poker players, con artists, and gods share in common, thought Alex. Then J. J. smiled a smile of regret and embarrassment.

"Skeletons. I have a few. They're not the skeletons of J. J. Jones. As J. J., I'm cleaner than Mr. Clean."

Alex recalled Victoria's briefing on Jupiter. The philosophers of old had carped on his philandering—something about moral ambiguity and absence of leadership. Then there were the sexually uptight Christians who passed judgment on him. For someone like Jupiter, godliness must have lost some of its fun. As if reading his mind, J. J. went on.

"I know you think it was the womanizing, the everlasting chase of the next nymph. And of course there's my castrating grandmother, Gaia. But none of that will ever concern Angela," said J. J., who then paused for a long moment, before adding, "but all of it will be of concern to you."

Alex's head spun with the cosmic possibilities of this ambiguous afterthought. Was J. J. going to hit on Victoria? Sensing the meeting was drawing to a close, he wanted to leave on the best of terms, short of signing a contract. "We appreciate your candor J. J., and you've given us much to think about."

"I'm confident that you and Victoria are the right mortals to help me, Alex. I know I still need to win your commitment."

J. J.'s words triggered a question that had concerned Alex during the meeting with Angela Cooper. "Does Angela know you as Jupiter or just J. J.?" he asked.

"You and Victoria are the only humans who know the real me, and I know the two of you don't know what to think of me."

"What about Argie?"

"I've programmed him to be completely loyal to me. I'd like to do the same with humans if I could," said J. J., who then paused to let his words sink in. As Alex frowned and pursed his lips as if to speak, J. J. resumed, "I love the look in your eyes. Just kidding, I understand free will is important to you guys. As for Argie, the Imagen staff love him. He'll be the center of attention at the staff party tonight. They try to stump him with any question; his android brain loves it. By the way, no one has had any success yet."

"Well, you've given us a lot to consider," said Alex, still looking for a way to get out without committing to any agreement.

"Look, I have an idea that might help you two decide. My Imagen group leaves tomorrow. Why don't the two of you come for a dinner party, Sunday evening? Meet your prospective students? Then, you won't be able to say no."

Alex gave the man, who claimed to be a god, credit for doggedness. Still, he wanted to confirm their original understanding.

"And you will be OK with whatever path we choose?"

"The choice is yours, consultant, prophet, dreamer, all futures will work," came the reply with the ever-present smile.

Alex looked to Victoria, who winked at him and then nodded to J. J., giving him a thumbs-up sign. After a brief pause, she said, "Sounds great. It's just been a dream so far."

Alex looked out to the ocean waves again, his anxiety level rising as his stomach churned. He wasn't sure any progress had been made.

TWELVE

Whether a man is burdened by power or enjoys power; whether he is trapped by responsibility or made free by it; whether he is moved by other people and outer forces or moves them—this is of the essence of leadership.

—Theodore White

Seven o'clock Sunday morning in Toronto's financial district projected the coldness of a cadaver. The sun struggled awake; the streets were quiet, the buildings ghostlike. Lonely pigeons dined as sidewalk gourmands, eagerly gulping down scraps of pizza crusts and forsaken French fries discarded from the previous night's partying.

In contrast, Gerry Schilling's executive conference room emitted the same controlled energy as any other day of the week. The group of individuals of five days earlier was again at the conference table, all in regular business attire: Gerry, James Waite, Ann Horowitz, Larry Kirkpatrick, and even the young treasury analyst, Ted Allaby.

In another time and place, a group dressed like this would be on their way to church. But not this group. Gerry had never bought into casual Friday or casual any other day. He felt casual dress was the first step to casual thinking, and casual thinking was the first step to a second-class business. His ideal was Thomas Watson senior, the godfather of IBM, which had become interchangeable with the term "Big Blue," the nickname for Watson's army of well-trained salespeople who followed his strict dress code of navy blue suits and white shirts. Gerry did not go this far, but he did require formal business wear at any company meeting, regardless of day of week, time of day, or place in the world. And so it was this Sunday morning.

Waite had called Gerry the night before to tell him that Ted Allaby had identified the stealth buyer. Gerry had requested a full briefing for the morning.

"I want to thank each of you for coming on such short notice," said Gerry opening the meeting, while Waite fiddled around with the computer linked to the screen on the wall. "I've always been proud of the caliber and commitment of our people, and the group of you lead the way. And special thanks to you, Ted, for such speedy detective work. So what do we have, James?"

Waite flipped a switch on the computer and moved into the presentation. Gerry found himself looking at his nemesis on the oversize screen. The man had the air of a pirate, with a tan, full, dark mane of hair, trimmed beard, dark eyes, and flashing smile of sparkling teeth. Gerry wondered if he had had cosmetic dental work.

"J. J. Jones was the silent partner in Genetech in its founding years," said Waite. "Something like Paul Allen, who was Bill Gates's founding partner in Microsoft. He left Genetech as a billionaire several times over in the mideighties. Since then he has set up several companies, the most successful of which is Imagen. He is a very private person and avoids the media. Associates claim he's a genius and unnaturally lucky in business. And seemingly a real people person, if you're on his team."

"You sound like his cheerleader," said Gerry grinning a humorless grin. He didn't know whether to feel threatened or flattered by the man on the screen, or both. He went on, "Tell me more about Imagen."

"It's been a success almost from the day it was formed. It has five products with revenues over $500 million yearly. More importantly, they have several exciting drugs in the final stages of clinical trial that should be approved next year. But the rumored blockbuster in the mill is an anti-aging treatment."

"Is it a match for Pharmaglobe?"

"J. J. Jones obviously thinks so, because he's buying our shares," replied Kirkpatrick. "And Ted's preliminary analysis agrees that it's a good match. No, make that a potentially great match."

Ann chimed in, "Jones has done his groundwork on this, Gerry. We're an established global company, with excellent marketing and distribution, exactly what Imagen needs. They have one of the leading research programs in the world, and it could kick-start our struggling efforts of late."

"Any drawbacks?"

"The biggest one is no surprise. Different styles. The cowboys versus the riding set," said Allaby.

Gerry looked at the previously shy Allaby with some surprise. What did the kid have for breakfast?

"Thanks, Ted," said Gerry. He smiled and went on, "Perhaps we should thank Mr. Jones for narrowing our search for a partner to merge with."

Gerry leaned back and continued to stare at the screen. Like many things in life, this match was so obvious it hurt to have someone else point it out to him. It bugged him that Jones had figured it out and had made the first moves. But that was OK. It's how you deal with the unexpected that defines the character in a person. Gerry was a long-distance runner. He was at his best against a strong opponent.

"Do you want us to develop an antitakeover strategy?" said Ann.

"Hell no. I want you to arrange a meeting for me with J. J. Jones."

"Sir?"

"Just the two of us. The only two people who can make a deal."

"But ...," interjected Waite.

"No buts. We'll seize the moment. We were looking for a partner to merge with. Turns out they were looking for us. James, please get me anything and everything there is to know about Jones and his key people. Check filings, track record with the SEC and FDA, and any issues," said Gerry, who then paused for a moment, looking triumphantly around the room, feeling energized now that he knew who and what he was dealing with. Now he could act: "And Larry, develop a scenario of a merger of Pharmaglobe and Imagen, strengths and weaknesses, pros and cons. Then arrange the meeting as soon as possible."

Gerry pushed himself back from the table and stood; he put his hands on his hips and stretched his shoulders back while he reviewed the next steps. He felt a merger story would play better than a takeover story, preserving his public stature as a leader. It would reduce the risk of too many questions about Pharmaglobe's research and its financials, questions that Gerry preferred to avoid being raised in public, if possible. Public stories could get out of control.

He finished stretching and opened his hands to the group: "Great work, team. I want to thank you again. Please enjoy the rest of the day. And please, take your loved ones to a favorite restaurant for Sunday brunch or dinner, courtesy of Pharmaglobe."

*   *   *   *

Gerry sat alone in the conference room after the others had left. Strains of Beethoven's Fifth played softly. He needed time to think. There were two big reasons he had to keep control of Pharmaglobe. First, and most importantly, Pharmaglobe was his creation, his child, and his lover.

Gerry scanned his famed "biography" wall, a wall covered with framed magazine covers and stories that had featured Gerry and his rise as a superstar CEO over the past twenty years. His eyes focused on the two in the center of the display. The left one was the front cover of the University of Michigan's alumni magazine. It showed Gerry shaking hands with the dean of business at the ceremony announcing the Hannah Schilling Scholarship Fund. It was a million-dollar trust fund to provide scholarships for students of merit in the Detroit area entering the business program at the University of Michigan who otherwise would be financially unable to attend the university. Gerry had set the fund up in memory of his mother.

To the right of this story was a *People* magazine cover that showed Gerry at the bedside of his wife Susan, who had been left an invalid by a massive stroke five years earlier. The headline on the picture said, "Gerry Schilling: A CEO With Compassion." It described the extraordinary steps and expense undertaken by Gerry to care for his wife. It told of his fund-raising efforts for the American Heart and Stroke Foundation, as well as his generous gifts of Pharmaglobe stock.

*   *   *   *

Born into one of the poorest families in Detroit, Michigan, Gerry Schilling was the only child of German immigrants. His father had died in a car accident four months after he was born. His mother, Hannah, never remarried. She worked as a house cleaner in the homes of automobile executives to support herself and her young son. Diligent and frugal, she stuck to the German community and never learned more English than necessary to get by. Gerry learned English in nursery school and the playground. They lived with friends until he was five, and then his mother bought their first house. It had been a day of joy and celebration, a place of their own in this great place called America.

Gerry excelled at school, although he did not join in readily with the rough playground games, preferring to watch at the edges. Hannah did not approve of unsupervised play. By high school, he was consistently the top student in his class and worked out enough to make the school basketball team. By his senior year, he was a little over six feet tall, and his voice had changed to a deep resonating baritone that was as distinguishing as his stone gray eyes. His friends used to say that Gerry's eyes could freeze the water on Lake Michigan. During high school, he became aware of how humble and poor his background was. Although he could make friends easily, he had found friendships faded when his richer class-mates found out about his mother's job and where they lived. His best friend, Paul Dabbs, whose father was a successful insurance executive and lived in the most expensive part of the city, harshly judged Gerry's rickety frame house with its sparse used furniture and stopped hanging out with him.

Hannah was his greatest supporter, his confidante. She mentored his dreams and ambitions. Her dream was for Gerry to succeed where she and her husband had not. Gerry came to understand that they had sacrificed everything to create an opportunity for him. Hannah had pushed Gerry. When he came home with straight As on his report card, she demanded to know why they were not A pluses. But she was always there for him.

In his final year of high school, Hannah was diagnosed with breast cancer. It was an aggressive case and well advanced when it was discovered. Within weeks, it had spread to the rest of her body like an invading alien force, consuming her life, cell by cell. Within another week, she was dead. On her deathbed she had told him to carry on, that she would look over him. On a more practical level, she told him where to find her papers, including her life insurance policy. To Gerry, it was guilt money. Some part of him felt responsible for Hannah's cancer, that her efforts for him had ruined her health.

*   *   *   *

He had been glad to get to the University of Michigan. A basketball scholar-ship supplemented Hannah's life insurance payout and ensured that he would not have to worry about finances. UM was a giant melting pot. Backgrounds were irrelevant. No one needed to know and no one cared where he lived, what his parents did. It was like starting life over. Again, his academic strength and athletic skill served him well, giving him campuswide recognition.

By chance, a roommate had set him up with the friend of his girlfriend, and it led to the romance of his life. For Gerry, it was more like winning a lottery ticket than falling head over heels in love. Susan Worthington turned out to be the daughter of Tommy Worthington, who headed his own drug company, which bore the family name. They were rich beyond any measure that Gerry had ever imagined. Susan fell hard for Gerry, and Gerry fell hard for all that Susan's family represented—wealth, status, refinement.

Gerry was torn. He liked Susan but did not love her. On the other hand, marrying her would provide a fast track to everything he needed to fulfill Hannah's dream for him. He hit it off with her father, and by graduation time Gerry had agreed to work for Worthington as a graduate trainee.

Yet Gerry did not rush into marriage with Susan, a calculated delay, as he did not want to reveal his deep wish for the instant prominence and wealth that such a marriage could bring. Susan, on the other hand, was smitten. She persisted in finding out where Gerry grew up and who his parents were. When she found out, she was nonjudgmental. She seemed genuinely interested in his life, his growing-up years, and the trials of his parents as new immigrants. But he always waited for the accidental slip that his credentials weren't good enough, given what she and her family had.

Susan persisted in her pursuit of Gerry. Their career ambitions reflected their needs to escape their pasts. She had gone into social work, wanting to help and nurture society's underclasses, while he scrambled to get topside and never look back. Gerry sometimes wondered if he were her personal charity case—a marriage of penance for the wealth into which she had been born.

They finally married when both were set up in their careers. Gerry had felt the time was right. Susan's father had urged him, Susan had urged him, and it could not possibly look like he was taking advantage of her.

For the next fifteen years life was good. Gerry rose to president of Worthington, while Tommy stayed on as CEO and chair. The company grew at a steady but not spectacular rate.

Gerry focused on the company, keeping just enough connection with Susan that she would not complain to Tommy. Meanwhile, he learned to nurture Tommy, taking up golf, joining the same clubs, and smoking the same brands of cigars. And, not surprisingly, he became the chief implementer of Tommy's vision for the company.

Not that Gerry didn't have a vision of his own—seeing Worthington among the top ten in the world, maybe the top five, pharmaceutical companies. He started to get edgy and bored, not wanting to wait until he was sixty or seventy years old to become CEO and chair. By then it would be too late.

One sunny fall day in October, circumstances changed in answer to his wishes. Tommy suffered a massive stroke and died within twenty-four hours. The board of directors was shocked. The founder and leader of a business for almost forty years was dead. The board looked to Gerry as the natural successor. It seemed that this was Tommy's wish. And it was Susan's too as the chief share-holder.

Over the next two years, Gerry's sense of triumph slowly turned to a growing apprehension as Susan took her role as chief shareholder more seriously than he had expected. Although she supported his elevation to chair and CEO, she had exercised her right to become a member of the board. She felt a duty to keep the company moving in the vision and direction established by her father. She turned out to be a quick study in corporate governance. Armed with this knowledge and steeped in the values formed in her youth and nurtured from her years in social work, Susan became a shackle around the neck of Gerry's dreams. He recalled her first board meeting.

*   *   *   *

"Why are drugs so expensive? How much profit is fair? Shouldn't moral standards apply to drug pricing for the poor, all the poor, Americans, Africans with AIDS?" asked Susan in her little girl voice. She had been greeted with polite smiles and patronizing nods of support from the other board members.

"Excellent questions," said Gerry, quick to assure her that she wasn't out of place.

"Yes Susan," added Eleanor Holmes, a senior board member appointed by her late father and a friend of the family. "Worthington is one of the most active members of the Pharmaceutical Research and Manufacturers Association of America."

"What's that?" Susan had asked.

"The group that represents the country's leading pharmaceutical and biotechnology companies, the ones inventing medicines that allow patients to live longer, healthier, and more productive lives."

"Sounds like a plain old self-interest lobby to me," said Susan gently. "I don't think it addresses my questions."

"I'll arrange for a corporate task force to review the issues and report to the board," said Gerry, trying to give Susan enough face-saving recognition before moving to the next agenda item. "Worthington's corporate citizenship program is recognized as best practice, but it may not be enough,"

Concerned, he spoke with her that evening before bed.

"Susan, you seem increasingly resistant to my vision for Worthington."

"That's not true Gerry. It's just that I don't like the word 'global' for my father's company unless, of course, it becomes a crusading, reforming global drug company. That way both of our dreams can come true."

"Come on Susan, you sound like a bleeding heart liberal, a latter-day Don Quixote tilting at imagined windmills. Worthington is a business, not a social service agency."

"Is it always one or the other, Gerry? Can't it ever be both?" Susan had replied. He didn't respond. If his vision was to survive, he had to keep her neutralized, yet satisfied.

He asked board members with solid business experience and sympathetic to his vision to mentor her in the intricacies of market dominance. She seemed eager and a good listener, according to them. Susan's zeal for her director's role increased with each passing month. She read all reports that went to the board for approval. She asked questions. She wanted to become chair of the strategy and governance committee of the board. Susan had become an impediment to his greater ambitions. Their different visions took an increasing toll on an already diminishing relationship.

Then one afternoon in May the problem resolved itself when Susan suffered a massive stroke. It left her an invalid, a vegetable. And it left him in control. In the five years since, he had grown Worthington into Pharmaglobe through a series of takeovers and mergers. He had moved the head office of Pharmaglobe to Toronto. He wanted the advantage of a big city, but he wanted to emphasize global by getting beyond the borders of the United States. He was thinking of the next steps of expansion. Pharmaglobe was knocking on the doors of the top ten pharmaceuticals, an industry that was going through significant change itself as biotechnology and drugs started flirting with each other. No one knew when the dance would end and who would end up with whom, but it was a heady time, and Gerry Schilling was viewed as an emerging star.

Now someone else might interfere with his agenda, might take his one true love away and threaten his commitment and his priority. He had to preempt any takeover move. He had to stay in control.

THIRTEEN

We do not see things as they are, we see them as we are.

—Talmud

"I'm glad you've arrived," said Argie, greeting Alex and Victoria at the door to J. J.'s mansion as if they were his best friends. Then he added in a worried tone, "I find J. J.'s family strange." The irony did not escape Victoria, but they had both agreed to enter into this twilight game until one of them shouted "Stop."

"Didn't they recognize you?" asked Victoria.

"Yes, perhaps too well. They're astounded by my likeness to the real thing."

"And Juno is pleased with you?"

"At first she was delighted," said Argie. Then, after checking around for eavesdroppers with his myriad eyes, whispered, "But then she looked at J. J. in a strange way and asked if I were a gift for her or a spy for him."

"So your status is unclear?" asked Alex, in a sympathetic tone.

"Somewhat. Mercury has been following me around as if he intended to kill me. I feel like a piece of meat. I much prefer humans."

Alex laughed. Victoria was less sure. She gave full credit to J. J. as a man of surprises. She was curious to see who or what could trouble a precocious android.

"Let's get some food first," said Victoria. "I'm starved, and we may not get a chance once introductions start."

"No problem. Follow me folks," said Argie, adopting the manner of a graceful maître d' and leading them through the house to the deck.

It was early evening; the tide was out and the breezes gentle. A six-foot ice sculpture of Jupiter and Juno rested on a concrete pedestal at the far corner of the deck overlooking the ocean. Victoria felt the display was needlessly extravagant, given the semitropical heat of a late Carolina summer; the melting ice couple looked as if they were covered in satiny high-gloss lipstick. She doubted that it would last to the end of the party. Under a canopy nearby was a table covered with a lavish buffet of tropical fruits and an assortment of seafood dishes. Argie led them to the table, and said, "Feast while you can."

Alex heaped a plate with freshly steamed prawns. Victoria settled for gravlax and several slices of melon. She wanted her food easy to eat while she focused on her main curiosity, this collection of so-called gods. She and Alex had agreed that they would split apart and talk to as many of them as possible, one-on-one.

About twenty people milled about, evenly split between the sexes, wearing luxurious, flowing togas that displayed key body parts to strategic advantage: pecs, biceps, six-packs, and cleavage. The golden rays of the setting sun brushed their radiant skin and glistening hair. The scene could have been an exotic photo set for tanning products and hair conditioners.

Victoria caught J. J.'s eye, and he came over to greet them.

"I'm glad you're here. I want to introduce you to everybody," he said, shaking their hands. Turning to his android, he continued, "Argie, get the group to stop their gabbing for a minute. I want to make an announcement."

Argie sounded a bell. Or did he make the sound of a bell? Victoria couldn't tell, but it got everyone's attention. J. J. introduced them as the special teachers who would do their makeovers, adapt them to modern humans, help them arrange an identity, and be their friend. Victoria sensed unease among the group with their concentrated stares at Alex and herself and the occasional side whispers. J. J., as usual, finished his remarks on an upbeat note.

"This evening is informal. Alex and Victoria want to mingle and meet with each of you for a bit. But be on your best behavior. They will help me decide who joins me first on our great adventure."

With that he turned to Victoria and Alex and, taking each by the hand, drew them toward the tall voluptuous woman who was standing to his other side and said, "Juno, my love, I'd like you to meet Alex and Victoria." Juno surveyed the two with skeptical eyes, remaining silent. In an effort to get some conversation underway, J. J. said, "Victoria has a real interest in our Olympian ways and would like to ask you some questions."

Then, taking Alex by the arm, J. J. pointed to an older man standing on the other side of the pool and said, "I'd like you to meet one of my oldest friends, Pan."

Victoria overheard the remark and looked in the indicated direction. Alex winked good-bye to her.

*   *   *   *

Victoria found Juno had the commanding presence of a private school head-mistress, head held high, with strong cheekbones, strong eyebrows, dark eyes, and flowing auburn hair to her shoulders. It was obvious she mesmerized J. J. and possibly intimidated him.

Returning Victoria's gaze, Juno narrowed her eyes and said, "I don't know why we need your help. It's never worked in the past."

Her words spilled out like the little cubes from an ice machine. Clever, thought Victoria. This Juno disagrees with her husband and wants to undermine his plans, if possible. If this was a practical joke, it was a complex one. If Victoria could get this Juno person on her side, then she might be able to find out the facts behind the fanciful charade that J. J. had produced.

"How do you feel about the role Jupiter has cast for you?" said Victoria tact-fully, wanting to the leave the door open for Juno to share her views, but able to close it if Juno felt she was sneaking around.

"He never knows when to leave well enough alone. But the sooner we get this behind us and over with the better," said Juno, sighing with frustration.

Her response perplexed Victoria.

"Get what behind you?"

"This crazy idea about making a comeback."

Well, thought Victoria, at least they agreed on the crazy part.

"So you don't agree with it?"

"No, I don't agree with it. Nevertheless, I'll bide my time while this game unfolds. And you, my mortal friend, would be wise not to venture too far into a foolish cause."

Victoria paused. Historically speaking, Juno was known as a jealous and argu-mentative goddess. Had Juno just threatened her? She changed the subject.

"I love your eye shadow. What is it?"

"Saffron, the finest saffron, I'm glad you like it," said Juno, the flare of her eyes softening; she showed the faintest smile.

"Oh yes, the color complements your necklace," said Victoria. She had scored a minor victory.

"And my sandals," added Juno as she held out her right foot in the manner of a ballet dancer. Victoria glanced from the amber and gold necklace to the golden sandals as Juno went on, "And I have it added to my perfumes as well."

"How clever, I must remember that." And not a bad historical touch, Victoria thought. How might this Juno find modern cosmetics, if she were the real thing?

*   *   *   *

"You two seem to be getting along well," said J. J., approaching his wife and Victoria. Taking Victoria gently by the arm, he said, "I'm sure Juno won't mind, but there's someone else I'd like you to meet."

J. J. was playing the good host, Victoria thought. Rule one, don't let your guests get stuck in conversation with the family bore. Victoria excused herself with external politeness and inner joy. Juno gave an imperious nod in her direction.

J. J. led Victoria to a young man sulking by the edge of the shallow end of the pool, introduced him as Cupid, and then quickly headed off again. Victoria decided this was his modus operandi for this evening, dump and run. Again she scrambled for words.

"Cupid, you seem unhappy," she said. Victoria, whose imaginative curiosity was increasing with each encounter, found this youthful god pleasing in looks but glum in manner. "What's wrong?"

"I thought there would be more female mortals here, you know, a wilder party." He measured his words. "Don't take this the wrong way. You are most beautiful but you are taken by your associate, Alex, and if not him, then Jupiter. We can all see that."

Victoria reacted quickly. She did not like strangers to view her as taken or owned.

"J. J., Jupiter, has asked Alex and me for help in his work. It is a business arrangement."

"That's how most of these things start," said the young man with sarcasm.

Victoria opted not to get drawn in by Cupid's baiting, smirking manner. She had outgrown guys like this before she finished high school. Besides, it was all acting. She continued, "Alex and I are just good friends."

"Well, the two of you could be more than that," said Cupid in a manner suggesting mischief, adding, "Would you like some help?" Victoria decided she didn't like Cupid, at least not tonight, perhaps not ever.

"No thanks. I prefer the real thing, no enhancements, no helpers."

"I'm really good."

"No thanks."

"Well if you change your mind, let me know. I'll fire one of my love darts at him for you."

"No thanks."

"And if you want to get rid of him I also have resistance darts. He'll never want to be near you again."

"Absolutely not. But it's good to know you have a range of talents."

Victoria excused herself. She wandered over to the buffet table, musing on Cupid's comments. There was a time she would have jumped at Cupid's whimsical offer to get Alex. It complied with her belief that sending energy messages into the universe can produce desired results. In college, she and Alex had been everyone's most promising couple. His intelligence and style attracted her. His career had started so well with McKinsey. Then he became preoccupied with religion. However, now he seemed to be on the right track again. She wanted to help him win her on her terms, not with some rinky-dink matchmaker.

FOURTEEN

As different streams having different sources all mingle their waters in the sea, so different tendencies, various though they appear, crooked or straight, all lead to God.

—Swami Vivekananda

The bell-like tones caught Victoria's ears as she gazed over the palmetto garden near the ocean side of the deck. A light and soothing melody came from a corner of the garden, where she beheld a man sitting on a bench, playing a golden seven-string lyre, shaped like an open shell. Absorbed in his music, he sang softly, plucking its strings with a golden pick, oblivious to his surroundings and Victoria's gaze.

"Apollo," whispered Argie who had joined her.

"I know," she said. This interactive antiquarian show just kept getting better. After Jupiter, Apollo was one of Victoria's favorite Roman gods. He was the favored son; he was the sun god, the god of prophecy, of musical and artistic inspiration, of archers, and of healing. As she listened to this master musician, who seemed so balanced in physical and psychic splendor, a crow landed nearby, as if it too was entranced by Apollo's music.

"Aah, the crow, Apollo's bird, just as the eagle is Jupiter's," whispered Victoria, trying to beat Argie to the punch for a change. Although she admired his knowledge, he had the maturity of an eleven-year-old, much too precocious for his own good. It had become a game, could the android outdo the human? Perhaps she would suggest to J. J. that he have his scientists program some humility into this marvel of silicon and plastic and do something about his looks as well.

"That's true, but not of this particular crow," said Argie, chuckling.

"What are you talking about?" said Victoria, equally impressed by how he was programmed to make the right sounds at the right time.

"I've seen this one in action. Watch this," said Argie, as he extended his arm toward the crow and fired a laser light out of his forefinger, growling, "Get lost you smelly old bird."

Turning, the crow grew several times in size as it defiantly expanded its wings. It then flew at him with its claws open. Victoria closed her eyes. When she opened them a blond-haired goddess, resplendent in a shimmering white robe, stood before Argie, staring angrily.

After an awkward silence, the goddess said, "How dare you insult me in front of the honored guest, you soulless fool."

Victoria stepped back, her heart racing, fearing for Argie. She thought the goddess might be a hologram, like the one in the movie *Vanilla Sky*. By now she was open to all possibilities. The movie scene was a catered birthday party for the Tom Cruise character, a filthy rich Manhattan publisher, in his magnificent apartment in the Dakota. A hologram of '60s jazz great John Coltrane, performing "My Favorite Things" on saxophone, provided entertainment. It had been the best part of the movie, but the hologram before her now was even better.

"Fair goddess, I had no idea it was you," said Argie in deference to the blond, his head bowed and his countless eyes showing remorse.

"Of course you didn't, you lower than mortal drone. Get lost yourself, and let me speak with our guest alone." Argie nodded to Victoria and waved good-bye as he moved away in haste.

"Who are you?" asked Victoria, perplexed. This cold-eyed beauty, formerly a crow and who knows what else, had the manner of a Viking warrior.

"My name is Morrigan. Some call me the Phantom Princess."

"But you're not of the Roman family?" said Victoria, thinking Ice Princess might be more appropriate.

"Absolutely not. Those days are gone, lost in mortal if not moral, history, as Jupiter knows well."

"Why are you here?" asked Victoria, wondering why J. J. was shoving an outsider in the faces of his Olympian family. Was he doing his own corporate shake-up by bringing in new blood?

"To help Jupiter, or J. J., as you call him."

"Why?" asked Victoria.

"Because if he succeeds, then I succeed. 'Hitch your chariot to a star' is my philosophy," said Morrigan.

Victoria nodded. Morrigan acted more positive than Juno and every bit as determined.

"What do you want of me?" Victoria asked, holding her breath in fear of what might follow.

"Simply this. J. J. will ask your advice on whom to select for his first team. I must be on that list," said Morrigan. Victoria felt a reprieve as she heard these words, but lost it, as the so-called Phantom Princess continued ominously, "For my sake—and yours."

Victoria's hands involuntarily crossed her chest over her heart. She gasped, "Mine?"

"Get a life. You need an ally," said Morrigan, with an a sigh, one hand resting on her hip, the other pointing at Victoria, looking like an older sister speaking to a naïve younger sibling. "You will have no choice but to choose Juno. She is a jealous wife with much anger, which she usually vents on mortal females who she suspects are dallying with her god."

Victoria reflected on these words. So far, everyone she had met thought she was involved with J. J. in some way. This was just another part of the charade. She didn't have to stand for it and burst out indignantly, "But I'm not. Don't degrade me based on his reputation."

"I know, sweetie. But life is all about perceptions, and Juno perceives too much based on imagination. She doesn't trust you."

"And what about you?"

"She doesn't like me either, but she hasn't figured out my powers yet. And she's jealous, because I am closer to a grand goddess than she." Victoria liked Morrigan, whoever or whatever she was. She seemed about the same age. She was direct in saying what she wanted and why. Of all the so-called gods that Victoria had met so far, Morrigan was the first one other than J. J. to whom she could relate on a personal level.

"Thanks for the inside advice," said Victoria, dipping her head in a deferential bow.

"You're welcome. Remember our conversation," said Morrigan, and then, without warning, dissolved into a crow and took immediate wing, flying to a nearby palmetto, where she perched. Victoria contemplated her new friend. Clearly Morrigan, as the dark bird, sat in the treetops to gain perspective on the party, observing who talked to whom and about what. What was her back-ground? What mythical group did she belong to? If Jupiter wanted to make a comeback, then what were all the other old gods up to? Golfing? Bridge? And why did J. J. go outside his family of Roman gods? As she thought about this J. J. wandered by.

"How're things going? Ready to sign up?"

Victoria laughed as she said, "I'm not ready to talk about that yet, still gathering information."

"Isn't that what consultants call paralysis by analysis?" he teased. "I need you and Alex in Toronto by Wednesday of next week. I'm closing my business deal with Pharmaglobe."

"No answer tonight, J. J., and you know that," said Victoria. Then she laughed again as she looked across the pool at an attractive man.

"Who's that?"

"Which one?"

"The taller one with the special smile for the ladies, the kind of guy I'd like to have at all my parties."

J. J. caught his eye and waved him over.

"Victoria, please meet Mercury, my special messenger," said Jupiter, and then he turned to Mercury and smiled. "Victoria is interested in your social calendar."

Introductions complete, J. J. again took his leave.

Victoria found herself on her own, face-to-face with that special smile.

*   *   *   *

Breaking the silence Mercury said, "Aah Victoria, you have the radiant beauty and elegant manner of the deathless ones."

"And you are as smooth as melted butter," was what Victoria wanted to say. Instead she smiled and looked down, embarrassed by his steady, brazen gaze. At least someone had finally commented on how she looked. She had worn white tuxedo pants with a satin stripe that trimmed each leg and a white halter top with a shapely fit, though fully lined. It also had a satin trim. White satin sling backs with straps adorned with rhinestones completed the outfit. Simple but chic. "Thank you, I'll bet you say that to all the mortal girls you meet."

"Trust me, you are the only one I have met in a while," he said and then in a more serious tone, added, "And at Jupiter's request, your wish is my command."

"I'll give it some thought, but I hear you're just a charismatic trickster who's been hounding Argie all evening," mocked Victoria.

"He's tempting all right, and he keeps such a careful watch on me," said Mercury as he nodded toward the corner of the pool, where, sure enough, Victoria saw Argie with several of his eyes on them. "He has nothing to fear, though. I'm just having fun."

Victoria thought of a good test for this charmer. "Rumor has it that among your other marvelous talents you can travel to the dead. Is that true?"

"Without a word of a lie, usually for special assignments," said Mercury, and as if reading her widening eyes, he went on. "And you are, without doubt, special. Jupiter said to treat you so. Is there someone that you wish to see?"

His reply caught Victoria off guard, but if there was a good way to challenge this endless practical joke, this must be it.

"Yes, my grandfather, Dev Mikhail, he died two years ago of a heart attack—I was his favorite grandchild, and I didn't get a chance to say good-bye," said Victoria, flushing and slurring her words as she let this personal information out to a stranger.

Busy on a major contract, with a deadline that was measured in days and hours, she had no time for mourning. Flying home to Boston on the morning of the funeral, she had returned to Washington that evening. Since then, she had not discussed her grandfather's death with anyone at work and had not given herself any time to work through it either. Now her emotions stirred, when she least needed to deal with them.

"Would you like to see him to say hello and good-bye?" asked Mercury.

Victoria laughed without hesitation. Even James Van Praagh and John Edwards, the celebrity spiritualists, didn't promise this much. They only talked to heaven. And any time she had seen them on TV, it seemed they always got a faulty connection, like somebody yelling at you from the bottom of a swimming pool. They always needed the help of a caller or a member of the audience to clarify the message. James Van Praagh would say, "I'm hearing something about mud, a lake, something murky. Does that mean anything?"

"Oh my God," a caller would say, "My Uncle Jake, he drowned in a mud puddle. Oh James, what is he saying?"

Van Praagh would then look at his pad, stare hard into the middle distance of the TV camera that presumably had the red light flashing to signal that it was the one for him to pay attention to. He would frown, write on his pad, and then speak rapidly, barely moving his lips in his best stream of consciousness manner. "Smoking, something about smoking."

Out of nowhere the caller would shriek. "Incredible. This is so incredible, James. That's him. He was smoking marijuana when he drowned. Oh thank you, you are so wonderful."

At this point, Van Praagh would become animated and explain how he was just a humble medium and that he was glad to be of help. Sometimes the words would have no meaning to the listener at all, in which case James would blame it on a bad connection.

Communicating with the other side was not always easy. Victoria smiled at the thought. Now this marvel man before her offered to take her literally over to the other side. Her giddiness surprised her.

Mercury interrupted her thoughts. "Well, yes or no?"

She looked straight into his eyes, "In my dreams always, but you know that can't be done. What game are you guys playing?"

Mercury continued, unaffected by her skeptical tone, "No games. Jupiter told me to help you in any way that would give you confidence in who we are. He thought you might make such a request."

Victoria felt both exhilaration and terror, but she managed to gasp, "Well, carpe diem."

"You speak Latin?"

"No, it's just a popular expression, 'Seize the day,' the moment in this case. I'm willing if you are."

"Let's go then. My steed awaits."

Victoria stifled a laugh at the thought of a magical steed appearing amid this conclave of the rich. Mercury guided her to the stairs that led from the deck down to the beach. Shadows were growing with the retreat of the sun; the breezes caressed the shores, lulling this part of the world to a peaceful sleep.

FIFTEEN

*Personally, I would be delighted if there were a life after death, espe-
cially if it permitted me to continue to learn about this world and
others, if it gave me a chance to discover how history turns out.*

—Carl Sagan

As they reached the pathway between the dunes and deck, Victoria asked, "Are
we going far?"

Mercury looked puzzled, and replied anxiously, "Have you changed your
mind?"

"Definitely not, but walking in this sand is difficult in low heels. Just a second," said Victoria, stooping over to take off her shoes. She placed them neatly
by the steps. "I can get these when we return."

Mercury waited until she finished and then he whistled. Victoria heard a rushing noise and looked out on the water to see a large wave forming. The wave soon
crested and curled over on itself and then, like a roll of fine fabric, unraveled to
display a wall of sparkling silver before crashing into luxuriant mounds of surf.
Out of this surf came a glistening golden stallion at a full run. It galloped across
the sand toward them and stopped at the feet of Mercury, bending its head
toward him, announcing his arrival.

Struck by the sheer boldness of the scene, Victoria breathed out softly, her
mouth partially open in a smile of awe. Unformed words struggled in her throat

only to produce a small cough. Mercury did not notice and said, "This is my great steed, Traveler. He helps carry my guests across the boundaries of time."

He turned to Traveler, patted his nose, and said, "Say hello to Victoria, boy— she wants us to take her to her grandfather."

Traveler lifted his head high, and snorted and whinnied, as if this was the best news he had heard in a while. Mercury turned to Victoria again. "Are you ready to leave the sand and water and time temporarily?"

Victoria simply nodded her agreement. Mercury helped her onto Traveler and then got up behind her. "Hold onto his neck and mane as tight as you can. I'll hold you secure."

This was a more intimate riding arrangement than she would have preferred. But her anticipation and curiosity was greater than any discomfort she felt. Mercury took the reins and signaled Traveler that it was time to go.

Within minutes, Traveler's mane flew back as he charged along the sands of the beach away from the sun. The clear evening gave way to a mysterious mist that descended like a change of mind. Victoria could no longer see the sand below, the waters, or the shoreline, just the fine pearls of mist hitting her face. Traveler picked up speed. She squinted, and all she saw were swirling grays and white of the shapeless wafts of mist that quickly grew darker. The aqua musk of the sea filled her lungs. The roar of the ocean gave way to an even greater howl as if the waters and winds of the cosmos were charging at them. Her lungs felt full; her ears were splitting. And just as it seemed her body was about to be forced off Traveler by the winds, it all stopped. The sounds, the smells, the swirling forms of air, all went away.

She heard no sound. She had no sense of motion, no sense of smell. She could feel neither Traveler beneath nor Mercury behind her. She had a vague sense of light and warmth but could not tell if it was real or a state of mind. Then she became aware of her companions once more as she felt the fine velvet mist reemerge to cover them. Within minutes a sliver of light came into her sight in the distance, and Traveler made his way toward the brightness.

When they passed through the opening, Victoria saw that they were no longer on the beach. In fact, she could no longer hear the gentle lapping of the waves. The humidity had died down, the air was light, the temperature moderate. They were in a garden, a familiar garden with evenly planted rows of carrots, beets, and lettuce. The black soil had the texture of a lush thick carpet. At the end of the garden she saw a man in casual white shirt and khaki pants sitting on a bench with his back to them.

Mercury whispered to her, "I'll let you get down here. You can go over to the gentleman and tell him who you are looking for."

Victoria wasn't sure where she was. She wasn't sure who Mercury was. She didn't know enough about weather formations to understand what had happened with the mist. Where had they traveled? Was this a teleportation to a different time? She walked across the garden path. Just before she got to the man on the bench, she looked over her shoulder to see what Mercury was doing. He was gone. Traveler was gone. They had disappeared without a sound. Her thoughts turned to the man on the bench. She needed this guy to help her get back to the party.

"Excuse me sir. Could I bother you for a moment?"

The man turned. Victoria screamed a cry of anguish that gave way to joy.

"Poppa?"

"Vicki? What's wrong?" he said, holding out his arms to take her in and hug her. "I haven't seen you in such a while."

She hugged him, kissed him, pinched his skin, and pulled his hair like a small child testing the strength and durability of a new doll. She asked him to whisper a secret in her ear like he had when she was a little girl.

He guided her to the bench. "Please sit down. We have so much to talk about. I want to know how you're doing, your job, your loves, your hopes and dreams. Do you like living in Washington? Do you have a boyfriend? What happened to that nice boy Alex? How's the rest of the family?"

They laughed and cried. It was too good to be true.

*   *   *   *

"Alex, come here. You must see this," said Argie, who was standing near the side of the deck by the windscreen. Alex excused himself from Pan and joined Argie. As he approached, he detected a delicate floral scent, but its source was uncertain. He did not recall a flower garden from his first visit. When he finally stood beside Argie, he saw a sunken garden that was just beyond the deck, hidden by the windscreen. This private area of the property could be accessed through a narrow corridor of rich foliage.

They stepped into the corridor and approached a horticultural smorgasbord of blooming azaleas, camellias, dogwoods, wisteria, and yellow jasmine. His eyes feasted on an endless array of inspired contours and shapes, twisting, folding, spiraling in an endless outburst of colors—golden yellows, sensuous fuchsias, creamy whites. Some colors were pure, others mixed. Multileveled small petals rivaled for glory with singular large ones. Some were opening, some were closing, others were reaching out

"There is Venus walking in the garden," Argie pointed to the figure fewer than forty feet from them. Alex had no trouble looking. It was hard not to gaze. The goddess strolled unaware of them, examining each flower and plant.

"Isn't that amazing?" said Argie. His enthusiasm intrigued Alex. Why was an android so excited by a beautiful woman? Was there more to his artificial intelligence than he had let on?

"Yes, she is stunning."

"Not her looks Alex. Lower your eyes. Her feet! Look at what happens when she moves." Alex looked down. With every step she took, new flowers—impatiens, tulips, and wild atamasco lilies—sprang up spontaneously. She was creating the garden as she walked. She transformed the plain by her simple nearness.

Argie sighed, "You are so unobservant."

Venus continued her walk, oblivious to her private audience.

Alex nodded agreeing as they watched her and whispered, "I wonder how she does it."

Argie shrugged. "Beats me. I could find nothing on the Internet. This has been a tough night for me. Wait until I report to J. J."

"Somehow I don't think this will surprise him." The anxiety that had plagued Alex since he had met J. J. had given way to awe at this party and, at moments, an awe of pleasure in witnessing such natural beauty.

"But I want an upgrade," said Argie. "I can't be fully effective if I don't understand all of J. J.'s worlds."

＊　　　＊　　　＊　　　＊

Victoria heard the stomping hoof of a horse and turned around.

At the end of the garden she could see Mercury atop Traveler. He motioned with his arm for her to join him. Victoria sensed that this was the end of her waking dream visit. It must be well after midnight. Her long absence would worry Alex. But he would surely understand when she told him why she had been gone so long. She turned back to Poppa Dev. "I have to go Poppa. Tell me what I should do."

The old man took her by the hands, "You must forget the past, forget the future, and forget the present. You must find a new path."

Victoria knew her time was limited. She did not have time for riddles and puzzles. "What path is that?"

Poppa Dev held her hands and smiled. "Follow your heart and steer with your head, and you will find it."

"That's all?" cried Victoria in distress.

Poppa Dev put his finger in front of his mouth to quiet her, then whispered with a gentle smile, "And don't linger too long on any mountaintops."

Victoria laughed. This was an old joke between them from her university days, when she had toyed with mystic philosophers and the idea of withdrawing from day-to-day life in a search for truth on some Himalayan mountaintop. He had always told her truth could only be found with others in the everyday world of work and play.

She closed her eyes and hugged him. Then she stood as Traveler whinnied again. As she took her first step toward Mercury and Traveler, she heard her grandfather's voice. "And Vicki."

She turned. "Yes, Poppa Dev?"

"Don't wait so long for your next visit."

*   *   *   *

The return trip followed the same pattern as before. The white pearled mist descended as Traveler's gallop quickened, and his mane flapped at her hands on the saddle horn. Soon the wind in her face and the motion of the ride emptied her racing mind. She was at peace again. Mercury held her to make sure she was safe as they passed through the howling, screaming winds and waves of time and space that had marked the start of the adventure.

At last they returned through the clearing to the beach, and she saw the setting sun was almost in the same position, maybe a little further down. How long had they been gone? Had it been a full day? They returned to where they had first met Traveler and dismounted. Mercury patted Traveler on his nose, saying, "Thank you, boy, for a job well done."

The stallion raised himself on his hind legs, giving a final whinny, before heading off into the surf and finally disappearing behind the translucent curtain of a falling wave. In silence, Mercury and Victoria located her shoes by the stairs and returned to the deck. To Victoria's astonishment, she found the party essentially the same as when she had left it.

She saw Alex standing by the bar and ran over to him. "I'm so sorry—I lost all sense of time."

Alex looked at her with a mystified expression. "What are you talking about?"

Victoria instinctively placed her hands on her hips. She could not believe his insensitivity. "Weren't you worried about me for being gone for so long?"

Alex now took her hands. "Are you feeling all right? You were only gone about ten minutes. What happened? You look like you've seen a ghost."

Confounded by the time reference, Victoria gathered what inner reserve she had left. Their aim had been to get as much information as possible, to chat to as many of these people as possible. Then they would compare notes tomorrow. Her mind drifted back to the last few hours. She felt the unworldly glow of her time with Poppa Dev. It was such a delicious feeling. At least to her it had seemed like hours.

And then a chill snuck up on her. Her brain was full, overflowing. Recalling their agreed-on signal, she said to Alex, "It's time."

"Is anything wrong?"

"Dumb question, Alex. Always slow on signals." Eyebrows arched to their maximum, she repeated herself, "It's time."

Recognition lit in his eyes. "Yeah, right. I got it."

He took her hand and led them to J. J., where they gave their thanks, said their goodbyes, and hastened out the front portico.

SIXTEEN

Passion is universal humanity.
Without it religion, history, romance and art would be useless.

—Honore de Balzac

With typical feline curiosity, Max watched Alex pull a blanket over the sleeping form of Victoria. He then jumped up on the end of the bed, positioned himself at her feet, and kneaded the blanket until it was just right to lie down himself. Purring throughout, the cat finally plopped down and looked up at Alex with a sleepy-eyed invitation. Although tempted, Alex demurred.

Although the last few days had gone well between them, they had yet to make up fully from their separation, and he did not want to take advantage of her vulnerability. Turning off the bedroom light, he headed to the kitchen, opened a bottle of red wine, poured a glass, and retired to the lounge chair on the balcony. The sound of the ocean, the stars of the night, and the magic of the wine massaged his body and his mind. What had happened tonight? Who could tell? Victoria would help him deconstruct the party tomorrow morning. His consciousness crumbled like a sand castle caressed by the advancing tide.

"What do you think you're doing slouching like that. You could fall asleep," boomed a voice above him.

Alex looked up to the source and rose right away from the chair as if yanked up by the sight. Before him stood a ten-foot giant with the head of a crocodile and the face of a man. Wearing a kilt embroidered in gold sequins, he stood with his hands on his hips. His mismatched, open tunic of linen revealed a muscular chest and a six-pack stomach. On his feet were sandals, one gold, one green, and on his left hand a decorative glove of corresponding gold and green. Recovering a portion of his senses, Alex realized the crocodile head was a bonnet that enclosed the giant's head except for his face. His upper and lower eyelids were painted with kohl eyeliner that extended in a line out to the sides of his face. A red cream exaggerated his full lips and high cheekbones. The fingernails on his right hand were yellow and orange, and his skin glistened with perfumed oil that had the scent of sandalwood. Could it be that he was an escapee from a Michael Jackson music video?

"Who are you?"

"Call me Stan."

"Who are you, Stan?"

"A friend of Jupiter's. He only allows me to appear in dreams. Thinks I'm too kinky for prime time."

"Where are you from?"

"I am Sobek, the crocodile god. At my peak, most Egyptians worshipped me as God of the Nile, and many others bowed before me as the great creator. Then flashy Jupiter and his Roman boys, Caesar and Mark Anthony, showed up, had their way with Cleopatra, defeated her armies and before you know it, I'm yesterday's divinity. But I got a nice severance package. And I go back and do contract work for Jupiter now and then, like tonight. He's a very civilized guy, you know. But call me Stan. It's easier."

"What do you want?" asked Alex.

"You know about dreams, Alex. I'm here to help you with the unresolved conflicts of your waking life, your romantic life to be specific."

Intrigued by Stan's connection to J. J., Alex decided to play along. If this is a figment of some misfiring neurons, unhappy with the vintage of the wine, it meant that he was the author of this strange conversation and, more to the point, the creator of Stan the crocodile god. Freud asserted that every dream was an attempt to fulfill a wish or deal with an anxiety. Residue of the day mixed with repressed wishes produced the fictions of dream work. And they were full of symbols that were puzzles in themselves. Freud claimed the meaning of the symbols varied by individual, but his errant disciple, Jung, argued for a collective unconscious made up of archetypes common to all humanity. Either way, Alex could not think of any special significance of a giant wearing a crocodile hat and decided there must be other dream material to pass the night away, so he prepared to make a polite exit.

"You want to get together with your girlfriend in the other room. What's her name?" said Stan.

"Victoria."

"Right, Victoria. Anyway, to get back together with Victoria, the way you would like, will need much groundwork and continuing sacrifice. From you to me, that is."

"I understand your offer, but I don't have the time for a lengthy conversation."

"Don't give up before you hear more. I'm flexible. Tell me more about you and Victoria. Do you still love her? Want her back? Did she bicker and complain? Women do that, you know. Did you fall out? Have you eaten meat recently? When did you last have sex?"

"Slow down, slow down," said Alex, stifling a laugh. Stan sounded more like his grandmother from his mother's family, whose prime focus in life was the link between men and women: how to make them succeed, what broke them up, what would mend them. "And I'm not sure I want to answer all of your questions. Some matters are personal."

"OK, OK. I hear you. But if you really want to rekindle Victoria's affection, I can give you the *je ne sais quoi* of attraction. It's an easy but powerful spell. But first you need to be in a state of purity. You'll need to go to the public baths, wash thoroughly, and dress in fresh linen."

"No way on public baths," blurted Alex. "I have my own shower. And no linens. Besides, I've haven't got all night."

"Alex, relax my boy. This is a dream where years can pass in a second. Got it?"

Alex paused. Stan spoke with an independence of mind that suggested he was the dreamer and Alex the illusion. He nodded and waited for Stan to go on.

Stan paced about on the balcony, looked out on the ocean, and then turned back to Alex.

"We'll keep it simple, then. All you have to do is bring me some of Victoria's hair and clothes to get me started and a quick shower for you. However, I'll expect a little more of a sacrifice from you."

"Sacrifice?"

"Stay cool. I only meant that you'd put in a good word with Jupiter for me. And maybe put me on your Web site. For those seeking old-fashioned religions with a water theme and a bite," said Stan who then paused and gurgled at his own cleverness.

Alex decided to hunt down Stan's credentials when he awoke. He didn't want to run the risk of J. J.'s ire. "What background do you have in making spells?"

"In my day I was big, huge, some might say colossal, in Egypt at least. I spent my days creating. I created the earth that made their bread; I made their trees grow. Always did cool god stuff. Fitting to time and place, of course. You know, making bulls mount cows and letting calves be born. In those days my eyes were fire and my fingers were serpents."

"Why the change?"

"Would you listen to me if I looked like that?"

"Probably not. Now, about your requests. I showered earlier this evening before J. J.'s party," said Alex.

"OK, OK, I'll overlook that," said Stan, in a conciliatory tone, "I wouldn't want you to overdo it. Anything else I should know?"

"Yes, there's no way I'm getting samples of Victoria's hair and clothing. How about a photograph?" said Alex reaching into the right back pocket of his pants for his wallet. He pulled it out, opened it and removed a small thumbnail size picture that he handed to the crocodile god.

Stan grimaced in dismay at Alex's words as he took the photograph in hand. He studied it for several minutes, first holding it close to his eyes as if counting pixels, then holding it as far as his extended arm would allow, squinting at it and then smiling.

"Nice-looking girl. Hmm, I guess it's worth a try. Get me a beer while I get to work in the living room."

Alex led Stan through the French doors off the balcony and into the living room, where he left him to make his preparations. Where could this possibly lead? What were the risks? He headed to the kitchen thinking about his predicament. Dreams don't need to follow social convention or physical logic. Although this one had certain tangibility; it felt real, it sounded real, and he could smell the perfumed oils on Stan's skin. He couldn't recall smelling anything in any other dreams, which were more like movies, sight and sound, but no smell. How about a "lucid dream"; was he having a lucid dream? To Frederik van Eeden, who coined the term, it meant mental clarity. Lucidity usually begins in the midst of a dream, when the dreamer realizes the experience is not occurring in physical reality, but is a dream. Often the dreamer, noticing some impossible or unlikely event, such as flying or meeting the deceased, triggers this realization. Certainly Stan was an unlikely visitor. Having convinced himself that everything experienced with Stan was occurring in his mind, Alex realized that he was in no real danger, and that he was asleep and would awaken shortly. But while he was here he might as well have fun, enjoy Stan. He might learn something. And he might get some insight into how to make up with Victoria.

A beer in each hand, Alex returned to the living room to find Stan at work over a wooden table that was new to the room. On the table were three bowls, containing ointments, a jug of milk, two pieces of paper with writing on them, and a green bar of soap. Alex handed him the beer.

"Here's to us my friend, I've mixed the potions and prepared the magic," said Stan, holding his bottle up to signal cheers. Picking up the bar of soap, he pulled out a Swiss Army knife from the pocket of his tunic, opened it and proceeded to draw a falcon-headed crocodile on one side of the soap and his name on the other. Alex's full attention produced a sheepish smile from Stan.

"My name and sign on the soap. Gotta manage my brand you know," he said. Holding the bar of soap out to Alex, he continued, "If you wish to win Victoria back, lick this soap and the power of the spell will be yours."

It's dumb and disgusting, but it's a dream and harmless, mused Alex, as he took the bar and licked one side of the bar and then the other, when, suddenly, he started to foam at the mouth. Stan's smile showed that he was pleased with the display of obedience, and obviously it was enough for him. He took the half-licked bar from Alex, dropped it into the bowl of milk, poured in his remaining beer, drank half of it and gave Alex the rest so he could drink the power of the spell.

Alex made a face as the liquid ran over his tongue and down his throat. Although he was unsure of the spell, there was no doubt about the foul, ammonia-like, soapy taste of the mixture.

"Good boy, we're ready for the next step," said Stan as he picked up a crude figurine of a naked woman, kneeling with her arms tied tight behind her back. All over her body, with a fine brush, he had written in tiny letters the names of Jupiter and his gods. Apollo on the breast, Mercury on the sole of her left foot. It was the image of Victoria. Alex felt ashamed, embarrassed, and shocked at the sight, but found himself transfixed despite or because of these feelings. In any event, the process was under way. Next, Stan took one of the pieces of paper on which was written the magic spell and fastened it to the figurine by piercing the body with several tacks.

"At first sight of the moon," he said, "we'll bury all this in the tomb of a male child who has died before his time, so his uneasy soul may carry your message to the powerful spirits of the dead."

Alex shuddered at the thought. Stan's performance was over-the-top, suitable for a David Lynch movie. Stan led them out on to the balcony, took a healthy gulp of his beer and then, looking up toward the moon, in a low, melodic voice whispered his spell. He then gave Alex the other piece of paper.

"Here, now you have to say it,"

Alex looked at the page of writing and groaned. But, sensing they were near the end, he began to read it aloud.

"I call on you, great Jupiter, ruler of the cosmos, victor of the night, who travels through the air. Order your gods and goddesses to go after Victoria, pull her by the hair, by the feet, so she is in continuous fear of phantoms, hungry, thirsty, sleepless because of her passion for me, Alex Webster. As a result, she comes to me in my bedroom, a burning need in her soul, a frenzied passion in her mind."

"I call on you, great Olympians, do not allow her to eat, drink, go out, or sleep apart from me, Alex. And I appeal to you great Jupiter and Juno and your entire court; bind Victoria so she is not fucked, buggered, cunt-kissed, or given pleasure by any other except me, Alex Webster. Drag Victoria by her hair and her entrails to me, Alex, and make her inseparable from me until death, head-to-head, lip-to-lip, belly-to-belly, thigh-to-thigh, sex-to-sex. Now, now, quickly, quickly."

As Alex finished, Stan took up his Victoria doll in his left hand and, with the other, plunged bronze needles into each of her vital parts. Alex's cheeks burned with embarrassment. Stan's actions mesmerized his eyes, while they churned his insides in revulsion. Yet he tolerated it because he had employed the old god to provide an urgent service. Besides, it was a doll in a dream that he could shut down at any moment, a dream with pornographic overtones of intense sexual passion and violent excitement. He continued to stare as Stan plunged needles in the doll's belly, genitals, and feet, thirteen needles in all, and as he pierced each one, he chanted: "I am piercing Victoria's hands, so she thinks only of you Alex."

Chant complete, Stan prepared to leave.

"Well Alex, it's all up to you now. I will bury the doll in a grave before dawn to seal the spell forever."

"Thanks, Stan."

"And remember me to Jupiter. He may need me again," said Stan with a wink.

"If this works, I'll not only do that, but also mention you on my religion matchmaker Web site, when I build it."

"You'd do that?" said Stan, obviously touched. Out of his tunic, he withdrew a small blue bottle.

"Here, take this,"

"What is it?"

"It's a perfumed massage oil for love and romance, when you and Victoria are ready to reconcile as lovers. You will both be pleased with the results."

Alex took the bottle, looked at it, studied it. When he looked up, Stan had vanished.

Shaking his head, Alex made his way to the bathroom, placing the bottle in his cabinet. Finally, Alex returned to the leather sofa in the great room and collapsed. The time for dreams was done.

SEVENTEEN

If there were no God, it would have been necessary to invent him.

—Voltaire

"You can't believe how much I appreciate this," said Victoria as she busied herself in Alex's kitchen, turning on his stovetop. "Where you do keep your frying pans?"

"Bottom cupboard on the right of the sink, top shelf," said Alex, still waking, "What are you making?"

"My favorite dessert, Oreo cookies fried in butter."

"I thought you wanted to talk about last night."

"First things first. This is my favorite comfort food when I'm stressed," said Victoria, speaking quickly as she sliced a huge hunk of butter into the pan. "I'm using two bags of Oreos. Do you want some?"

"I'll pass for now, thanks," said Alex, thankful he had remembered to stock up on her preferred sweet treat. He waited in silence as she finished her culinary masterpiece.

"You know that could probably kill your typical, middle-aged American male, clogging his arteries instantaneously."

"I might try it some time," she said, adding playfully, "Maybe starting with J. J. Jones."

"What are you talking about? Did he come on to you?" asked Alex, suddenly anxious.

"I wish it were that simple," she said, before taking another mouthful of dripping Oreo ooze and flushing it down with a glass of milk.

"Have you tried table cream instead of milk with that?"

"You're just jealous."

"Isn't it time to tell why we made the dramatic exit last night?"

Victoria placed her creation on the coffee table, leaned back in the tan leather sofa, took a deep breath and said, "OK. I'm ready."

*   *   *   *

"Awesome, simply awesome," said Alex shaking his head. His response was trite, but he could think of no other words to describe Victoria's story. As surreal as everything had been since his first meeting with J. J., her experience took it one step beyond. He had no intention of telling her about Stan.

"Had you ever thought about what being in the presence of a god would be like?"

"Not until earlier this week," said Alex, shaking his head slowly. "One of my religion professors used to tell the story of the little girl who was drawing a picture of God. Her mother came in and asked her what she was doing, so the little girl told her. The mother, trying to do the right thing, told her daughter that no one knew what God looked like. To which the little girl replied, 'They will now.' My profs said this was ageism, adults dismissing the views of children."

"What do you think?"

"He felt children viewed the divine with a natural sense of awe and terror. My feeling is that modern thinking has thrown an intellectual blanket over the divine. And now J. J. has pulled that blanket off of you and me."

"So you're still convinced that we're dealing with a group of out-of-touch gods?"

"Yes. I mean, I don't have any other reasonable explanation for now, but I won't give up looking for one. I do realize one thing, though, and that is that J. J. is not the god of myth, who can make things happen just by willing it so. He is a god of great powers and awesome power, but limited expectations."

"I agree with you. He could be humbled by his experience of defeat and reflection."

"Or it could be that gods are not the all-powerful entities envisaged in history. Perhaps there are limits to their powers. They don't know what is going to happen next."

"And thus they need humans?"

"Well, if J. J. is any example, they do. Perhaps the final result is based on a partnership of gods and humans. Who knows?" said Alex.

"Well, for sure, I don't. I'm excited, yet horrified at where this could take us. At the same time, I have this sense of inner peace from seeing my grandfather. It's as if it doesn't matter where all this will end. But still," said Victoria, hugging herself as if she felt a chill, "what do you think J. J.'s trying to do?"

"Something simple. He's trying to rebrand himself to become acceptable to a mass audience again. Think of him as IBM. It started out as a company that made cash registers, then it became known as a monolith that only sold mainframe computers and so on. At critical junctures it had to transforms itself to survive. That's J. J.'s challenge—transform or die."

"I don't get it. J. J.'s a god."

"Exactly, a lesser, forgotten god in the religious marketplace. Religion is like any other market, survival of the fittest. Look at the successful gods of today such as Allah of Islam. People are willing to blow themselves up for him. By comparison, J. J.'s ambition to take over a corporation is very modest."

"A niche market."

"Exactly. We have the choice of declining. J. J. will purge our memories of all that we have seen and heard, and we can return to normal."

"Amazing isn't it?" said Victoria. "It's as if he'd have us drink from the water of the River Lethe, the River of Forgetfulness, where, if thirsty souls drink its water, they forget about their previous lives."

"Exactly, but to go back to the way we were would be a form of death and reincarnation," said Alex, pausing only slightly before adding, "And given what I know now, I could never forgive myself for choosing a lesser path."

"Since when is a successful career and a happy family, without interference by some ambitious god, a lesser path?"

"You know what I mean Vic. You couldn't go back either, given what you know now. It would be like choosing to become a lower form of intelligence. Reverse evolution. So, no matter how frightening, I'm going to go with J. J.," said Alex. He paused again. "It's a personal leap of faith, so to speak, but I'll understand, if you choose not to."

Long seconds passed, and Alex's heart began to sink, simply based on the fact that Victoria needed time to think about it. Finally, taking a deep breath, she said, "Well, I'm with you. That was Poppa Dev's advice. Go with my heart."

"I'm glad you're joining me. A true joint venture."

"What a story. Two former lovers, bound together in fear and trembling, start a new business," said Victoria in her most somber business voice. Then, smiling mischievously, she added, "Besides, I'm a better negotiator than you. What terms and conditions do we want? How many of these gods do we want the first time around? How will we do it? When will we do it? Who would we like to work with? And would they be best for J. J. now?"

EIGHTEEN

"No talk shall be of dogs," said he, "when wolf and gray wolf meet."
—Rudyard Kipling

Gerry Schilling entered the crowded elevator to get to the fifty-fourth floor of the Toronto Dominion Tower for his lunch meeting with J. J. Jones. He hated elevators. He had never told anyone about this fear. He regretted giving Jones his choice of place for the meeting, as others squeezed around him. But it was a small price to pay for appearing flexible.

Was Jones onto his phobia? Probably not. Jones had selected Canoe, one of Toronto's finest restaurants, always popular with the business crowd. It was consistent with Jones's profile to choose the best. Coincidence? Whatever. He could hardly refuse the location for their first meeting.

Except for that concession, Gerry had planned every detail of the meeting, including time of day and day of week. Thinking through every scenario, he had developed and then acted out test scripts with an actor, who played J. J. Jones. He even hired actors to play restaurant staff to rehearse his response to embarrassing scenarios, from bad food, to personality mismatch with restaurant staff. For Gerry, an unscripted moment in a face-to-face business meeting did not exist. Every measure of J. J. Jones, the man who threatened his control of Pharmaglobe, needed to be assessed: his body language, his choice of words, his voice inflection, but most of all his eyes. Gerry needed to see into the eyes of J. J. Jones. And looking into those eyes, he desperately needed to persuade him that a merger was in their mutual best interest.

His only disappointment so far was that Waite's people had yet to come up with any real dirt. Waite's briefing on Jones had yielded no fire, not even smoke: no angry ex-wives, no girlfriends, and no questionable deals. However, he was patient. Everyone had skeletons. Even if they had to be created.

The doors of the elevator closed, and his body tensed; he felt imprisoned in a windowless cage. The fact that the elevator was full further increased his heart rate. He felt the first dribbles of sweat under his arms. His face flushed. He took a deep breath, closed his eyes, and started counting. It was an involuntary apprehension, something he could control, should control, but he never got around to it. He didn't want to let his doctor or some specialist know about a weakness. Staring straight ahead, stony, silent like a prisoner on his way to execution, he prayed his stomach didn't turn before they reached the fifty-fourth floor. He breathed deeply. He wanted to appear relaxed when he joined Jones. As the elevator rose, he continued to count, up to ten and then back down to zero. He could not let the gremlins of fear out of their cave.

The elevator jolted to a stop as it arrived at its destination. The door started to open to reveal the floor of the elevator about six inches lower than the floor of the fifty-fourth. Someone touched the close button, and the door jammed shut with an authoritative clunk, and all of Gerry's counting plunged back to zero.

"Jesus H. Christ," he muttered. This was a scenario he had not envisaged. He was just about to drown in a wave of anguish, when the door started to open again. Mumbling apologies in the form of commands, he shoved others aside to get out of the box before anything else could happen.

*   *   *   *

"J. J. Jones's table" requested the gray-eyed, stone-faced man to Carmen D'Angelo. Maître d' at Canoe for ten years, Carmen D'Angelo knew most of Toronto's established Bay Street stars and kept note of the aspiring financial gladiators. One person he hoped would become a regular was J. J. Jones, a man of warmth and graciousness. Jones always greeted Carmen with a wide smile, inquired about his family and interests, asked his advice on food and wine selections, and always wanted to know if any noteworthy guests would be lunching that day. Carmen had felt important in his presence. J. J. Jones was a man who knew value.

Today was special. Mr. Jones had arrived early to inspect his table overlooking Toronto Island and Lake Ontario, one of the most dramatic aerial views of Toronto possible, without leaving the ground. Pleased with the table and its setup, he accepted Carmen's final recommendations for lunch, wines, appetizers, and entrées.

"Your guest must be important to you," Carmen had remarked, his voice rising on the word *important* to create a tone that was somewhere between a question and a statement. Jones had just winked, smiled, and said, "His name is Gerry Schilling."

Now the *important* guest stood before him.

"Aah, you must be the esteemed Mr. Schilling," said Carmen deferentially.

"Right," said Schilling in a clipped response and then in anger continued, "and you should do something about that elevator soon, before someone gets hurt."

"But, of course, sir," said D'Angelo, quickly scanning this statue passing for a human. The eyes were dead, the tone unfriendly, the lips thin and unsmiling. In fact, the only redeeming feature of the man, in Carmen's view, was the fine Zegna black pinstriped suit, the cream white shirt, and silk tie with a gold and black weave. Unimaginative, but pricey, thought Carmen. What a contrast to the outgoing Mr. Jones. He could only speculate on what could bring two such different men together. He hoped the lunch went well for J. J. Jones.

As Carmen led the way to Mr. Jones's table, he noted his follower straightening his tie and clearing his throat. When they reached the table, Schilling had brightened, smiling like a television news anchor. Holding one arm up in hail greeting, and the other out to shake hands, he boomed, "J. J. Jones! I'd recognize you anywhere."

*   *   *   *

Gerry felt on top of the world as the elevator reached the ground floor. The merger was in, the takeover was out. And he found Jones a worthy opponent and a good listener, something rare in successful entrepreneurs.

His opinion of Canoe had softened. He could see himself returning to it, if there was a private elevator that he could arrange for himself. He liked its design—clean, simple, and unpretentious, yet stylish. He even complimented the maître d' on his recommendations. They had started with a baby spinach salad with prosciutto, mustard, and sherry dressing. The main course consisted of grilled Alberta strip loin done medium rare, with king oyster mushrooms, broccoli and russet potato hash, enhanced with a green peppercorn sauce. A perfect lunch for a meat-and-potatoes man, he had joked with Jones. The busboys served as magic elves, whose uniforms matched the colors of the wall panels so well that the young men seemingly appeared out of nowhere and then disappeared, wordlessly and unobtrusively.

He even allowed himself dessert, a vanilla bean panna cotta with fresh wild blueberries. He did not have wine, as he normally avoided liquor at lunch to set an example for all Pharmaglobe employees. However, with the deal complete, J. J. insisted that he relent to enjoy a postlunch, Canadian-content coffee infused with Yukon Jack, Canadian Club Rye, and topped with crème fraîche. He deserved it.

The conversation had moved from business to global economics and foreign policy. He felt he had found an intellectual peer who thought on the same grand scale that he did.

"What are your views on religion?" asked Jones, bringing him out of his reverie.

This was a topic Gerry didn't have much use for.

"I'll be frank," he said, "Life begins at birth and ends at death. If most people on the planet understood this they would live their lives differently. The world would be a better place and more productive."

Gerry looked around the room, making sure no one was within listening range, and then leaned forward, lowering his voice. "I'm skeptical of those who always try to find religion or some other mysterious force to fill out their inadequacies. Heaven and hell are here on earth, every minute of the day."

Gerry stopped. He recalled from the briefing file that Jones had met recently with some young religious scholar and, trying to retreat, said, "I hope I'm not offending you?"

"Hardly, it's an area that interests me, and I like your forthright assessment. It helps me in my own thinking. And it helps me get to know you. You're the man of mystery, you know," replied J. J.

"Look who's talking," said Gerry and laughed. They both were playing the same game. He liked being a mystery. It was part of his philosophy of life. "Being a mystery has its advantages. No one ever takes you for granted. When people know you, the relationship becomes predictable in every respect. We become clichés to one another, and that's the point at which you stop living. So once you know someone, it's time to move on, because there's nothing left to discover. It's all repetition, reruns without the payoff of residuals."

Gerry could not read the expression on Jones's face, but the gap, since his last word, was growing. Had he touched a nerve?

"Well put," said J. J. finally, his smile resurfacing. "I wish I had thought of that myself. It could have saved me years of grief."

*   *   *   *

Gerry had called his driver just before he left J. J. at the restaurant, and he was relieved to see him when he stepped out of the TD Centre on Richmond Street. The car was a new Mercedes S500 sedan. His driver wore a plain black uniform and held the door for Gerry.

Gerry slowed his pace to allow passersby to look at him and his luxurious car. He had enjoyed the recognition by the maître d' at Canoe when he arrived. Sometimes he wondered if he should have his driver hand out business cards so they would be able to tell their friends whom they had seen. Maybe his business card with a small token, like the latest quarterly report brochure for Pharmaglobe. Even better. He would get public relations looking into it. After all, it could be an innovative way to touch base with current and future shareholders.

A little old gray-haired woman sobered him with a sneer as she walked by the car. Maybe he would drop the idea. Shareholders might not like their investment spent on luxury cars. Anonymity had its privileges. He didn't view the driver and limo as a perk so much as an essential business tool for executives of his caliber. James Waite saw it as a risk management tool. Waite had given the driver his personal clearance. He was trained as an executive protection specialist and covered such details in Gerry's schedule as times, daily pickup points, transport, and evening events. Plus he was trained in defensive and evasive driving to help ensure the safety of one Gerry Schilling. Also, no time was wasted fighting traffic and looking for parking. The driver did not speak unless spoken to and kept his eyes averted in Gerry's presence, another royal touch that he liked.

Gerry reflected on the details of the meeting while his driver made their way through the afternoon traffic. Overall it had gone well. He had what he wanted from Jones. But there would be some critical issues to sort out. He liked Jones. He regretted that they had to be rivals. Everyone knew there was only one leader of a corporation. That is why the chair and CEO positions so often went to the same person. It was the only way the company worked efficiently. Splitting the positions between two people confused everyone—shareholders, customers, and employees. People liked hierarchies simple. A single vision represented by a single leader like Jack Welch at GE, Bill Gates at Microsoft, the Watsons through Lou

Gerstner at IBM. For now he could live with the split in roles. It was the price of a merger on his terms. If J. J. were close to retirement, it would be a different story. It could have been fun. But J. J. was too close in age to him with too much energy and too many ideas. Conflict was unavoidable. So the first order of business was how best to take down Jones in a civilized way. He decided to allow a year to achieve it.

Then there was the nuisance issue of the visit to Susan. Jones had agreed that Susan would have a seat on the board of directors of the merged company and Gerry would have the proxy vote for her, as long as she was unable to attend. To this point the meeting had gone well. Then Jones spoiled the mood by asking personal questions about about Susan. How was she doing? Would she recover? Could he visit her? Why on earth did Jones want to do that? Visit a vegetable? Indeed. Well, no harm in that. There was nothing she could say or do. And if it bought the advantage of an extra board vote that Gerry could use to advantage, so much the better. Going into this arrangement he would always have the deciding vote if it became necessary. And in his script, it would become necessary when they voted to remove Mr. J. J. Jones as chair. The thought of it gave Gerry a warm rush.

NINETEEN

Adopt the pace of nature; her secret is patience.

—Ralph Waldo Emerson

Sitting across from J. J. and Angela Cooper, Alex felt he and Victoria were at the Indy 500, next to the engines of two powerful race cars, primed and ready to go. J. J. was enjoying himself in direct proportion to Angela's annoyance.

"Be patient, Angela, the top job will be yours in time," said J. J. in a buoyant voice. He had invited Alex, Victoria, and Angela to meet him for dinner and a debriefing at Truffles, the restaurant in the Four Seasons Hotel, where they were all staying on this Toronto trip.

Angela looked up at the soaring ceilings. She then glared at her boss over the candle on their table. From Alex's angle, it appeared he was about to be burned at the stake.

"What is, *in time,* J. J.?" she said.

"Within a year."

Focusing on the flame, Angela nodded her head in slow motion. Alex speculated on the boundaries of friendly banter between the two. Did both know how far they could push the other? Most people found it after the fact, unable to bring back the words that could destroy a partnership. Then Angela spoke. "A year? A year of fighting in the trenches with that sleazeball Schilling? Is that my reward for loyalty, J. J.?"

J. J. tried to engage her. "I can tell by the flames in your eyes that you're not happy."

"Gee, J. J., you could be a psychologist. You read people so well," replied Angela with a roll of her eyes that sent waves of pure fury in his direction. "You think I'm not happy. I wonder why?"

"Yes, I wonder why," J. J. appeared genuinely puzzled.

What an act, thought Alex. He knew J. J. was too street smart not to know why. But J. J. managed to give his little boy hurt look. Angela wasn't buying it. "Let me give you a few hints," she said.

She clenched her fists around her knife and fork, as if they were her weapons of choice. She leaned into the table, shoving aside her appetizer, a mille-feuille of fingerling potatoes with chanterelle mushrooms and sweet garlic froth, whose cooling aroma now appeared to make her nauseous. "You know what you and Schilling remind me of with your big-time dealing?"

"No."

Angela pointed to the two whimsical sculptures of Uffizi boars that adorned the gated entrance. "See those? That's you two pigging out in style on the backs of your shareholders and employees, and most of all, me."

J. J. looked, considered the sculptures, and then teased. "You're always so creative in your anger. Not many people can do that. But I think you're taking this far too personally. Now what specifically are your concerns?"

Angela forced a smile. It was clear to Alex that she didn't want to use up all of J. J.'s patience, so she put her venting into a special little compartment that she used for such occasions.

"OK, my big concern is how we get through this year. Let me review my notes based on what you've told me so far. The deal you agreed to is more than fair to Schilling. You are chairperson, he is CEO. Pharmaglobe and Imagen will each get six members on the new board of directors. An extra board seat will be reserved for Mrs. Schilling, who is well cared for, but for all practical purposes vegetative and unable to speak. Meanwhile, as long as she lives or, by some miracle, recovers to take her seat, Schilling has her proxy vote on the board, thus giving him the deciding vote on any issue. Why do that? It seems suicidal to me."

"Let's come back to it; finish your summary."

Angela looked down at her notes again. "Now for my favorite part. Head office of the new company will be in Toronto, using the existing space of Pharmaglobe. Which means I have to give up my new house in Atlanta. Plus the winters here are dull and gloomy."

J. J. brightened. "If that's your biggest worry, consider it fixed. We'll be keeping our Atlanta offices, and we'll revisit the head office location once we work through the next year. You can keep two offices. Many people do that."

She wrinkled her nose and started out in a sarcastic tone. "I don't know about lots."

"Meantime, the company will pick the tab for a lakefront condo for you in Toronto and cover your commuting expenses from Atlanta.

Angela sighed with some relief at his words and then smiled. "Hey, thanks J. J., you sure know how to sweet-talk a girl."

"I thought you had just moved," said Victoria.

"I did. On Peach Grove Lane in an older section of Atlanta. I love the city in the spring when I can feel like a Southern belle living in a city ablaze with blossoms of white dogwood, pink azaleas, and the ever-present white magnolias."

"Toronto might be a break from the brutal humidity and languid days of summer in Atlanta," said Alex.

"And decorating a lakefront condo would be a fun way to occupy your down days, more likely hours, few as they are," added Victoria.

"I like it," said Angela.

J. J. called the server over to bring their entrées. Within minutes, the server presented Angela with a steaming dish of lobster à la nage with summer vegetables. The aromatic broth of the lobster whetted her appetite, and she started to sample her food.

Alex noted that J. J. had chosen well, as usual. They had much space between their table and other guests, so he did not worry about them being overheard. Large bay windows overlooked the handsome mezzanine lounge. And the high ceilings and stylized murals of French formal gardens gave a light feeling to a place that was well ensconced in the bowels of the hotel.

"So tell me, what's Schilling like?" asked Alex. He wanted to get J. J.'s first impressions of the man who would be king.

J. J. paused and looked to his side, a habit Alex had noticed when J. J. was organizing his thoughts and choosing his words carefully. "Gerry Schilling is a very bright man, and he was very well prepared, had all the facts and possible scenarios for a merger. He was clear in what he wanted."

"Sure, sure. That's why he's head of Pharmaglobe. What did you think about him on a personal level? Your gut feel impression," said Victoria.

"Polished, cool, perhaps too cool for my style, but that's no reason not to like him. He reveals nothing of himself, neither facts nor emotions. He had no obvious sense of humor. And again, you can say 'No surprise,' it was all in Angela's briefing notes," said J. J., using every opportunity to get back in Angela's good books. "So I decided to push the envelope."

"How?" said Angela, "How do you push the envelope of a black hole that sucks in energy and lets none out?"

"I asked him about his wife, how she was doing."

"Nice touch, given the exposure he has had as the caring, thoughtful husband," said Victoria.

"Yes, and he played it by the book. He said all the right things. However, my sense was that he has no real feeling for her now."

"Given the heartless automaton that he is, you mean," chimed in Angela.

"No, Angela, I want to be fair. Susan Schilling has been an invalid for five years, with almost no hope of recovery. To Gerry's credit, she receives top-notch care; he notes all developments, clinical trials, and frontier thinking that might be able to help her."

"So how did you push the envelope?" asked Alex.

"I asked him if I could visit her. Said I understood her condition. Said I wanted to do it because she would be a member of our board. And as a personal gesture of support for his sacrifice and trials over the past several years."

"And?"

"Caught him off guard. Not that he choked or coughed or anything like that. No, he stayed quiet, just staring, the way Argie might with a tough question. I had hit on something. Anyway, the silence went on for several moments. Then finally he said, that it was very thoughtful of me, unnecessary but thoughtful. When I insisted, he looked at me again, distrust peeking out from the dark pupils. The look of a wolf guarding its young."

"Or maybe eyeing its kill," said Victoria.

J. J. smiled and continued, "Well, you might be right. However, he agreed to alert the nursing care in charge of Mrs. Schilling of my visits and changed the subject."

"He didn't offer to come along?" asked Alex.

"No."

"Obviously. Why should he? She's unable to speak, so there's no worry of a slip of the tongue," said Angela, unrelenting in her distrust of Schilling.

"Interesting. A crack in the mirror?" asked Victoria.

"Possibly, but no more than that, and not enough to draw conclusions from. So let's keep an open mind on Mr. Schilling."

"Body language?" said Alex.

"Nothing. This man has control. Remember, he's been in the public spotlight for years; he has appeared as a witness before Congress and the Food and Drug Administration. His mask is on so tightly he may not be able to get it off, even if he wanted to."

"Just to let you know, I checked with my contacts at the FDA and SEC about Pharmaglobe," said Victoria, jumping in. "Officially, their record is clean, but my contacts have an uneasy feeling about the company."

"Why?"

"Well, all the submissions and results have been in order, but they appear too neat, too well-ordered. The natural cynicism of career regulators."

"Well, you will have a chance to find out," said J. J.

"Meaning?"

"I want you to help Angela with the transition. Schilling and I agreed that Angela and Waite should head the transition team to bring the companies together over the next twelve months and complete the due diligence."

"I have dreams about that man, but not the kind anyone wants," said Angela, returning to the fray.

J. J. smiled knowingly.

PART THREE
DISCOVERING SCIENCE IN RELIGION

TWENTY

*If A equals success, then the formula is A equals X plus Y and Z,
with X being work, Y play, and Z keeping your mouth shut.*

—Albert Einstein

Alex, Cupid, and Argie swaggered through the bustling crowds, exploring Savannah's historic City Market like the three musketeers of urban hip. They were on their way to Club One, the city's hottest dance club. For the past month, the three had ventured out on Friday nights for fun. Although Alex had avoided the club scene when he was at university, he felt like a latter-day Margaret Mead, studying the urban natives who emerged only at night on the islands of make-believe known as clubs.

Club One had it all—dance club, gay bar, cabaret for America's leading drag queens. The Midnight in the Garden of Good and Evil Book Tour featured it because it was where the colorful drag queen named Lady Chablis, whom the author, John Behrens, had befriended, performed. It offered guests a smorgasbord of social and sexual choice mixing young and not so young, straights, gays, and preop transsexuals. They all came together on the multiple floors, to dance and let dance, to tease and be teased, until they faded away into the vapors of the early morning hours.

The main floor dance club was their destination of choice with its wraparound mezzanine and pulsing lights. Alex found that he enjoyed it more than he should have and felt like when he was eight years old, sneaking cookies before dinner. It was a perfect place to go with his two partners, an android and a made-over god, who blended in like extra vegetables in an already exotic stew.

This weekly trip to sample Savannah's nightlife had started as a celebration of completing Cupid's makeover. Victoria had dragged them out on the pretext of mentoring Cupid in social and mingling skills. Cupid was cast now as Carmen Cupido, red curly hair and midtwenties, although he looked a little older with his two-day beard. His dimpled chin and the constant gleam in his eyes added a touch of rogue mischief about him. Victoria and Alex despaired finding a suitable persona for Cupid. For now, he was cast as a contract software programmer and aspiring screenwriter. Cupid thought he would be a natural writer and producer of hit screenplays. The profile played to his inability to settle down and take anything too seriously and gave vent to his creative ways of having fun. The only areas he had to learn with expert skill were swearing, drinking, and shaving every third day.

His idea of fun for the last four weeks had been going into the clubs and befriending some shy, socially awkward young man, who typically had difficulty with the opposite sex. Cupid saw himself as Doctor Love to these forlorn males. He would ask the young man which girl would most likely make his life complete. After the man chose, Cupid would fix his eyes on the intended target for several seconds and then suggest to the young man to go over and say hello. By the end of the evening, the beauty would be draped over the shoulder of the tongue-tied young man, nibbling on his ear, stroking his hair, while his face and lips toggled between ecstasy and disbelief. Cupid would smile with smug satisfaction, while sipping at his favorite drink, a specialty of the bar called The Red Headed Slut, made of equal parts tequila, Compari, white and red vermouth, with a touch of Tabasco sauce.

Alex had no idea how Cupid performed these love transformations. He had pictured Cupid from his childhood as a cherub flying through the air with a bow and arrows, tipped with a secret love potion. In the club, he had never seen Cupid with any arrow, dart, or any other instrument. Nothing, except for the intensive gaze that lasted mere seconds. Was it a form of telepathy? Was it perhaps one of J. J.'s more experimental inventions, a love laser beamed from Cupid's eyes? It all seemed harmless fun that brought brightness into someone's life and a few laughs into others. But what happened after the couple left the bar? Was it like Cinderella? When the clock struck twelve did the spell disappear with the young man's dreams, when the young woman recovered her mind and realized who she was with? Could it be forever? He meant to ask Cupid just how long these spells lasted.

Completing the threesome was Argie, sporting a new physical persona. Victoria felt that with the forthcoming merger and the other makeovers, Argie should appear more normal so that he could fit in more readily with Pharmaglobe staff and the population in general. Argie embraced the idea of being able to merge more readily with the group in his new design. He was given final choice subject to J. J.'s approval. His choice had transformed him from the hideous multiple-eyed creature into a Brad Pitt look-alike.

Alex felt like a celebrity when he went out with Argie. Such was the effect of the endless stares and smiles he produced from women. Sometimes he felt jealous of Argie, and sometimes he felt sorry for the women who did not know that Argie's sex appeal ended at his neck. Or at least he thought it did. He had never asked.

If Argie had merely leaned against the wall in the club, he would have been a hit. But, as with most human actions, Argie had been a quick study in the art of the club scene and, for an android, had an incredible sense of fun. On his first visit to the clubs, Argie discovered that he could dance, after Victoria, who loved to salsa, pulled him onto the dance floor and taught him the basics. He caught on with the speed that a new baby learns to breathe; he led clearly, like perfect diction, with smooth breaks, and Victoria mirroring his every move. He navigated their steps like the winning skipper in America's Cup. He didn't start a move unless there was room. He watched where he was sending her, just in case others may have seen the same empty space. Once there, he'd look around to protect her from dancing bozos. By the end of the evening he displayed expert swiveling Cuban hip motion with the spontaneous choreography of a dancing Zen master, all to the whistles and shouts of onlookers.

On the second visit to Club One, regulars started to call him the Salsa King, and women lined up for a chance to dance with him. Everyone else just stood back and watched. While Argie dazzled the crowd with his dance steps, Cupid would survey possible candidates to serve as his love prodigy of the night, and Alex would watch with envy, while sipping at his San Pellegrino bubbly water with lime.

This was fun. They were finally beginning to get some payoff from the makeover project of the last six months. Victoria was in Toronto working with Angela Cooper and J. J. to help make the new merger work. She had managed to ingratiate herself with both Gerry Schilling and James Waite. Even more amazingly, she had arranged, through her consulting firm, to have Apollo, now Doctor Abraham Apollo, appointed as chief of research for the newly merged labs. Juno had taken up residence with J. J. in a large house in High Park, Toronto. She was a PhD in classics, and Victoria's firm had arranged a teaching appointment for her at the University of Toronto. Morrigan was set to be a human resources consultant, modeled after Victoria. Mercury was being groomed as a communications and public relations specialist to serve as spokesperson for the new company.

They were still looking for an opportunity for Minerva to join Imagen-Pharmaglobe. In the meantime, she had enrolled at George Washington University to study corporate and international law. Given the success of this first wave of makeovers, Alex and Victoria were ready to take on a second round of gods from J. J.'s family. Alex planned to fly up to Toronto and brief J. J. on the results of the makeovers and to discuss the next steps in the takeover struggle with Gerry Schilling. For now, his focus was on having a good time and starting work on his presentation tomorrow. At least he would be able to update J. J. on Cupid's steady progress. His Dr. Love routine would be good for a few laughs.

TWENTY-ONE

Love looks not with the eyes, but with the mind;
and therefore is winged Cupid painted blind.

—William Shakespeare

"Dudes," bellowed a voice from a dark corner. Alex turned toward the voice. He recognized one of the nerds from Cupid's first love matches a few weeks ago. His name was Baird something or other. In a minute Baird was beside them with two friends in tow.

"Dudes, meet Ernest and Edwin. Ernest is in deep need of your help, Dr. Love." Alex looked at Baird and then at Earnest who was shortest of the group, slouching, hands in pockets, eyes averted, and a dumb grin on his face. He fit the profile of the tongue-tied love-lost guy whom Cupid liked to befriend. The second friend, Edwin, a tall African American, shuffled reluctantly behind the other two. A sorrier looking trio he couldn't imagine. Why would the door attendant even let guys like this in? They didn't have the looks, the body language, or the wardrobe. He held out his arm to shake their hands. Ernest's hand was cold and damp despite the heat of the club. Edwin's grip was firm and his eye contact direct.

Cupid responded with a smile and a nod, then zeroed in on Baird. "Where's your ladylove, Casanova boy?"

"Oh, she couldn't make it tonight. She has to stay with her parents for the next few days," came Baird's whiny reply, "So what do you say, Dr. Love, can you help my friend Ernest here?"

Ernest gave a limp smile.

"Why can't Ernest look after himself?" said Cupid, teasing, as he swirled his black swizzle stick in his drink. Ernest slouched like a whimpering casualty of the style wars, in his too-short Levis riding too high on his stomach.

"He's too shy, and he feels he's not good enough," said Baird and then with a nudge to Cupid, added, "he ain't never been with a decent woman, at least the kind that you can set up."

Baird's words fed Cupid's ego. Alex rolled his eyes in wonder. He despaired for people who spoke like Baird; he felt sorry for their social plight. They were the hidden poor of mating America. Where did people like this come from? How did they survive and reproduce? Was there a secret society they belonged to, a Ku Klutz Klan?

"Well, Ernest, who would you consider a decent woman around here?" said Cupid, sitting up with his back straight and his head high.

"Oh god, Mr. Cupido, I mean Dr. Love, Baird told me what you did for him. I'd sure appreciate it if you could help get me hooked up with someone as beautiful as his fiancée."

Cupid smiled. Alex recognized the smile. It was the same smile all people get when flattery starts feeding the brain, as if their favorite mirror had been placed in front of them. Their eyes grow sleepy, hypnotized in the pleasure of self-adulation.

"Do you see anyone who might be of interest? What are your preferences?"

"I want to meet a sweet, innocent, next-door-type girl, with a spunky personality and a great smile," said Ernest, greedily ambitious in his dreams of love.

"Whom does that remind you of Dr. Love?" said Alex trying to pull Cupid's leg. This was a good opportunity to check Cupid on his extensive briefing on popular culture. Alex found the gods were OK so long as they were familiar with a topic. The risks occurred when they faced unexpected circumstances and relied on old habits that were not always proper. Especially Cupid, who preferred spontaneous fun to deliberated actions.

"Somebody like Mandy Moore, right Ernest?" asked Cupid.

"Oh yes," blushed Ernest, looking around the room of dancers, watchers, and wannabes. The music pulsed through them as they waited until Ernest finally pointed and said, "Over there, over there. That one by the dance floor watching that fancy couple dance."

They looked over toward Argie and his partner of the moment, a sensuous, tanned Latino who had as many moves as Argie. The room was coming alive with the vibrations given off by the two. The Latino's hip motions were in active competition with Argie's footwork for the attention of the whistling crowd.

They focused on the girl Ernest had pointed out. She was Mandy Moore with soul, an attractive African American dressed in a white tank top, short leather skirt, and low-cut boots. She stood with her friends watching the show, her arms and hips revving in rhythm to the music, ready to dance.

"What would you like Ernest?" asked Cupid. He was playing this out, enjoying each moment of anguish that Ernest poured out as he looked across the floor, the pained look of unrequited love. He looked at Cupid.

"I'd like her to like me, maybe even fall in love with me."

Cupid looked at the young woman. He gulped back his drink while he held his gaze on her. Then he turned to Ernest and said, "Consider it done, dude."

Cupid spoke with an authority that immediately brightened the face of Ernest. Cupid gave him a little push, "Now go over and introduce yourself before I change my mind."

Cupid, Alex, Baird, and Edwin watched as Ernest made his way to the young woman. He tapped her tentatively on the shoulder to get her attention. The young woman turned and looked at Earnest. Alex expected her to brush him off before he spoke. But no, she gaped at him as if he were a rock star. Her eyes opened wide. A smile blossomed on her lips. She opened her arms, leaned forward and hugged him.

"God," said Alex, "I wonder what he said."

"No need to say anything," smiled Cupid and then he stood, took a bow and added with the conceit of those who have never known failure, "It's a sight to behold, isn't it, when a man and a woman find love."

Alex wasn't sure this was love. It looked like lust. It looked like magic

They watched as the new couple continued their embrace. Ernest's eyes were as wide as a little boy's on Christmas morning when he gets his favorite Nintendo game, and the young woman continued her tender coverage of him with her arms and hands and lips. Cupid inclined toward Alex and whispered, "I wonder if I should charge for this."

"I'm not sure what J. J. had in mind for your role, but I don't think this is it," said Alex, although he saw its potential. It would be interesting if it could work on a larger scale. Then he thought of Baird, who was now engaged to the first love match and asked, "By the way, how long does this effect last?"

"Forever, or at least until they die. Unless ..."

The potential outcomes jolted Alex out of his fun mood, and he turned to Cupid and asked, "Unless what?—Are you saying that poor young woman is glued to that loser for life?"

"Yes,"

"Even if Ernest gets bored?"

"He may; but she won't."

"Do you think that's fair?"

"Should I send a love dart into him as well?"

"What did you mean by unless?"

Baird interrupted by sticking his hand between them to give Cupid the high five. "Put her there, Dr. Love; you have made my day."

"Think nothing of it, dude," came Cupid's reply, as he slapped his hand into Baird's. "And give my best to your bride-to-be."

Baird and Edwin wandered off.

Alex wanted to continue the *unless,* with Cupid, when Argie came over and grabbed them both by their arms and pulled them up. "Time for dance lessons guys; you two are my star pupils."

TWENTY-TWO

The illegal we do immediately. The unconstitutional takes a little longer.

—Henry Kissinger

An hour had passed, and Alex was ready to go. Cupid stirred his swizzle stick in his drink absentmindedly as he studied the denizens of the club. Argie continued on the dance floor. Ernest was with his new girlfriend by the wall, embarrassing Alex by the open display of lust. She was shorter than Ernest and he had to bend to bring his head closer to hers. She clasped her hands tightly around his neck, pulling him closer, while Ernest wrapped his arms around her small waist. Alex watched as Ernest's hands ventured down, cupping the young woman's buttocks, and then squeezing them provocatively.

Dr. Love had struck again.

"Well, Cupid," said Alex, as he tapped him on the arm and nodded toward Ernest, "it looks like another guy is eternally grateful to you, although I still wonder what these poor young women are going to think when they come to."

"Alex, they don't need to come to. They're in love. They only need their man."

"I suppose," said Alex, unsure. "As long he continues to love her."

Before Alex could continue, a voice interjected, "Excuse me, gentlemen,"

Alex looked up. Cupid turned around. Standing before them was the silent partner who had been with Ernest and Baird. He no longer looked like a retiring

wallflower. He eyes were narrow, his expression mean. He held out an identification card from his wallet.

"Allow me to introduce myself," he said.

Alex squinted but couldn't make it out.

The man continued, "Cleve Morrison, Detective Cleve Morrison, Savannah
Police Department, Sex Crimes Unit. I'd like to have a word with you two gentlemen."

Cleve Morrison delivered the request in the form of a command, as if he had
the full authority of the U.S. government behind him.

"How do you do sir," said Cupid, extending his arm in greeting, and adding
cheekily, "what kind of name is Cleve?"

The detective shook Cupid's hand warily. "Full name's Grover Cleveland
Morrison. You know, after the twenty-second and twenty-fourth president of the
United States."

"Were you related to him?" asked Cupid, as Alex's mouth dropped open.

"Son, does the color of my skin look white to you?" said the detective. His
manner was tired but patient, a man who knew he had the final power and could
afford to be humble. "Obviously it was my parents' idea. Anyway, I hated
Grover. Sounded more like a dog's name. So I used my middle name starting in
high school. Soon, everybody called me Cleve."

The history of Detective's Morrison's name gave time Alex to consider their
circumstances. His heart pounded in his ears; his pores opened like floodgates.
What had they done? The young woman. It must have something to do with the
young woman. It must have something to do with Cupid's play. What had he
missed? He had to stay cool.

"What can we do for you, Detective Morrison?" said Alex, wanting to take
control, if that were possible, before Cupid intervened with any more questions.

"I'd like to have a little chat with you and your friend here if you don't mind,"
said Morrison with seeming patience. He paused for a long moment while he
stared first at Alex and then at Cupid and then continued, "I don't know what
drugs you two are dealing in but I can assure you you're in a truckload of trouble.
Based on the behavior of that young woman over there I have enough to book
the two of you and take you downtown for questioning."

The implications of Cupid's Dr. Love routine exploded in Alex's mind. How
could he have missed it? He had been so caught up in the romantic, practical joke
of it all that it hadn't struck him how it might look to an outside observer. Attractive young women falling for unlikely, nerdy guys, making fools of themselves as

they submissively followed these mousy guys. It might well look like Cupid had done something to those poor young women.

"I can assure you we're not dealing in drugs of any sort. We don't use them. We don't deal with them," said Alex respectfully. His only advantage was the absence of physical evidence linking Cupid to the young woman. He hadn't touched her. He hadn't touched her drink. In fact, he had never spoken to her. Except for shaking hands with Ernest, there was nothing physical there either. They might be able to bluff their way through this accusation if they remained cooperative and discreet. Morrison would not believe the truth anyway. Alex prayed that Cupid would keep his mouth shut until necessary and then follow his cue.

"You won't mind then if we step outside and do a quick body search. And depending what we find, we just might have to take it further," said Morrison.

"This is a big mistake officer. We'll do anything we can to help," said Alex. What was the detective getting at? A judge's order? A search warrant for his house?

Thankfully, Cupid remained quiet, though Alex could see a faint smirk emerging on his face. He hoped Morrison didn't pick up on it.

"Damned right, a big mistake," snapped the detective. "Please follow me outside to our mobile command center."

As they started to follow Morrison, Alex leaned over to Cupid and whispered quickly, "If there's any way that you can undo what you just did to that young woman, do it now, do it fast and don't say another word and don't ask why. I'll explain later."

Alex wasn't sure if Cupid even heard him in the din of the club. He prayed first that he had heard him and prayed even more that Cupid was able to reverse the spell. While he was concentrating on his next steps behind Morrison, he heard a scream. Alex looked in the direction from which it came. It was where Ernest and the young woman had been. The young woman had stepped back from Ernest; her eyes were large as a dog ready for attack. Alex saw her just as she threw a solid punch into the nose of Ernest and as her voice carried above the music, "Get your hands off me, you fucking freak."

Alex felt immediate relief. That answered the "unless" question. Thank God for step one.

Morrison looked over, rolled his eyes, and otherwise seemed unperturbed as he said, "This way gents. Let's not get distracted. Looks like your handiwork doesn't last on everybody."

*   *   *   *

Once outside, they were directed to an unmarked police van. As they got in, Alex saw that it was a well-equipped surveillance control center. He looked at the command post, where he saw several laptop computers, but he could not read the screens.

What are these guys expecting? Alex scanned the communications gadgetry and said, "What a setup."

"Impressed? Besides, we also have three law enforcement radio frequencies," said Morrison with the satisfied grin of a man who took pride in his knowledge of technical detail and liked to tell others of it. He held out his hand like he was introducing his best friends as he continued. "The 16-channel mobile radio communications unit includes the radio frequencies of local fire and emergency medical services. There is also a portable weather monitor, a Coast Guard marine radio, an 80-channel programmable scanner, and a citizen's band radio. We are ready for anything."

"I'm glad to hear that," said Alex. He nodded in dismay as he glanced at the electronic listening equipment and photographic and video equipment. On two of the monitors he could see the inside Club One, the camera focused on the table where he and Cupid had sat. They were color monitors and the resolution was lifelike digital quality. They must be in deep trouble.

Once inside, Morrison's partner frisked them down, and then asked for their driver's licenses and Social Security numbers. The partner then took the cards and sat down at a laptop to type in the basic data. Alex's heart made an Olympic bid jump. He did not know what would show up on Cupid's identification. What if Cupid appeared as an illegal alien? Alex regretted leaving these details to Victoria. He didn't doubt that she had double-checked everything. Her strong suit was detail, thoroughness. But still, he should have gone at least to watch some of the what-if simulations that she had conducted with the gods so he could anticipate what would happen next. He tried to hold his breath. But he couldn't do it for that long without looking guilty and feeling faint. Instead, he concentrated on the slow breathing technique he had learned in stress management classes in university.

The door to the van opened and Ernest climbed in, breathing hard. Morrison glanced at him and then at Alex and Cupid.

"I'd like you to meet Detective Alphonso," said Morrison. "You met him earlier, I believe, as Ernest."

Alex felt his heart sink as he stared at the smirking Alphonso.

Morrison continued to question them.

"So what drugs you boys dealing in? Rohypnol, aka the Forget Pill, Trip-and-Fall or Mind Eraser? Or is it GHB? Sometimes known as Easy Lay, Woman's Viagra, Grievous Bodily Harm, Thunder Nectar, and Ink Jet Cartridge Cleaner. Or Ecstasy? Or maybe some special drug cocktail you've invented yourselves?" said Detective Morrison, the tone of his voice growing with a cold anger as he listed the various drugs used to ensnare unsuspecting young women. All the drugs were tasteless, odorless, and colorless. "You can make my job and your life a lot easier if you are just straight out and up front about things."

"Sorry Detective Morrison. As I told you before, never used drugs, sure don't deal in them," said Alex deferentially. He did not like the way Detective Morrison's cheek twitched as he stared at them.

"People like you make me sick. Playing with the lives of young women. If I find even a hint of any controlled substance you guys are going away for a long, long time.

The officers completed their search of Alex and Cupid. Finding them clean, Morrison clenched his fists so tightly they turned white.

"I have to admit you guys have a neat maneuver here. I watched you closely. Detective Alfonso watched you. We have you on tape. We have you on audio. And I'll admit, we haven't been able to figure out how you do it. But we'll find out. You think you're smart-asses, but sooner or later sickos like you trip up. And when you do, I'm going to be there, and I'm going to shove it right down your lying throats."

Alex didn't like the tone or the tenor of Morrison's voice, but he was unsure of how to continue. They were free of drugs; nothing had been seen. That was the plus side of the equation. On the negative side were the young women—smitten, silly, head over heels in love with the least likely men in the state. That was the hard evidence. That was an unpleasant track record. In addition, there were many witnesses to Cupid playing Dr. Love. And worse, Cupid had reveled in his growing celebrity in the club underground. Alex could only cross his fingers at what Cupid might come up with when questioned. He only hoped Cupid realized the trouble they were in.

"So tell me, Mr. Carmen Cupido," said Morrison. He turned to Cupid and continued, "Or Dr. Love, as you prefer. Do you care to share your secrets about what you've been up to in there?"

Cupid smiled and said, "All I do, Detective Morrison, is a simple thing. I give these young men confidence. As everyone knows, when a woman sees confidence in a man she turns to putty in his hands. Just look at Ernest."

Alex was impressed with Cupid's improvisation. He was a natural con, effortless, smooth, and convincing. But not for everyone. Morrison punched the side of the van, the twitch in his cheek now extending to the corners of his mouth and his eyes narrowed even more as he spit out, "You expect me to believe that bullshit?"

Cupid shrugged his shoulders and said, "I'm only trying to explain what I did. I didn't mean any disrespect."

Alfonso aka Ernest came over and whispered something in the detective's ear. Morrison listened and then turned to Alex and Cupid, looked at them with a cold smile.

"I just got the results from computer searches on your IDs," he said and then paused to study Cupid's face. He resumed, "Any idea what's showing up, Mr. Dr. Love?"

Alex held his breath. This was the scenario that they had talked about and performed in the makeover role-plays but to which he had not paid much attention. The scenario of what happened if one of the gods was pulled over, even for a speeding ticket and had to show their new IDs. How good were they? How genuine were they? He had relied on J. J.'s multiple connections to produce suitable documentation to back up the invented personae. As usual, J. J. claimed he knew best. But this was a best that Alex didn't want to know about because none of it could be legal.

Victoria had handled the multiple details and testing. What if the police stopped them? What if they ran their IDs through a computer? Would they even show up? And if they did, what would it say? That they had been dead for ten years? Or that it was an identity theft? Or that they have a criminal record? Would they have any record? Speeding tickets? Credit ratings? What electronic track record existed? He hoped nothing that was trouble.

Victoria had assured him their records were clean, perfect. No surprises. Even so, he could not recall a scenario of a hostile cop grilling them on suspicion of criminal action.

He could not forgive himself for being so stupid. He hung his head. His shoulders sagged. His legs felt weak. Date rape, drugs. God, it wasn't that he hadn't seen the sordid stories on the news and in the papers about women who had been victimized by body hunters of the night. Most of the abductions took place in the clubs. And now the Savannah Police Department suspected him and

Cupid of being among the dark stalkers. He had let J. J. and Victoria down. Would they survive this early test? His thoughts cleared as Cupid started to speak.

"Can't imagine you'd find anything there, detective," said Cupid with utter confidence. He was playing his smarmy self with a touch of respect, an aspect of himself, until now, unrevealed. It dawned on Alex that the gods had sat in on the detailed testing, which he had skipped. Serendipity. He didn't have to carry all the responsibility. And Cupid adapted with suitable behavior, respectful even, while assertive in his knowledge of the details of his mortal persona and his rights.

"My record is clean. I'd be happy to tell you my life story from when I was a little cherub if you want."

"Right you are Mr. Cupido. Just checking to see how well you know yourself. Spare me your childhood. But what is a Canadian citizen doing spending weeks in Savannah?"

"Canadian winters are cold. I'm a contract programmer, so my work follows the sun, or at least climates that I enjoy, like Savannah and, until half an hour ago, the club scene here."

J. J. had suggested they vary the backgrounds of the gods, some with American, some with Canadian, and some with British citizenship. It was easier to get valid Canadian citizenship documents.

"How about you Mr. Webster? Do you have any idea what your record says? It isn't quite as clean as Mr. Cupido's."

Alex's stomach turned. What the hell was Morrison talking about? His record was cleaner than Mr. Clean.

"I'm sorry Detective Morrison, I thought my record was blemish free as well," said Alex, hoping that his voice did not betray the revved up twin engines of guilt and fear that were roaring inside him.

"Well, it will be, once you clean up those parking tickets from the city of Savannah, Mr. Webster," said Morrison.

Relieved, Alex tried again to plead their case. "Detective, this whole episode is based on some misunderstanding," offered Alex. Cupid nodded and performed a slight bow.

"That may well be, Mr. Webster and Mr. Cupido. However, I must tell you there has been a complaint filed against you. One of the first young women who swooned at the confidence of one of Dr. Love's protégées, Mr. Baird, who you recognized earlier, turned out to be the daughter of one of Georgia's senators, Dwayne Burbidge. And the senator is unhappy that his dear daughter, product of private schools, student of Yale, would fall for the riffraff that she met in this club and plainly wants to marry and have babies with. Senator Burbidge leaned on Baird to disappear from his daughter's life. Baird, being a smart boy, understood the usefulness of money and the threat of power. He was ready to disappear. But the daughter. The daughter despaired at the thought of no Baird. She spoke of suicide. At this point, the senator can do nothing with the daughter. Baird claims he is innocent. Said it must be courtesy of Dr. Love's mentorship."

"I agree with the senator. Baird is riffraff at heart. You can't believe him," said Cupid. Was he being cute or baiting the detective?

Morrison shrugged him off and continued, "So the senator now believes someone has drugged, hypnotized, or otherwise taken his daughter by dark forces over which she has no control. Now I'll confess we have run every possible drug test on her. And we're going to test that young woman tonight even though she has come out of whatever state she was in."

"You are wasting the state's health budget on unnecessary tests," said Cupid as Alex winced.

"And if I find so much as a hint of anything like a foreign substance in her, you guys are toast. And you had better get your lawyers. As a matter of fact, I suggest you start thinking of lawyers anyway, if the senator's daughter doesn't soon snap out of her love malaise. Besides, I don't buy your story of giving them confidence."

"Are we finished detective?" asked Alex patiently. Morrison's briefing had given him time to pull together his nerves that had initially scattered like a sand castle with each kick of the detective's words. They had to get out of here. And if Morrison insisted on keeping them, he was going to demand a lawyer.

"For now, you're free to go, but don't travel too far. The long-term weather forecast for Savannah is real nice," said Morrison.

Cupid stared into the eyes of Morrison and then turned to focus on Detective Alfonso.

Alex recognized the look and took him by the arm, praying for a quiet exit. They walked away from Detective Morrison. After a minute of walking, Alex stopped and, like Lot's wife, chose to look back at the mobile unit.

He felt a chill.

Morrison and Alfonso were locked in a passionate embrace, deep-kissing in the middle of the sidewalk outside the van. Passersby had slowed to stare.

Alex turned back to look at Cupid. He thought he detected the ever-present smirk.

Cupid started walking again.

Alex said nothing.

TWENTY-THREE

To see and to be seen, in heaps they run;
Some to undo, and some to be undone.

—John Dryden

Alex and Cupid made their way back to Club One, a half block away, Alex feeling his future darkened by the last hour. He would have liked to go back to the beginning four weeks ago. Why hadn't it occurred to him that Cupid's powers would be socially unacceptable in the club scene? Probably any scene. The first order of business was to assess the damage. To this point, Morrison had not charged them with anything, had not asked for any search warrants, and the police were not following them, at least not that he was aware of.

"Are we in serious trouble, Alex?" asked Cupid, as they arrived back at the entrance to the club. The security guys at the door recognized them and let them through the velvet rope. One small break.

Alex walked a few more steps before he said, "Stay quiet and follow me. We have to get Argie."

Angry and confused, he said no more to Cupid. They wouldn't be in this predicament if it weren't for his obsessive need to show off and draw attention to himself.

Inside, the club had lost its magic, its allure. The music was merely noise. It was too loud to think, and the people appeared as monkeys in a zoo, prattling and posing to attract a soul mate or a sex mate. He went to the mezzanine surrounding the dance floor so he would be able to spot Argie more quickly. One of the male go-go dancers winked at him and waved; Alex nodded back, tight smile on his face. He remained polite. He didn't want to publicize the circumstances they were in. The place had filled up, a sign that Lady Chablis had completed her show and the crowd had moved down to the dance floor level.

Alex leaned over the rail and had no problem spotting Argie. There, among the flashing lights, he continued to dance as if the night would never end.

Alex went over to Shaun, one of the bartenders, and asked him to arrange for one of the servers to get Argie off the dance floor and bring him over to them.

*   *   *   *

"What's up, guys," said Argie with his ever-cheerful smile as he approached Alex and Cupid. As he reached them and took a closer look, his smile faded, replaced by a quizzical expression. "Alex, what happened? You look sick. Too much salsa and soda water?"

"We have to leave right away," said Alex. "I'll explain when we get to the car."

And so the three amigos made their way out of Club One, Argie smiling and waving at everyone he saw, Cupid looking perplexed and following Alex, whose dour expression matched his slumping shoulders.

As the three of them made their way along Richmond Street, Alex and Cupid briefed Argie on what had happened. Alex was thankful that Detective Morrison had not included Argie in the questioning. Morrison would have found something sinister about a high-powered android as an accomplice to two suspected drug dealers.

As they reached the car, Alex had finished briefing Argie. They opened the doors and got into the car in silence. Alex slid into the driver's seat, shut his door, and leaned onto the steering wheel resting his head on his forearms.

Argie started to ask Cupid questions, "Why don't you tell me in your own words what happened."

Cupid shrugged his shoulders, "Beats me, I mean I was only doing what I had always done, in a nice way even, matchmaking."

"And?"

"So suddenly the world is anal about everything," said Cupid.

Alex felt even worse with Cupid retelling the story. He had covered himself in a blanket of doubt. He barely listened to Argie and Cupid as they babbled on. There he was sitting in his car, on the worst day of his life, and with an android and a retread god chatting as if it were just another day, another discovery, and a new problem for them to solve.

"How long do your spells last?" asked Argie.

Alex's ears picked up like sonar detectors alerted to signs of life in a remote areas of the ocean floor. This was the "unless" question. Cupid had reversed the one in the club. How flexible were his powers?

"Forever," responded Cupid, "unless, of course, I undo them."

"You can undo them?" said Argie.

"I can undo them or I can change their intensity. In fact, not only can I make people fall in love, I can reverse the intensity and make them hate."

"It's that easy?" asked Argie.

"It's that easy for me, plastic boy," came Cupid's reply. "Except I have to be able to see the recipient of my signal. I have no idea who those young women were."

"I do," said Argie. "We know the senator's daughter, Jade Burbidge."

"Sure," said Cupid, "but there were three more."

"Well, I might do you a favor if you learn some manners," said Argie. "All three of them were fans of my dancing. Before you had cast your spell they had all come up to me and whispered their names and gave me their numbers."

"So, what are you going to do? Call them up? Tell them they are under a godly spell and you'd like to come over with Dr. Love to reverse it. Please tell how to get to your place?" asked Cupid.

"No, my dumb one, nothing like that. I too have talents."

"What do you mean?"

"I mean, you forget I'm fully wired. Let me display. OK, Anthea Prior, the young brunette with the long shimmering hair, manicured nails, and pink lipstick, from three weeks ago, lives in a beach house on Tybee Island."

Alex did not want to breathe for fear of interrupting.

"How did you do that?" asked Cupid.

"Exceedingly straightforward," said Argie. "I take her telephone number and use the reverse telephone service to find her address. Then I plug into a map service for detailed directions. I even have a satellite picture of her place if you want. Very simple. Alex can drive. I'll navigate. And you can do penance."

Alex perked up like a chirping baby robin whose mother has just arrived with a juicy worm and said, "How about the others?"

"Well, Michelle Costalato lives in the Victoria district, on Martin Luther King Jr. Boulevard. Elaine Entwistle lives in the historic district in one of the student housing complexes owned by the Savannah College of Art and Design. And Jade

Burbidge is at her parents' home in the golf community, The Landings, on Skitt-away Island."

Alex turned to Cupid with the unabashed enthusiasm of a pig in a trough, "And you said you can undo these spells?"

"If I can get close to these young women."

"Do they have to see you?"

"No, but I have to see them. However, I can enter their houses as discreetly and softly as a spring breeze."

"That would be a welcome change," said Alex.

"Are you thinking what I am thinking Alex?" said Argie.

"Probably," said Alex, energized at the thought of escaping their predicament. He went on, "You navigate, I'll drive us to each place, and Cupid will go into their houses and inconspicuously remove his spell. And we'll do them all tonight. You OK with that, Cupid?"

Cupid was wise enough to know there was only one answer. "Anything you ask, Alex, if it'll get us out of this state of affairs. Want me to make them hate their young men?"

"No," said Alex, "that might make things worse. Just getting them back to normal would be best or back to normal and maybe liking the guys a little bit so they won't lay charges or anything."

"Good as done," said Cupid.

"I need a coffee before we start," said Alex. He sensed it was going to be a long night, and he needed something to perk himself up.

*   *   *   *

Alex pulled up to the Dunkin' Donut drive-by window and almost immediately had second thoughts about the coffee. The server was a middle-aged woman with big hair that had seen too many dips in the peroxide pool. She was chewing gum with her mouth open as she leaned out the window, held out the coffee for Alex, and said, "There you go, hon, one large double, double. That'll be a dollar fifty."

Alex's heart sank. How could anyone screw up a simple order of coffee? He noticed her name tag on her uniform placed tactically over her left breast and tilted upward. He leaned forward and squinted as he tried to make out her name, paused briefly as he read it and then said, "I'm sorry, Debbie Sue, but I ordered an extra large coffee with two sugar twins and extra milk."

"Are you one of those health nuts, no sugar, no cream?" said Debbie Sue. "And by the way don't stare at my chest."

"I was not staring at your chest, I was only checking your name tag," said Alex. The night was continuing like a nightmare, where he had a lead role as an alleged sexual deviant. The accusation was bizarre. Why was he on the defensive? He continued, "I'm only trying to clarify my order."

"That fake sugar causes cancer, hon."

At least they were back on the subject of the coffee. He now went on the offensive, "And I said extra large, not large."

"It's better to have a little real cream in your coffee. Milk isn't right you know."

"Some businesses put the customer first," said Alex, regretting in an instant that he had allowed himself to show irritation. He had put himself at a disadvantage. Not a good idea with people like Debbie Sue.

"Sometimes the customer doesn't know what's good for them, hon."

Take control. Change the subject. Appeal to her sense of service, "I have an appointment that I have to get to."

"I always try to do what's right for people, you know what I mean, hon?"

"I think I understand," said Alex. He wanted to appear reasonable. But he also wanted to escape.

"All this fussing by you has caused a lineup. You're making others unhappy. They have to get to places as well, you know," said Debbie Sue, who then pursed her lips and blew a small bubble, which burst immediately.

She knew how to get him, pushing buttons he didn't know he had. He became argumentative. "I didn't create a lineup. I only want what I ordered."

"Some people are born whiners. Nothing is ever good enough for them."

Several cars honked their horns. Alex heard angry yells from the car behind him. He checked his rearview mirror and saw a man shaking his fist. He saw tattoos on the arm. A mean, unshaven mug, in need of dental work.

"How much do I owe you?" said Alex.

"One dollar and fifty cents, and it better be exact change."

Alex looked in his wallet, felt for change in his pocket, glanced at his two partners who only stared at him and shrugged. He looked out with his best nod of atonement given his angle in the car seat. "I'm sorry, I only have a twenty."

"Holy Virgin Mother. What did I do to deserve this?" said Debbie Sue, her voice rising.

"Honest. This is all I have," said Alex.

"Some people think I'm a bank machine. I think it's a form of sexual harassment."

"Isn't this a little extreme?" asked Alex. "After all, I'm going to take my coffee with sugar and cream. Believe me, I'm trying to help out here."

"I think I'll call my manager, or maybe 9-1-1."

Alex heard more honks; the guy in the car behind him opened his door, got out and yelled over to Debbie Sue to see if she needed help.

"He's been leering at me since he got to my window," she replied.

Alex wondered why Cupid had not stepped in to help. He glimpsed over to see him with his arms crossed, with his lips contorted into a shape that looked somewhere between a pout and a smirk.

"Alex," said Argie, "it is fight or flight time. The price of escape is twenty dollars. Actually eighteen eighty, and Cupid can drink the coffee."

Cupid winked at him.

Alex nodded, leaned out the window and said, "Look Debbie Sue, why don't you just keep the change for all your trouble."

"Why ain't you sweet after all, hon," said Debbie Sue, suddenly smiling again. "You all have a nice night"

Alex returned a weak smile and drove off.

"See Alex, you can manage on your own," said Cupid. Alex turned to look into the gloating eyes of his godly protégé and felt the loathing that one reserves for a colleague who could help out in a time of need, but for reasons of going one better, declines. Circumstances had defeated him for the second time this evening. Could it get worse?

TWENTY-FOUR

Science without religion is lame, religion without science is blind.
—Albert Einstein

Alex decided they would start with Anthea Prior on Tybee Island. It would be easy to check if anyone followed them as they made their way down the lonely twenty-mile stretch of Highway 80 passing through several traffic lights, over Bull River Bridge, and through the Fort Pulaski National Monument to their target. Within a half hour they crossed over Lazaretto Creek Bridge with no sign of pursuers and were on Tybee Island. Alex felt growing confidence in their plan. They had not seen a car in the last ten minutes.

Tybee Island was a small island, two and a half miles long and two-thirds of a mile wide. It was an eclectic place comprised of a growing community of writers and painters and a unique laid-back style. Although only four thousand families lived year-round on the island, it was a growing resort area, and the houses ranged from beach huts to million-dollar homes.

It took them only minutes to find the hut of Anthea Prior. Alex parked about a half block away, doused the lights, and turned off the car. He turned to Cupid and asked, "You're sure you can do this?"

"No problem," came the quick reply.

"As we agreed?" said Alex.

"Don't worry Alex, everything will be OK," said Cupid, placing his hands on Alex's shoulder. "I will go in, remove the spell, and return. There will be no trace, no sound, no sign that I was ever there. Watch me as I leave."

With that Cupid reached for the door handle, opened the door, and got out. He had not taken two steps when an evening breeze scooped him away into the night air as if he had never been there.

"Boy, I wish I could do that," said Argie.

"You've done enough," said Alex. "If it hadn't been for you we wouldn't be here for Cupid to use his magic to solve our problems. You've been the real life-saver. I wish I knew how Cupid manages to do what he does. It does act like a drug."

"It is effectively a drug. These young women are love addicts," said Argie in his usual knowing tone.

Alex started to feel sick again.

"What drugs?"

"Phenylethylene and opioids are the two main ones. Cupid knows how to kick-start a person's brain to produce these drugs internally when in the presence of a love object, usually another person. He is simply building on people's natural capacity to fall in love," said Argie.

Alex paused for a minute; Argie's explanation had an air of believability to it.

"I'm not a scientist."

"A weakness with all you dreamers, but I digress," said Argie. "Neuropsychologists have shown that infatuation is associated with increased levels of phenylethylene, an amphetamine-related compound. Interestingly, the same biochemicals are also found in other animal species like birds. However, it appears that this emotion wears out when it happens naturally."

"Why? People would bottle this if they could."

"And plainly Cupid can do that," said Argie. "But for most couples, after a buttery-haze period of attachment, the brain's receptor sites for the essential neurochemicals become desensitized or overloaded, and the infatuation ends, setting up both the body and brain for separation or divorce. This period of infatuation lasts for about three years."

"Which is why studies show divorce most often occurs in the fourth year of marriage," volunteered Alex. He may not know the science, but he knew the results.

"Exactly," said Argie. "The brain also produces chemicals called *opioids* when a person falls deeply in love. They are similar to addicting opiates. So what Cupid is doing is giving an indefinite supply of self-produced drugs. These young women are addicted to love in the same way others are hooked on crack cocaine."

Alex mused on the poetry of it all. The mythical god who uses scientific methods beyond the bounds of current knowledge.

*   *   *   *

Anthea Prior slept restlessly. Her dark hair traced a random pattern on her pillow. She had not slept well in the three weeks since she had met Tino Lopez at Club One. Her life had changed the moment she had seen him. The only moments worth living since then were when she was with Tino. She did not understand it. Her friends did not understand it. They told her she was mad. That she was too good for Tino. That he was a lowlife. A high school dropout. A dead-end job in the shoe department at Wal-Mart. But none of that mattered. This was love. This was passion. How else could she explain the urge to see him every minute of the day?

He made love like a dream. He touched parts of her no other man had ever touched. She could barely make it through the day without seeing him. She only felt calm and complete when she was with him. When he was away, she could hardly eat. She felt anxious, sick. She had never dreamed that love could be so beautiful. He had called her every hour of every day for the first week.

She sighed as she felt a gentle breeze caress her skin. If only that was Tino, she thought.

The breeze passed.

The air was quiet.

She felt in control of herself for the first time in weeks.

What time was it?

What had she been thinking about?

God, she needed to get some sleep.

Her boss was dropping hints that she had been distracted and had complained about her calling in for three sick days in three weeks. And thank God for digital recorders. Although she was a good court reporter who rarely missed a word, she recently had missed full sentences and took twice as long to complete transcriptions because she had to triple-check the audio record.

She needed to catch up on her rest. Maybe she would stay at home after work and in the evenings for the rest of the week and use the weekend as well to catch up. Why had she arranged to see that Tino guy every night? The sex was tolerable, but he wasn't her type. And he had that dead-end job.

She would call to cancel her dates with him in the morning. And then she would buy some chocolate and concentrate on her job. Time to get back in her boss's good graces again.

*   *   *   *

"Will this solve our problems?" asked Argie.

"I hope so," said Alex. "As these young women return to normal feelings and behaviors, there's less reason for Detective Morrison to continue the case. And I gather if the senator's daughter breaks her engagement to our friend Baird, there will be no pressure or incentive for Morrison to continue. Let's stretch our legs while we wait. We've still got a ways to go tonight."

Alex opened his door, got out, raised his arms to the sky, and stretched back. He felt he might return to the land of the living. He bent over to touch the ground with the tips of his fingers. As he did so, a sudden gust of breeze delivered Cupid before him.

"What are you guys up to? Doing your yoga while I do all the work?"

Alex looked up. He was glad to see Cupid had returned. He did not want to know details. He assumed this god knew his business of spells. He had a new respect for how advanced Cupid was. He had seen more than enough evidence of the results; the challenge was to make sure they used it in the right way at the right time. Most of all, he wanted to avoid a repeat trip to the murky side of applying their gifts.

Only three more stops to free the other young women from Cupid's gaze on this longest night of his life. They would leave Detectives Morrison and Alfonso to enjoy each other for a while.

PART FOUR
SURVIVING THE FITTEST

TWENTY-FIVE

I'm impatient. I get twitchy. When I get that feeling
I just go out and make something happen.

—John Cale

As usual, the game was close on the North American court of the Cambridge Club in the Sheraton Center on Richmond Street. Like a high-tech exercise machine that gauges muscle strength and responds with suitable challenge, Waite kept Gerry on edge in the squash court. Gerry leaned forward and tensed as the ball hit the wall; he anticipated the angle of return. With his Muscle Weave C-Max Titanium Dunlop racket, he slammed the ball into the left corner of the backcourt wall at a sharp angle. Perfect placement. It felt good. Waite lunged for the return and just missed the streaking ball. He stood bent over for a moment staring at the floor, then straightened himself and walked over to Gerry.

"You win again," he said, grinning as he held out his hand.

"Thanks," said Gerry slapping the hand of his foe of the courts, forcing a smile as he reached for his towel nearby on the floor. Wiping his dripping forehead and sodden hair, he didn't feel like he had won. He never felt he had won when he played against Waite. Instead, he felt used. He looked at Waite and marveled at his fitness and muscle tone. If he didn't have a six-pack, he at least had a four-pack. Not bad for a man of fifty. And what motivation did the man have to stay in such remarkable shape in middle age? He often wondered why he was masochistic enough to go back to the court time after time with Waite.

The two men had played squash since Gerry had first hired him. It was a passion that both men shared. With over forty-seven thousand squash courts in the world, they had tested their bond in every country where Pharmaglobe did business. Deep down, he felt Waite was more like a coach, a mentor in the squash court, helping him improve his game, but always two moves ahead of him. His only comfort was when he and Waite won the club's over nineties doubles championship last year, an annual doubles event in which the combined age of the team must be ninety years or over. But that was not enough. He had recently joined the Granite Club in North Toronto and had arranged for one-on-one coaching with a world-class squash player. His aim was to beat Waite decisively. He wanted to see surprise in Waite's eyes and, more importantly, surrender. Meanwhile, these games felt like the scene of a psychological mugging, conjuring up emotional storms from each previous bout and creating new mental scars layered on the old ones. Seeing how easily Waite was breathing while he felt his own heart pound, sweat escaping from his pores, reminded him of his own failure. He did not feel like a winner.

"Kill or be killed," gasped Gerry as he looked at Waite. This is how he reminded himself every day of his commitment to his mother Hannah to succeed. He read all the business biographies he could, Lou Gerstner of IBM, Jack Welch of GE. Someday he would write his own or at least get a ghostwriter to get it down. He had started to jot down his thoughts. He wanted to avoid the clichés of the other business leaders' books. Was it their words or their lives that were cliché? His voice rose in a rasping chant, "Win every minute, every hour, every day. Never let up. Eat your enemy or he'll eat you. That's the law of the marketplace."

"Sounds more like the Discovery Channel's credo for the insect world," mused Waite. Gerry let the comment slide. Waite never liked the slogans of the marketplace, yet he was the fiercest competitor of all Gerry's employees. The projects of the Bronx, in his teen years, had taught him street smarts. A tour of duty in El Salvador as a young officer had built up raw courage and endurance; one year as a POW, after capture when trying to save a friend who had lost a leg after stepping on a mine, had built inner stamina. Operation Desert Storm, where he was a junior general, serving as a special assistant to General Norman Schwarzkopf, had added tact, diplomacy, and savoir faire.

Waite cleared his throat and added, "People are only spawn in the food chain of destiny."

"Do you think?" asked Gerry, pausing to take a deep breath while he stared at Waite. He had chosen him because he saw a fellow traveler who could clear the back roads that would not be fitting for someone of Gerry's stature. Gerry sometimes wondered what Waite had tried to get on him; it was his nature to snoop. "Do you still have that fascination with insects and poisonous spiders?"

"You will learn more from army ants than from all the collected drivel of retired CEOs," said Waite.

"I'm always fascinated by what captures the imagination of James Waite," said Gerry. Waite never displayed much interest in the product lines or services of Pharmaglobe or its competitors. He was more like the perfect mercenary. He had gone to the highest bidder out of military service. But he had also demanded challenges equal to someone of his talents. So far Gerry had managed to provide them.

"Besides, competition is not about people. The creative destruction of the market applies to technology and products, not people," said Waite.

"Aren't we the philosopher today. Losing must make you humble," he said, watching Waite closely. "And you know you're dead wrong, don't you?"

He let his words linger, wanting Waite to get antsy, like his little friends. Why wasn't the threat obvious? Waite sensed it was a rhetorical question and stayed silent. After a long moment Gerry said, "You know how mergers work. Everyone making nice. Joint this. Joint that. Sharing. Respect. Face reality. Within a year only one of us will survive, either J. J. Jones, with his lead groupies Mss. Cooper and Malik, or us."

Waite's eyes sobered, a sign of progress.

"Now we've done this before. You know the drill. This is our golden ring, becoming a major global player. But we must get rid of Jones, Cooper, and Malik."

Waite frowned, then said, "Jones I understand. Why Cooper and Malik? Why not try to build a larger team. They have talents that complement ours. Surely the new company is big enough."

Anger and resentment on dark wings flew out of Gerry's heart. His eyes flashed.

"Psychologists call it the halo effect. Are you a victim, James?"

Waite held out his hands defensively as he replied, "Don't get me wrong, Gerry. It's your call. My point is simply that it might be worthwhile to get a feel for these two, assess the choices, and explore the possibilities. Malik is a real find. She could be useful to us."

Cooper and Malik. They are Jones loyalists and don't forget it. You know the leopard and spots routine better than I do."

"Let's shower and dress," said Waite. "Then I want you to review a proposal; I've reserved a table in the club dining room."

*   *   *   *

Gerry studied the briefing notes, and Waite watched.

"Sarah Orenstein looks like our powder keg. I can see Jones being smitten with her, making a fool of himself over her," said Gerry as he held up an 8 by 10 photograph of a young attractive brunette. "As usual, you've outdone yourself, James."

"We searched the country for this one," replied Waite with satisfaction. "There is no one who really came close to Sarah Orenstein."

"I love the way you have summarized her, brilliant, aggressive, attracted to power. Doctoral student in cell biology and genetics at UCLA, Jewish, feminist, atheist," said Gerry, reading from the briefing note.

"A 90 percent likelihood of some form of scandal with Jones," interrupted Waite.

"Yes, yes. And a pet turtle named Lucinda," continued Gerry from the list. "Where do you get this stuff?"

"Everything on the first two pages comes from the horse's mouth—Ms. Sarah herself, in various interviews."

"Likes Axl Rose," said Gerry with a frown. "Who the hell is Axl Rose?"

"You know how people define their lives by the music of their teens."

"Like the Beatles and the Stones?" said Gerry.

"You got the idea. The summary of our analysis is on page three."

Gerry flipped through the next pages, tapping his teeth with his pen as he read.

"Who is this Marcus McQuillan guy? Is he relevant?"

"Ms. Sarah's current love interest, and the icing on the cake, if we are lucky; he's better than a suicide bomber. I have a separate briefing note on him," replied Waite, handing Gerry another folder.

"What do you mean?"

"He's one of these nutcase activists, an antiglobal, antibiotech, tree-hugging fanatic," said Waite. "And, to boot, he is also a jealous fool in love."

"The philosopher Waite strikes again. And?"

"He will be our other instrument of destruction. Real destruction. All we have to do is lead the horse to water," said Waite. "But just to make sure, I've made contact with McQuillan, though he doesn't know the connection to Imagen-Pharmaglobe. He just thinks of me as a rich benefactor, James Watson, who supports his insane cause. I have already hinted that Imagen's research lab and executives are a threat to his vision of the world."

"Won't he check on you?"

"Not a chance. One, he's inadequately paranoid. And two, he's greedy."

"Good, James. Very good. Be sure you're as efficient when you plan your measures for Ms. Victoria Malik." Gerry smiled. He liked Waite's style, his sense of elegance in letting people arrange their own demise. All acts had effects. What Waite was good at, and Gerry approved of, was arranging affairs so the victim was also the designer, perhaps diviner, of their own demise. There would be no paper trail, no culpability that could lead to Gerry. The likely winner of a prison term, if there was one, was Marcus McQuillan. And the collapse of J. J. Jones would be his World Trade Center hit, total surprise and total destruction. Imagen-Pharmaglobe would be Gerry's New York City, the surviving beacon to the future; J. J. Jones would be ground zero, a vaporized site of rubble.

*   *   *   *

After Waite departed, Gerry had the server refill his coffee. He needed some time to think. He hadn't bothered to brief Waite on the fact that J. J. Jones was visiting Susan more frequently than he had anticipated. And he almost always brought Dr. Apollo with him. Why should he worry, though? She was no more than a vegetable. Ever since that afternoon in May, five years ago, when they were returning from a board meeting. It had been a tense meeting, and they had been on opposite sides of an issue. Afterward she had been remote and complained of an intense headache. That didn't stop them from arguing once in the car on their way home. Gerry recalled the scene. He had played it back many times.

*   *   *   *

"Gerry—I plan to hire an independent consultant to advise me on your proposed merger strategy—I want you to know before anyone else." Susan's voice was soft, but Gerry saw in her eyes that the intent was firm. He could not believe it. The new strategy would more than double Worthington's value within two years. Gerry attacked her as if his life was at stake.

"You've got no business raising these issues—we've had lots of consultants support my proposal, Wall Street analysts love it," said Gerry. His eyes narrowed and his lips grew thin as he went on. "All you ever do is slow down the board's business. You embarrass me and everyone else, and we're tired of indulging you."

"Excuse me, Mr. CEO, but I am a board member, I am the chief shareholder, and I have the right to hire independent experts if I want to test management's claims."

"You're just a stupid rich bitch who's an idealistic fool," said Gerry. The words had rushed out too quickly, not waiting for permission, not waiting for review. He felt regret the instant they were out. He felt instinctively their marriage was over. His life was over. He had failed Hannah.

Susan grew silent, but Gerry felt the anger simmering within her, sending waves of revulsion to wash over him. She held on to her head with both hands as tears welled up in her eyes.

When they got home, he opened his door, got out, and went around the car to open her door. As he opened it, Susan fell out onto the driveway. The live-in maid witnessed the fall from the study window and rushed out to help. Gerry asked the maid to stay with Susan as he went inside to call for assistance.

On the way to the house, he made a decision. He knew from Tommy's stroke that time was of the essence with a stroke or a heart attack. Getting Susan to a hospital was critical.

Gerry considered himself a moral man. But even with morals, life forces you to set priorities, make choices. His priority was his commitment to Hannah. He had to make a decision. His choice was to take his time.

He called the family physician first, Dr. Samuel Estate. It would take him at least fifteen minutes to come to the phone. No one ever hurried old Sam.

By the time the paramedics arrived, over an hour had passed since Susan had fallen silent. It turned out to be a massive stroke. Although they were able to save Susan's life, she had remained paralyzed down her left side and was unable to speak coherently. Gerry displayed the outward signs of a horror-stricken spouse; he was the ever-vigilant husband on the outside. Inside he was buoyant, especially when the specialists indicated that Susan might never progress beyond her current state of recovery.

Gerry arranged for their house to be modified to accommodate Susan in her now dependent state. He hired a full-time nursing staff to meet her every need. And he arranged to have her position left open on the board of directors, unfilled, as a way of recognizing his wife and expressing the hope that someday she might recover to take her place at the table once again. This served to reinforce the image of his devotion to Susan and the hope of recovery; it also gave him additional leverage with his own agenda on the board, as the other members deferred to Gerry as her proxy vote. Susan had become his bird in a cage.

He followed every advance in treatment; he became a leading fund-raiser to help stroke victims. And down deep, he kept his fingers crossed that things didn't progress too quickly.

Gerry held the keys to his future, his fortune, and his fame. He did not have to worry about divorce. He did not have to worry about loving Susan. He just had to pay to keep her caged and cared for. He sent the children to private schools. He was independent. He was in control. The world was his to conquer, and that is what he set out to do. His commitment to Hannah was secure. That is the way it had been since that day in May.

But still, it would feel even more secure with the demise of J. J. Jones.

TWENTY-SIX

They see me as the rebel, the man who hated the establishment, the guy who did Easy Rider and caused a lot of executives to lose their jobs.
I'm sure they looked at me in all other kinds of ways too.

—Peter Fonda

Marcus McQuillan stared in his bathroom mirror. He liked what he saw. Jet-black hair, stylishly long to his shoulders, mustache, partial beard, trimmed. His hair glistened from a fresh wash and shower. He used only the best conditioners. He arched his eyebrows in approval. In another time, ancient Rome perhaps, this would have been the look of a patrician senator like Cassius, or a senator's son, or a famous orator like ... like whom? He had never been much for history and names. At the least he should have been alive in the 1960s, the era of free love and flower power. The age of potential. Timothy Leary. Jane Fonda. H. Rap Brown. The Doors. He could be Jim Morrison reincarnated. Now, almost a half-century later, the minions of the marketplace strangled the true spirit of the earth. Many of those minions had once espoused the power of love. They were turncoats. They had sold out. Marcus would never sell out. And he planned to take special revenge on those who had.

He, Marcus McQuillan, had launched a one-person crusade to save the earth from the sewage of market globalism.

Marcus dressed slowly, purposefully. Black turtleneck, the black leather blazer, the black Levis, black cowpoke boots. He walked out of his bedroom to the full-length mirror in the entrance to his apartment. He looked again at his image with shameless admiration. Ironic, he thought; though he dressed in black, his mission was simple, to act as the force of light against the darkness encompassing the earth. He chose action over routine, challenge over comfort, nature over materialism.

Although he didn't hear voices, only nuts heard voices, he had a feeling, a calling, and a destiny. Day by day that destiny became clearer. His position of assistant professor in the environmental science department at Oregon State University in Portland, Oregon, gave him the financial independence and career flexibility he needed to chase his dreams. He taught a course called Environmental Activism in the Modern Era.

His one-bedroom apartment suited his spartan style as a man of destiny. After years of study and intellectual debate with peers, students, and third-rate dregs representing corporate America, Marcus considered that ideas were without meaning if they did not lead to action. Every documentary he saw, every book he read, and every idea he studied told him the path of globalization and free markets was wrong. It was a philosophy of plundering by the haves of the have-nots, a plundering of the poor and underdeveloped, a plundering of the environment. Marcus hung out in Internet chat rooms of international antiglobalism groups and over time decided there was a need for a broader vision, a vision that someone like him could provide. A duty he did not take lightly. Gradually his ideas came together.

He would organize. In three years he had grown a new international movement, still below the radar screens of popular media, but growing. He had set up his own Web site and gave his nascent organization a name that he felt captured his vision, a vision that went back to fundamentals, origins. He called it Gaia Only Development—GOD for short. On his heady days he fantasized the great goddess Gaia had somehow chosen him to restore her reign on earth. The movement had grown rapidly and now had membership in the hundreds.

But for all his growing support, he still had heard no voices, received no sign. No, he couldn't say that entirely. Some events were a matter of interpretation. He sometimes wondered if meeting Sarah was his sign.

Beautiful, sensuous, brilliant Sarah. She had an IQ of 180, perfect breasts, full lips. They had met in his final year of postgrad studies at UCLA. She had just entered grad school. The moment he saw her across the room with her sparkling smile, his heart split open like the San Andreas Fault. He felt his body shake; he felt tremors in his chest. His mind lost its rational footing; logic slipped to the floor. A primal notion of speech was all that remained. He jumbled his words when he spoke to her.

"Uh hi, name's Marc's McKillern, uh, Marcus McQuillan," he had introduced himself. How could he blow his own name? Strangely, thankfully, a similar magic had occurred for her when she saw him. It had been a simple wine and cheese reception sponsored by the faculty as a way of welcoming new grad students. They had left the reception early and gone to his room, not to emerge for two days. They had survived on animal passion, pizza, and cheap wine that he bought in four-quart containers and kept in his fridge. "Chardonnay-on-tap," he had told her.

Not only did they match in bed, but also in spirit. She shared his passion for the environment. She encouraged him to develop his movement. She would be his disciple, she said, or better, his muse. And that is when he wondered if she were a sign from the goddess herself. Sarah as an avatar of Gaia. That is why he was shocked, appalled, disappointed, indeed some might have even called it heartbroken when she told him she had accepted an internship with Imagen-Pharmaglobe—a company that was on the top of his list of corporate enemies.

The phone rang to interrupt his growing sense of disloyalty by the only woman he had ever loved. This was the stuff of all those country and western songs he liked to make fun of. Maybe there was something to them. Who was calling? He went over to the phone on his kitchen counter and checked the caller ID. It said "S Orenstein—Imagen-Pharmaglob*e*."

Stupid fool. Using her business phone to call him at home. A traceable call.

"Hi Sar, what's up?" he answered casually.

"Hi Markie, how's my favorite revolutionary?"

Marcus didn't like when she called him Markie. Didn't like her teasing.

"Getting ready to see you in Toronto."

"You're coming here?"

"Business Sar. Somebody who's ready to support me, us, with big dollars. And the bonus is I'll get to see you," bragged Marcus.

"Who?"

"Can't say," he demurred. James Watson, the mysterious benefactor, had insisted on absolute secrecy.

"How do you know I'll be available?"

Always teasing. Or was she? He tried to be objective. She was the personal assistant to J. J. Jones and Gerry Schilling, both leading agents who threatened his view of the world. She was with them every day. They were rich, powerful men. She was young, vulnerable, and naïve. Those beautiful breasts, lush lips, and adoring eyes were with these men. Without his protection. The idea ate away from within his heart. She had told him it would be good to get an inside view. She would be able to help him, she said. Besides, the money was good, and she needed that to help with her studies. It would give her connections.

"Well, I know you have your high-power executives to look after."

"Oh Markie, J. J. Jones is such a charm. You have no idea. And he has really exciting ideas about the genetics of life extension," said Sarah in a voice that contained the enthusiasm of a child who has just received her first bicycle.

Was he jealous? No, he was too much an objective, rational man to be jealous. Betrayed? Possibly. When one's most devout supporter enters the enemy's camp, one had to allow for any possibility. Perhaps this was a test by Gaia, and perhaps Sarah wasn't Gaia's agent after all. He had to think all of this through. Whatever the answer, J. J. Jones and company immediately moved to first place on his enemies list. He would have gotten there anyway with all of his meddling with genes and life extension. He and his research team would be the first target of his new strategy of environmental terrorism.

"Well, if you're too busy?"

"Oh Markie, I'm only teasing you."

"And Sar, next time, please call me on your cell phone."

"I have to run. J. J. is calling me on the other line. E-mail me your times so I can make plans for us."

"Right, bye," said Marcus to the sound of a click. He was no longer happy. He needed a little comfort.

He returned to the mirror in the hallway. He plucked a few hairs from his mustache that stood out unrestrained. Each pulled hair represented an enemy pulled out and tossed away. If you didn't fall into line, you would not exist.

Marcus liked order in all matters. It was important to trim it neatly. A perfect face. Marcus remembered the Che Guevara posters from the 1960s. He wanted to achieve the same look. Icon for an era. More polished. He had already taken some photographs to some friends in media to see what they could do with digital image enhancement. The results pleased him and found their way onto his Web site, a growing shrine to his presence.

His thoughts returned to Sarah and her daily presence with two filthy corporate pigs who probably fantasized about getting her into bed. And she was so vulnerable and so naïve. The idea munched away at his common sense.

"Violence in defense of natural life and the environment is no vice," said Marcus to the smiling image in the mirror. "Principles without action have no value."

TWENTY-SEVEN

For among my people are found wicked men: they lay wait, as he
that setteth snares; they set a trap; they catch men.

—(Jeremiah 5:26, Webster's Bible Translation)

Midnight drew near as James Waite entered the Pharmaglobe parking garage six
levels below the ground in the bowels of the bank tower. He took his ID badge
and swiped it through the slit in the electronic card reader. The light on the
reader turned green. He had ten seconds to open the door. It took him fewer
than five. Only the top thirty company executives enjoyed the use of the parking
area, courtesy of Gerry's philosophy of perks for his favorites. Access to the executive parking garage came with valet service and other treats such daily car wash
and cleaning and arrangements for any car maintenance. All the mundane actions
that eat time, Gerry preferred them to spend on Imagen-Pharmaglobe priorities.

Operating staff from Pharmaglobe's fleet department, a unit that reported to
Waite through several levels of intermediate bureaucracy, were the only other
people with right of entry to the garage. To go from the men and the women ser-
vicing the cars to James Waite was like navigating a multilevel computer game
where he was the final prize. Waite had always made himself available to the car
jockeys. He knew not only their names, but also the names of their spouses and
their children. They would chat about the executive car fleet, which executive
drove which car. What it signified.

Some people say that dog owners come to look like their dogs. James thought car choice revealed a lot about a person's personality. Just the color told a lot. For example, Bruce Bowmen, the company's chief auditor drove a brown Cadillac DeVille, the most boring car in the fleet. Brown car drivers were mean, cautious, and conservative, just like Bowmen. Gerry drove a black Mercedes-Benz CL Coupe CL 500. Black car drivers are ambitious, no surprise. Waite drove a metallic blue Volvo S80 T-6. He did not want to threaten anyone, least of all Gerry. Blue car drivers were consistent and conservative.

Waite made it a habit to check on the choices of the top staff, not only the car they chose but also how they kept it. So it was not an unusual order for him to have fleet staff arrange for him to test-drive the car assigned to Victoria Malik. She had chosen a silver 350Z. Interesting choice. Silver car drivers oozed class, representing speed, power, and success. Not bad.

The car was waiting in his parking space, an enclosed area within the larger parking area. Waite did not like people peeking in his windows, no matter how privileged they were.

After getting into the car, he adjusted the seat for his long legs. The wheel sitting in his lap made him feel trapped, reminding him of his El Salvadorian imprisonment, so he adjusted the steering wheel higher to a more comfortable level. He drove the car to the garage exit, lowered the window and swiped his card through the car reader. It was 11:43 PM according to the car's digital clock. Two hours was the upper limit to complete his task and return to the car, the typical period for one of his test-drives.

And Victoria would be picking up the car tomorrow.

She fascinated Waite. He found her like a border collie. A workaholic, she was happiest when she had a job to do. She was a quick, busy, high-energy person, bred for endurance. Waite admired her for that.

She would herd people into a meeting, her head lowered, eyeing everyone with an intense stare as if they were sheep. She noticed every movement of the players in a room, and she reacted to any threat by moving, at times imperceptibly, to counter it, to make sure the key players stayed onside, her side. Her style was always calm and steady.

Victoria guided Imagen-Pharmaglobe staff by "eye" rather than by nipping at their heels. However, nipping was well within her repertoire. Recruits were common targets of that behavior. Even Waite had felt a few nips when he once suggested less than full commitment to J. J. Jones and Imagen. At these times she could be a real pest.

Maybe Gerry was right. She was always underfoot, always making sure that no one got out of line so long as they were working on one of her deadlines. And she did watch him constantly.

It was ironic that an executive vice president of one of the world's largest companies had to rely on skills he had learned as a car thief in his teens. During a coffee break in one of the merger meetings, Victoria had told Waite that she liked to drive fast cars and had requested a Nissan 350Z. That was an extension of her personality. A smile crept onto his face as he recalled her upbeat enthusiasm

"Why such a small car? I thought you'd like a Lincoln Navigator to push people around."

"Forget it, James. They're for men with ego problems. I want pure sport."

"Meaning?"

"If I cut off a Mack truck coming off an on ramp, I don't need to worry. 70 MPH is only a pedal push away."

"I thought color was the key for the fairer sex," he teased.

"I want access to an engine that purrs, a stick shift that moves smoothly and easily in my hand, horsepower that can speed up at will with the slightest effort by me, and torque that gets the drive shaft moving smoothly for long durations, everything a young woman could want in a racing machine."

"You're sure we're talking about a car?"

Victoria ignored him and kept on going, "Performance, speed, and smoothness of ride, alternating with a touring gear that allows just the right feel of bumps and motion. I love a sporty car."

"Sounds like it turns you on just to look under the hood."

"You're pathetic, Waite. Make it silver. Now let's get back to real work."

*   *   *   *

The car handled well as it cruised along Richmond to University, then traveled north to Bloor, turned right, then right again onto Church. Memories of his beloved 240Z from the early 70s surfaced briefly. His right hand guided the leather shift from first to second to third gear as effortlessly as stirring a simmering stew. Beside him, on the passenger seat, were a pair of soft brown calf leather Sparco Super Pro racing gloves, a present for Victoria as a joking reference to her fondness for speed. Turning left on Shuter, he traveled eight blocks before slowing to a stop in front of an old, dirty brown brick building that housed Greco's Auto Repair and Sales. The streets were quiet except for the occasional coked-out hooker trying to wave down passing cars. He pulled up in front of the far left car bay next to the customer entrance, noting the sign at the side of the door:

Your One Stop Friendly Shop.

Repairs to All Makes and Models

Domestic and Foreign Cars, Vans, and Light Trucks

Class "A" Mechanic on Duty at All Times

Good Selection of New and Used Tires

Very Reasonable Prices.

He smiled. Not only reasonable prices but also reasonable hours for old friends. He blinked the lights on the high beam three times. After several seconds the bay door started to rise, clattering like an old trolley car on tracks in need of repair. He drove the car in over the hoist, turned off the engine, and got out of the car.

"You're late, bro," said a voice from the dark.

Lights switched on. By the panel on the back wall stood an African-American man in his midfifties, dressed in a well-worn blue jumpsuit. The name *Rufus* was sewn in black thread over the oval white patch on the man's left chest pocket.

"Five minutes is not late, Rufus. It's in the margin of forgiveness," smiled Waite.

"Ain't no forgiveness when you keep a man from his wife and children at this time of night," said Rufus.

"You're not even married and probably have no idea who your children are."

"So what's the deal with this little number?"

"I want a tire change."

Rufus circled the car looking at the tires.

"These are brand-new Michelin Pilot Sports, good as gold."

"Give them to your children."

"What do I replace them with?"

"A well-used version of the same, but not so used that an insurance investigator would get suspicious."

"I won't ask why. By the way, I got the other stuff you asked for."

"Smart man," said Waite, as Rufus went to the tool bench to get a pneumatic air drill.

Within minutes, Rufus was removing the lug nuts, while emitting an occasional needless grunt to suggest that he was working hard.

Waite looked at the tire replacements. They would look right to an inexperienced eye. He took a tire pressure tester from his jacket pocket and went to test each tire and then let air escape from each to achieve underinflation. If Victoria drove as fast as she said she did, then all he would need is a wet road. Just in case she didn't, he stuck a pin into the side of the right front tire. No ordinary pin, but the latest in plastic explosives.

He then checked the car's global positioning device, something he had placed on all Imagen-Pharmaglobe executive vehicles, unknown to the driver, including Victoria. It allowed him to track the car's activity. The system logged starts, stops, drive times, idling, rate of speed, landmarks, locations, routes, distances, and other significant events. In addition to the usual data, he had the 350Z's GPS programmed to page him when the car's speed exceeded 120 kilometers per hour and where the vehicle was at any given time. If Victoria couldn't do herself in, then he would help.

He had concluded that the best way to dispose of Victoria was at the wheel of one of her beloved fast cars. Many border collies ended life early under the wheels of a car. This would be an appropriate end to Victoria.

TWENTY-EIGHT

Ready are you? What know you of ready? For eight hundred years have I trained Jedi. My own counsel will I keep on who is to be trained. A Jedi must have the deepest commitment, the most serious mind. This one a long time have I watched. All his life has he looked away … to the future, to the horizon. Never his mind on where he was. Hmm? What he was doing. Hmph. Adventure. Heh. Excitement. Heh. A Jedi craves not these things. You are reckless.

—Yoda, *Star Wars*

Juno entered the room with her inimitable regal gait, head held high, eyes glancing imperiously down her nose. Alex saw her and barely managed not to laugh out loud. In counterpoint to her attitude was her workout attire, a black nylon and spandex top with tan cargo pants, a gold necklace, and hoop earrings with coordinated black sweatband, black sneakers with gold laces. In her left hand was a water bottle.

"I just got through my Pilates class so I'm fresh and alert," announced Juno as she danced about the room in her best Martha Graham imitation.

No one took note, least of all J. J.. Juno had joined a fitness club for women in an effort to remold herself into the self-image of her golden youth. Victoria had steered her to the club, as part of her efforts to help the goddess feel attractive for Jupiter. One evening after more red wine than even a goddess could manage,

Juno had teared up and confided in her. Victoria had later regaled Alex with the story.

*   *   *   *

"Being an old goddess is no fun, Vicky. Two thousand years have given me chronic back pain and lack of flexibility in my hamstrings."

"Can I help?" asked Victoria.

Juno had tensed, looked around the room to make sure no one could hear them and whispered, "This is just woman to woman. I'm telling you this as a friend and yes, I need your help. I want J. J. to look at me the way he did in Rome's early days. He used to be so romantic then. But when he started losing ground, he changed; he was off chasing every skirt in the universe,"

"I'm sorry," said Victoria. What else could she say?

"But it's worse than you imagine."

"It can be worse?"

"Worse than Bill and Hillary."

"Impossible."

"We only have sex every hundred years."

*   *   *   *

Alex looked around the windowless executive conference room, located on the lower level of the cavernous Fairmont Royal York Hotel on Front Street in Toronto. The room could hold up to twenty people and had all the necessary toys, screens, flip charts, markers, outlets for computers, and Internet connections. Morning treats were arrayed on a table by the back wall: fresh fruits—cantaloupe, watermelon, strawberries; juices—orange, grapefruit, apple; cold cuts suitable for morning fare, along with freshly baked breads. Seeing Victoria looking at him, he winked.

Pan stood in front of the buffet table, carefully studying the options.

"There are no Danishes, there are not even donuts, for crying out loud. What kind of breakfast buffet is this? Never book this place again."

He caught J. J.'s eyes and said, "How do you expect me to listen to this boring stuff if I haven't had any breakfast?"

J. J., Pan, Victoria, Argie, and Juno, plus the rest of the makeovers, made up his audience. As Alex glanced around the room, he felt as anxious as he had been when he had met Victoria's father for the first time. His anxiety was well founded. She was the only fellow human in the room. The rest were gods, except for one android. What if his presentation did not please them? Would they amuse themselves by changing him into a toad?

"I'll try to keep things brief," said Alex.

"Then consider stopping right now," quipped Cupid. Neither Alex nor anyone else paid attention, apart from Juno, who coughed in a weak attempt to suppress her laugh.

"J. J. once said that he felt like an old quarterback who'd been sitting on the bench for two thousand years," started Alex.

"So it's about time he got off his ass," said Pan, playing to the group.

"Thanks for the icebreaker, Pan," said Alex. Then taking a deep breath, he started his pitch. "As you know, our assignment is composed of two parts: makeover, which is simply helping the group fit into the human world of today. Now we have made great progress."

Approving nods and smiles came from all the group.

"But we still need a little more work."

The smiles disappeared. After another fifteen minutes, Alex saw the telltale signs of boredom, a stifled yawn by Pan, the drooping eyelids of Mercury, occasional glances by J. J. at his BlackBerry. He wasn't the only one. All this while, Victoria had remained silent. But now she spoke, without rancor, but with cool objectivity.

"Alex, I suggest we take a brief break. We need to stretch our legs, at least I do."

Alex caught the signal.

"Great idea. Let's break for fifteen minutes, and then I'll finish up."

Victoria and J. J. came over to Alex while the others headed for the door, apparently only too happy to escape. Victoria held her smile and her tongue until the three of them were alone, then let loose. "Alex, the presentation has been insightful and provocative. However, I fail to see its purpose. You've managed to both insult and bore the gods."

"Vic, it addresses J. J.'s long-term goal for a comeback," said Alex defensively. He didn't want to get into the details of Dr. Love. "The success of the takeover depends on the success of the makeovers."

"And everyone agrees we've made great progress, including you."

"But a little more time," said Alex, not wanting to go into the details of the Dr. Love episode.

"A little more time may put the takeover at risk," said Victoria.

Silence ensued, as they waited for J. J. to speak. After several moments, he smiled. "You've done a great job, Alex."

Alex brightened with a light smile at the recognition of his work. J. J. saw the wisdom of his position. He noted that J. J. was about to continue.

"However, as one of my business profs liked to say, 'Let not the perfect be the enemy of the good.' It's time to focus on the takeover."

Alex winced. Victoria smiled.

TWENTY-NINE

Yet if a woman never lets herself go, how will she ever know how far she might have got? If she never takes off her high-heeled shoes, how will she ever know how far she could walk or how fast she could run?

—Germaine Greer

Some women would have been angry; others would have been sad. Victoria was neither; but she was not happy with her business partner and former lover. Where was the mystery? Where was the romance? She did everything she could to support him, look out for his best interests, and periodically make herself available for deeper reconciliation. But the man, like most men, was tone-deaf to love.

At the airport, he had only just given her a lukewarm hug; his kiss had barely touched her lips. She had tried to maneuver him into one of the recessed doorways by the men's room for something a little more intimate. She had put her arms around his neck and crushed her breasts against his chest, but to little effect.

"It's a public place, Vic," he said, looking around as he pulled away. "And besides, Argie will be here any minute."

How could she deal with this high-achieving, exhausted lover, whose outdated sense of decorum always interfered with his hormones, whose squeaky-clean displays of public celibacy fought the sacred codes of love? So after he got his electronic ticket, she had taken her leave as quickly as possible. She would chase him until he caught her but she wasn't going to pamper him. If he preferred an android to her left breast, then let him test the differences. Let him sit for two hours in the executive lounge area prattling with an adolescent machine and reading magazines. She was leaving. She knew how to relieve stress. The night was young.

Wasting no time, she made her way to the parking garage, found her car, got in, and fastened her seat belt. As a final preparation, she put on her favorite Bryan Ferry CD, *As Time Goes By*. The gloves Waite had given her fit perfectly. Nice touch. Soft leather. Sense of humor. Maybe she was wrong about the man. The car's engine barely made its presence known in response to the turn of the ignition key, just a gentle hum, but all power underneath. Could it satisfy her? She would see.

She turned onto Highway 427 from Pearson International and traveled north to Highway 407, a multilane autobahn arching over the northern perimeter of the greater Toronto area. The best place to test the muscle in a car, according to Waite. Tonight she wanted to test the 350Z. She had just picked it up yesterday. Waite had promised her a car with guts. The roads were wet from a March mix of rain and wet, chunky snow. She had never experienced such sloppy goop before, though the traffic was moving well. Good. She wanted to release her energy through the accelerator.

Heading west toward Hamilton, she planted the throttle and let the tach swing north as the Z shoved her back in the seat. Alex could learn from this car. She felt the same thrill she had as a nine-year-old in space camp at the U.S. Space and Rocket Center in Huntsville, Alabama, when she had climbed into the 1/6th gravity chair. She had strapped up and then felt the acceleration pin her to her seat. She had loved it. After that experience, she had dreamed of one day becoming an astronaut, searching the stars. Surely a girl with this much energy was meant to travel beyond the solar system. At fourteen, she realized the gap between her dreams and the progress in space travel was insurmountable. Even Mars was beyond reach in her lifetime, and so she had changed her mind, feeling robbed of being born too soon.

She tested the acceleration and braking to get the Z's feel. It was pumped. It was buff. It was *The Matrix*'s Neo after he packs up and reloads to rescue Morpheus from the agents' grasp. The car cruised at 140 kilometers without any sense of excess movement. Overall, the steering was sharp and precise, though she would have liked more road feel. Bumpy corners taken at high speed set the tail skittering sideways, reducing control. The rear tires slipped too easily on the damp pavement, even with traction control. She tried it with the traction control off; the tires spun a bit more with slight fishtails, but easily regained balance. The overall the grip was solid, under control.

Waite had delivered. The 350Z could kick Porsche and BMW tail. She liked Waite. Too bad he worked for Schilling. How fast could she push it? No one was around; the risks were not great, and the car hugged the road despite the rain, showing no sense of hydroplaning.

After passing the Hurontario and Mavis exits, the traffic had grown even lighter. She was almost alone. Why not see if she could hit 160 kph before she saw another car, maybe even 200 kph? Sitting with her back pressed straight against the heated leather seat, astronaut Victoria Malik's left hand held the steering wheel. Her right foot depressed the accelerator, while her left foot and right hand coordinated seamlessly to shift through the gears. The acceleration, even from a base speed of 140 kph, was palpable—150 kph, 160 kph, 180 kph.

Still no one in sight. Should she push it?

Within seconds she hit 200 kph.

Liftoff.

What a rush.

Then a loud pop.

Spaceship Columbia was out of control.

Tire blowout, she was sure.

Quick rules of defensive driving. Don't slam on the brakes. OK. Let the car slow down gradually by taking your foot off the gas pedal. Done. But at 200 kph on a wet road this could be tricky. Work your car toward the breakdown lane or, if possible, toward an exit. Are they serious? She did not have time to steer. Like Columbia veering off course on reentry, the 350Z spun out of control on the wet pavement.

She felt she was part of a movie. In fact, she was the star. Was it a horror film? Was she going to die? Or just crash badly, with much blood and multiple fractures? Would she be impaled on a post? Decapitated by an oncoming transport truck like Jayne Mansfield? Crushed as the car slammed into a bridge abutment? The choices were endless. Except they weren't choices. She had no control. They were horrifying possibilities. How long was all this spinning taking? Where would it end?

She became aware of interior detail. The high doorsills and low seating position gave her a closed-in feeling, snug as the Mercury astronaut's cabin. The seat was built for viewing raindrops mixed by the windshield wiper. They blurred the dark road, the darker shoulders, and the indefinite shapes in the distance. The three-dial pod that moved up and down with the steering wheel dominated the dashboard. The speedometer, fuel, and temperature gauges flanked the large tachometer in the middle. The tank was half full, and the temperature was in the normal range. The audio and climate controls were within easy reach, but radio buttons were too undersized for her tastes. The leather upholstery felt rich. But the cup holder jutting out of the dashboard looked flimsy. Actually, the whole car felt flimsy now.

No time for popcorn as the Z became a child's spinning top traveling from one side of the road to the other, finally hitting the shoulder and taking flight over an embankment. It flipped over, landing on its roof and then skidding, for what seemed a long while, before making a soft landing.

Just as she thought the ordeal was over, a thundering detonation pinned her to her seat hanging upside down like a freshly butchered carcass. Pinned by a sound? Close. Air bag deployment. Right. She had been briefed in a defensive driving course.

*   *   *   *

"Your air bag is like sitting next to a time bomb," the instructor said. "It can cause serious injury, including acoustic trauma from the surprise assault of the sound of deployment. The pressure of 170 decibels will rip your eardrums."

"How loud is that," she asked.

"The threshold of discomfort is 120 decibels—a car horn, a chain saw, a jackhammer. The air bag deployment is much worse; it would sound like a 105 mm howitzer or a bazooka at close range."

*   *   *   *

Not being a weapons expert, the comparison had had no meaning. Now she knew. Fucking loud.

Then it was quiet except for the CD player. The 300-watt Bose sound system with its eleven speakers continued to give the bass and treble of Mr. Ferry's stylings a notable boost.

Feeling no pain and unable to move, she wondered if she was paralyzed. Or maybe even dead!

Her right hand was flattened against her jacket pocket. She felt a lump underneath. Her cell phone. She could not reach inside the jacket. Choices. What were the choices? After several minutes of concentration, guesswork, and experimentation she could identify two key buttons, power on and autodial for Alex.

Press one. Press two. As she pressed the speed dial button for Alex, she felt a wave of claustrophobic terror wash over her.

The pressure on her chest increased; a lump in her throat made it difficult for her to breathe; her heart pounded. She felt light-headed and nauseous and yet detached from her body. In microseconds she surrendered to Bryan Ferry's voice as he sang "Another Time, Another Place"

*   *   *   *

Toronto's Pearson International Airport reminded Alex of a European airport, especially Terminal 3. It was a big airport, and a rail shuttle would have been nice between terminals instead of the bus shuttles. Another annoying feature of this airport was that passengers needed a Canadian dollar coin to get baggage carts. He had wasted time on arrival trying to get change. At least he had prepared for the departure, carefully selecting three toonies and loonies. He couldn't believe what Canadians called their two and one dollar coins. Cartoon currency. How could you take the country seriously? Besides, carts should be freely available in baggage areas as at other major international airports. How cheap could you get? Someone should write *A Dummies Guide: How to Be a Great City* and present it to Toronto's mayor.

The airport's features aside, air travel was a burden to Alex. Because he was flying from Toronto to the United States he had to check into Pearson International three hours before departure. So much for the speed of air travel. He had fully charged the battery for his laptop as well. He had a copy of a favorite book on his iPod—*American Gods* by Neil Gaiman. It dealt with the interesting question of what happens to gods when they fade away. The book had been a disappointment. But this was before he met J. J. In Gaiman's vision, old Norse gods had become social lowlifes, posing as grifters, cons, and hookers living on the fringes of society. What had originally seemed far out and implausible now did not seem so far-fetched. Perhaps the Norse god Odin had contacted Gaiman. Alex wanted to reread the book and then contact Gaiman to explore the possibilities. He had also picked up a copy of this week's *Newsweek* and *US*; celebrity gossip was junk food for a tired mind. The wait in the terminal was almost as long as the flight back to Hilton Head Island.

He reviewed the last minutes with Victoria. She had been as touchy-feely as they had been years ago. When Argie showed up, and he had suggested that the three of them have a drink and review the status of the makeovers, she stood up abruptly and said her goodbyes

"You're working too long when you prefer androids to humans," she said.

"But this is Argie."

"Think about it, Alex."

He turned to watch Argie, who was working his way through the *New York Times* crossword puzzle, when his cell phone chirped. He reached into this jacket pocket to recover it. The caller ID said Vic. Ha. She's calling to apologize.

"Hi Vic, what's up?"

No answer.

She must still be mad. She did this sometimes. Called him just to give him the silent treatment over the phone.

Seconds passed.

He heard music. It sounded like Bryan Ferry. Maybe it was the CD he had given her for her birthday. Maybe the words meant something.

"Who's calling, Alex?"

"It's Victoria. But she won't say anything."

"Where is she?"

"I don't know."

"Give me the phone. I'll check."

Alex handed Argie the phone, and he immediately pressed a few buttons and then said, "I think something's wrong."

"What?"

"Her phone's coordinates place her off Highway 407 between the Mavis and Hurontario exits. There's no reason anyone would stop there. I'm calling J. J. and James Waite to get someone to her car right away.

Alex watched Argie morph into a no-nonsense security operative. Gerry Schilling had James Waite as his security guy, and J. J. had Argie.

"How'd you do that?" asked Alex as Argie got off the phone with Waite.

"Later," said Argie getting up, "Right now we're canceling our trip home so we can find Victoria."

*   *   *   *

Gerry looked at his watch. He was pissed off. What a strange expression, he thought. As a complex noun it meant an object or person that causes one to be angry. It sounded more like a contest that schoolboys might have at recess. Maybe it's in the Guinness book of records. He'd check tomorrow. As a transitive verb in the active tense, it could mean a mild version of fuck off, or else it could mean to make someone annoyed or fed up. In its passive tense that meant Gerry was either being mildly fucked or annoyed. In fact, it was both. That was what Waite was doing, he was mildly fucking around with him, and he didn't like it. It was annoying him. Waite had been gone for five minutes. Left after glancing at his beeping pager. Barely apologized before rushing out. What could possibly be so important? More than anything else, Gerry hated to waste time. He especially disliked waiting for others. And worse, he had no idea when Waite would return.

Two copies of a proposal for Imagen-Pharmaglobe life extension communities sat in front of him on his conference table. He had sold Jones on the idea because it built on Imagen's research. Jones would be the public face of the project. Though Jones was excited about the project, Gerry considered it at least a generation or two ahead of its time and fraught with economic and political risk. The idea was simple enough, secluded, secure communities in semitropical surroundings that pandered to the rich with life extension treatments that were on the forefront of Imagen-Pharmaglobe's research and clinical trials. Be first on the block to live one hundred fifty years or longer. Just sign over net assets of fifty million U.S. dollars or more. The man was crazy. If he were Jones, he would have had a subordinate handle it, probably himself. Someone needed to fall on the sword if it blew up. And there were many ways for it to blow up.

Waite reappeared with a big smile. The man walked across the room. No, he was swaggering. What a piss-off.

"This better be good," said Gerry.

"It is, it really is."

"Well?"

"No details yet," said Waite, playing coy. "Let's just say one of your prime aims is about to be realized."

"You better be right. Now for the skill-testing question. Where were we before you rushed out while I was in midsentence?"

"What's the prize?"

"Could be this year's bonus."

"I can start spending then," beamed Waite. "You're planning to set up J. J. as architect of life extension gated communities, on man-made islands similar to those off shore from Dubai that rich soccer players like Beckham and company purchased. Jones will float it publicly only to discover it's a Trojan horse. But too late because the board will have turfed him."

"And?"

"I will coordinate the negative media through a third party—including revving up Mr. Marcus 'Madman' McQuillan."

Waite's cell phone sounded.

"Boy you are popular tonight. Maybe you could ignore it for once."

Waite looked the phone and then at Gerry, "I'd better answer. It's J. J. Jones."

Gerry waved his hand in surrender.

"Hi J. J. How can I help you?"

Waite was smooth as spreadable cream cheese. Of course, he had to be if all their plans were to work. But still, Gerry felt resentment at Waite's easy cordiality with Jones. How easily could he switch sides?

"Yes J. J. I can send someone immediately. In fact, I'll come myself," said Waite, who now looked stressed. Color drained from his handsome face, his dark African-American features surrendering to tones of ash gray and taupe. What happened to the confidence of ten minutes ago?

"Give me about thirty to forty minutes to be on-site," said Waite as he stood up, closed his phone, and headed for the door

"This better be good," said Gerry.

Waite stopped at the door, turning to look back at Gerry for some signal of release.

"Go," said Gerry with a dismissive wave. "Piss off."

THIRTY

He bears an unmistakable resemblance to a cornered rat.

—Norman Mailer

Catering to a select group of rich older men of the Hugh Hefner generation, Club 22 was part of the Windsor Arms Hotel on Toronto's Thomas Street, just south of the high-end Bloor and Yorkville area. It had a separate cigar lounge to keep the air clean for the health-conscious models and cougars that hung out in the bar, with its suede-studded stools and a grand piano. For some, the place positively reeked of sophistication. For others it reeked of young models' perfumes. For Neil Spenser, it was nothing more than a Neanderthal's dream, a dark, small cave of retreat. He was safe here; no one could spot him, the place could have used usherettes to help its patrons find a table.

Eyes adjusting to the gloom, as he walked to the bar, he was able to make out a number of smart, older gentlemen engaged in intimate discussions with their "nieces." As his eyes became further accustomed to the darkness, he spotted a would-be uncle, balding, belly spreading over his belt, a man in his late forties, on a small dance floor, doing that sort of dancing that can best be described as akin to those embarrassing home-video wedding clips submitted to "You've been framed" style TV shows. The ones where someone's dad gets up to dance for the first time since 1974, and he's pissed.

Maybe he would send his own story into "You've Been Framed."

Advanced scotch and water therapy would transform him, relieve the ache at the back of the neck, and make the world a better place.

There was no way he was going down without Gerry Schilling coming along with him. He'd been set up. Schilling had applied incessant pressure to show results. Gerry had given him blanket authority.

"Gerry, you're asking the impossible."

"Neil, you're the man."

"Well, some creative accounting might help—you know, the Enron thing," started Neil.

"I don't want to hear details; just deliver results," said Gerry

He had written to Larry Kirkpatrick, Pharmaglobe's chief accountant, asking him for an interpretation from the external auditors. Would his proposals fly with the SEC? Were they consistent with generally accepted accounting practices? When he didn't hear back, he assumed it was OK. Silence was consensus. He had the authority to proceed. This was the way business worked. If he waited for a response on every question, he may as well shut down his business. Head office only reacted when he was too close to the line. Nevertheless, he got his local lawyers to write to Kirkpatrick for approval, noting that, unless directed otherwise, they would proceed according to plans. Kirkpatrick had passed the memo onto Gerry because the issue was beyond his authority to change company policy for accounting that could affect financial statements. In fact, only the board should approve the moves that he had proposed, as they would materially alter the bottom line in Pharmaglobe's financial statements. Gerry told him he didn't approve it because he knew the accounting was wrong. He wouldn't consider taking it to the board. What the hell was he up to?

Gerry wanted to buy him out. Have him go quietly. Told him there was no way he would ever authorize illegal activity.

"When I told you to get results, it went without saying that you were to do so within the bounds of the law, accepted accounting practice, and corporate policy."

"Bullshit, Gerry," said Neil, sweat beading on his forehead. "Everybody knows the old nod and wink routine."

"You've had your run, Neil. Give it up. I'll arrange a nice package for you. You can get on with your life," said Gerry as he examined his gold cuff links and straightened his sleeves, artfully dodging Spenser's eyes.

"I may not be as smart as you, Gerry, but I'm not stupid either," said Neil. "You think you can play high and mighty. This could be the end of my career. If I'm going to get a job this good again, I have to go out on my own terms."

"Meaning?"

"I stay until I line up something somewhere else."

"You have a month. I'll put you on special assignment."

"You ungrateful cocksucker."

They agreed he would come to Toronto in an interim position until his departure date was confirmed. That was as much of a compromise as Gerry was going to give him. He had sacrificed everything for the company, everything for his old buddy, his old teammate from Michigan U. When the word came in that he had crossed the line, he had met with his old friend, and those stone gray eyes had just stared back at him, lifeless, cold, unyielding. He may as well have been staring into the depths of a gun barrel. And, as far as he was concerned, he was. The effect was basically the same. The end of life as he knew it.

He decided to meet with the external auditors and then go public. Lay it all out for them. Tell them the pressure he was under. Tell them this wasn't an isolated case. He could name names and dates. They would see. They would understand that Schilling had given him implicit authority to do what he had done. There was nothing he ever did that wasn't in the rules of the game, as they were set out and approved by Gerry and the board of directors. He was a good soldier. After all, his record was sound in every respect. Almost. It was still his signature claiming that the books of Pharmaglobe Southwest were in order and met generally accepting accounting rules to the best of his knowledge. Everything would be gone if he left the company, because it would be clear that he was leaving under a cloud. And what way was that for a former class valedictorian, all-star guard? No, Mr. Schilling. If I go, we all go. Right to hell.

"You son of a bitch, you set me up."

"Come on, Neil, don't be silly," said Gerry. The words slashed through his heart, offended his business sense, as Schilling continued, "I never set anybody up, least of all you. I always give people freedom. Enough rope to succeed or hang themselves as the case may be."

"Hang myself with a gun to my head."

"You just happened to choose the latter, looking for a cheap score."

"Choose, my ass. You told me. You threatened me to do anything to get results."

"Anything within the law Neil—you know that—it goes without saying. I don't have to spell it out each time we speak. Have you taken a look at the company's code of ethics?"

"You taught me ethics by example a long time ago, Gerry. Remember what happened to that gay professor, who you outed, just because he gave you a B minus? How does his suicide rest on your ethical mind? Look what you did to my predecessor." Neil was struggling, thrashing about like a drowning swimmer as his one chance for survival started fading. One last lunge. "Maybe I'll use some of your tricks."

THIRTY-ONE

In this country, you never pull the emergency brake, even when there is an emergency. It is imperative that the trains run on schedule.

—Friedrich Dürrenmatt

Sensing Alex was the one person who needed assurance, the middle-aged nurse, with gray, short-cropped hair, looked up and smiled at Alex while she unwrapped the blood pressure monitor around Victoria's right arm.

"Your friend's vitals are good," she said. "No need to worry."

"When will she regain consciousness?" asked Morrigan, who had been at Victoria's side since she had arrived in the emergency ward at Toronto General Hospital. It was the same question that Alex had asked earlier of the neurologist.

"The first twenty-four hours are critical," said the coordinating doctor, who had slipped back into the room unseen. "There are no signs of spinal cord damage on the CAT scan or MRI of the brain, so this is promising. All the evidence suggests loss of consciousness at the time of injury, most likely from a violent shaking of the brain during a whiplash injury or from direct impact with a solid object. My guess is that it was the violent shaking."

"What is the prognosis?" asked Alex. Although he understood the information, he wanted some feel for the outcome, some insight that would lessen the leaden apprehension that bore down on him like an undiscovered gravity.

"Fortunately, most of the cognitive and memory problems associated with mild brain injury clear up within several weeks after injury. Occasionally, however, the residual effects of a brain concussion may last for months, years, or indefinitely. We need to watch your friend closely until she regains consciousness."

"This is all my fault," whispered Alex to no one in particular. "If only."

"If only, nothing," interjected Morrigan, reaching out to hold Alex's arm. "You know what Argie found. This was no accident. It's Schilling and Waite—I know it."

"Well J. J. wants us to stay cool, not to jump to any conclusions."

"Stay cool? What's that? It's time for action, tit for tat."

"When will Apollo be here?"

"Only if needed. You know what J. J. said, special healing only in emergencies."

"Maybe his definition of emergency is different from mine," said Alex leaning over Victoria and kissing her on the cheek. He had growing doubts about their deal with J. J., who didn't appear to be honoring his commitments. Alex wanted to give the god a piece of his mind, quit, and return to a normal life with a healthy Victoria.

THIRTY-TWO

In revenge and in love, woman is more barbaric than man is.

—Friedrich Nietzsche

Standing at his office window, all Gerry could see was the dark anger of storm clouds. Waite's failure hung over him, adding to the gloom of the cold March rains and biting winds outside. Without warning, an oversized, shrieking crow flew at the window. Startled, Gerry jerked back involuntarily to avoid the expected impact. At the last moment, the crow veered away, looking back in seeming disdain. His heart pumping, unable to concentrate, Gerry took the incident as a sign to surrender the rest of the day. He shut down his computer, gathered his papers, locked his office, strode to the elevator, and hit the down button. Even though he had half an hour until his dinner meeting with Neil Spenser, it was time to leave this personal prison of the Imagen-Pharmaglobe executive suite on the fortieth floor of the Commerce Court bank tower.

Standing before the elevator, his shoulders sagged, and his head hung down in defeat, dropping his 6 foot 1 inch frame by several inches. He felt under siege; first quarter earnings were down, the auditors were on his back. But most of all, J. J. Jones, chief shareholder, chairperson, and all-round bastard, was treating him like an indentured slave. Gerry knew J. J. was still in his office tonight as no employee, including Gerry, had ever seen J. J. leave before them. It amazed Gerry that anyone could manage such hours in middle age, but J. J. did. Not only that, but he also smoked his Cuban cigars, drank to excess, played with women less than half his age, and probably did assorted mind-altering drugs. Did his wife know? If he could only get some proof of any of this.

The elevator bell rang, and ice-cold air rushed through its opening door. He looked up as a stunning young woman in her late twenties stepped out, her delicate perfume refocusing his mind. Her raven hair was a feisty bob styled in a feathery look with trendy jagged ends and a few spiky bangs that fell on a flawless skin of alabaster white. Her sparkling ice-blue eyes locked into Gerry's eyes implying a connection that he couldn't quite place. Her full, high-gloss, tulip red lips framed a smile that probably had helped some orthodontist get richer.

"Hi," she said. "I'm looking for Mr. Jones. Am I on the right floor?"

"Yes indeed you are," Gerry offered, after a few seconds of staring. It figured. She must be J. J.'s latest conquest. Spellbound, he blurted out, "I know it's a line, but haven't we met before?"

"No, people meet me only once," she smiled and winked.

"My name is Gerry Schilling, the CEO, if you need any help," he added.

"How do you do, Mr. Schilling? My name is Morrigan du Morde, Morri for short, and in fact, Mr. Jones mentioned that he wanted me to meet with you when he called me," she said, handing him her business card.

The ache in his neck had suddenly disappeared. He straightened his shoulders as he looked at her card.

"Raven Human Resource Services, Principal," said Gerry, reading the card aloud. He looked up at her and continued, "So you must be the specialist in people problems Mr. Jones mentioned to me. Listen, Morri, he's busy right now, and if you have a few minutes, I can brief you on why we're interested in your services,"

They moved to Gerry's office. He felt restored. This du Morde person came with J. J.'s highest recommendation, although he had trouble believing J. J. would go out of his way to help him. Gerry needed perfection, no chance of failure, and Morri was so young, not what he expected. Well, at least J. J. was on board. She was his recommendation, so he had no worries on that count. But still, the results of failure would be disaster for the company and, more to the point, career ending for him.

"We have a problem, a rogue executive," he started. "Neil Spenser is his name. Until recently he headed our southeast U.S. operations. Was doing great guns; constant increases in operating profit. And then the auditors turned up some red flags, serious red flags. Spenser was goosing his numbers by cannibalizing our Latin American markets, which belonged to another sub's territory. And worse, he was financing growth with off-balance sheet debt, the smoke and mirrors accounting model that Enron made famous. You know the drill, borrow from yourself to invest in yourself and pay yourself huge brokerage fees."

"Where is Spenser now?" asked Morri.

"We moved him to Toronto four weeks ago to head our mergers and take-overs group," replied Gerry. "In appearance it's a promotion, but truth be told it was to get him out of San Antonio while we try to sort out the damage. So far it looks like it won't be fatal, but we could take a beating in the markets and the media."

"And let me guess; Mr. Spenser is starting to point fingers?" asked Morri.

"You got it. Spenser is scheduled to meet with our external auditors in two weeks. I met with him two days ago, and he hinted that if he goes down, he will take senior management and the board with him. Ugly stuff. Worst-case scenario is a bear run on share prices with investor losses in the billions, class action suits, regulatory investigations, and that's for starters. The chairperson also has close ties with the president and the prime minister, so as I'm sure you appreciate, it's politically sensitive," explained Gerry.

"Does Spenser have any credibility?" inquired Morri.

"Good news is, there is no paper trail. Bad news is, it looks bad. I hired him. He has a hot business record, and he's a favorite of Wall Street analysts and the business media. Just last month he was on CNN's *Moneyline*," expanded Gerry.

"So where can I help you?" asked Morri.

"I want Spenser out of the company within the week, for career or personal reasons or whatever, with no rumors, rancor, or recrimination," Gerry said.

"Nice alliteration to make a point," said Morri with a smile.

"Whatever," continued Gerry. "Spenser has to go in a way that doesn't come back to haunt us, and according to the chairperson, you are the only one who can make this happen."

"If I do it within the terms you describe, it will cost a flat fee of one million U.S. dollars, plus expenses," said Morri.

"Considering the potential risks, that's a bargain," confirmed Gerry. "And depending on your performance, there could be a longer term contract. Neil is only one of our problems."

"It's a deal, then, Mr. Schilling. I will have my office arrange for an electronic funds transfer payment of my invoice on completion," said Morri. "By the way, I have a 100 percent success rate, and I charge severe penalties for late payment."

"I'm sure you do. Done deal," replied Gerry with a touch of arrogance in his voice. He stood to signal the end of their meeting, extending his arm to shake her hand, adding, "Now I should let you get to the chairperson. And I have a dinner meeting to get to with Mr. Spenser."

Gerry watched Morri as she strode down the hall to J. J.'s office. Small clouds of doubt drifted into his mind. This was too easy, he thought. She didn't ask if there was any truth in Spenser's allegations, and he wasn't going to volunteer, but still, wouldn't it have been an obvious question for a human resource specialist? And what had J. J. told her? Was J. J. helping him or setting him up? That was always the problem with the son of a bitch. Nonetheless, he would sell his soul to the devil to get rid of Spenser, so one million U.S. dollars was a bargain-basement price. Besides, it was Imagen-Pharmaglobe's money, not his.

Now, if only his dinner with Spenser would go as well.

*   *   *   *

Gerry was barely into his office at 7:00 AM when his gray-haired, ever-serious executive assistant, Laura, asked him to take an urgent call.

"Gerry Schilling here," he barked into the phone.

"Good morning, Mr. Schilling, Morri du Morde here," greeted Morri on an upbeat note. "I wanted to tell you the Spenser assignment is complete. Just a reminder that payment's due by the end of the day."

"That was quick," said Gerry, the disbelief obvious in his voice. "I was with him until almost midnight last night, and not a pleasant time at that. When did you see him? How did you have time?"

"Check the breaking news on the *Globe and Mail* Web site for details," she directed him. "I've got to run, great doing business with you, and don't forget, payment due by the end of the day."

Gerry hung up as he powered his computer and called up the *Globe* site. The story had been posted a half hour ago, too late for the morning newspaper.

BUSINESSMAN KILLED IN FREAK ACCIDENT

A businessman was killed instantly early Wednesday morning when his Mercedes-Benz went out of control after hitting ice on the Gardiner Expressway near the Spadina ramp, flipped, and fell 20 meters onto Lakeshore Boulevard below. Neil Spenser, 52, was a senior executive with Imagen-Pharmaglobe. Fog and icy road conditions were contributing causes according to police. A witness reported seeing a large shrieking black bird fly in front the Mercedes shortly before it went of control. The businessman was alone in the car. Police continue their investigation. His wife and three children survive Mr. Spenser.

Gerry couldn't believe it. How lucky could he get? The gods must be looking down him with affection. His problem has disappeared just like that. Clearing his throat and suppressing a smile, he pressed his intercom for Laura.

"Yes, Mr. Schilling?" she asked with her head tilted forward in a Princess Di bow as she entered his office.

"Laura, Neil Spenser was killed last night in a tragic car accident."

"Oh my God. His poor family."

"Arrange to have a press release ready by noon."

"Yes."

"I want it to highlight how close Neil and I were, old college buddies, like family. Got it?"

"Yes, Mr. Schilling."

"And the usual condolences to the family. Send his wife some flowers. Call to see if there's anything the company can do to help in funeral arrangements."

"Anything else?"

"Find out why someone from our offices wasn't on the story earlier. Why do I have to do it all?"

As Laura left his office, he called Waite on his cell phone.

"Waite?"

"Gerry?"

"Spenser's dead. I want a special sweep done of his offices and home within the next twenty-four hours. Got it?" He hung up before Waite could reply.

And what a greedy, sleazy bitch du Morde was, so typical of the women that Jones went for, stunning but ruthless, without any sense of business ethics. Spenser has a freak fatal accident, and she wants to get paid. Forget it. His problem was solved, and he wasn't going to pay one million U.S. dollars for a coincidence.

THIRTY-THREE

If Nature denies eternity to beings, it follows that their destruction is one of her laws.

—Marquis de Sade

When Marcus McQuillan saw the Imagen-Pharmaglobe phoenix logo on the television screen, he pushed the increase volume button on the TV's remote unit and, smiling in anticipation, listened to the announcer.

> In a wide-ranging study published in the *Economic Journal* early this century, senior World Bank economist Branko Milanovic found that the richest 1 percent of the world has income equivalent to the poorest 57 percent. Four-fifths of the world's population lived below what countries in North America and Europe consider the poverty line. However, the poorest 10 percent of Americans were still better off than two-thirds of the world's population.

A split-screen display showed a luxury resort beside footage of a poor African village as the announcer continued.

> The world's richest fifty million people earn as much as the poorest 2.7 billion. They may soon be forced to live in heavily protected gated communities to escape. This week J. J. Jones, chairperson of Imagen-Pharmaglobe moved that vision closer to reality.

Stock footage appeared. J. J. Jones in a dark suit standing on a podium, smiling broadly, waving to his audience. He could have been a politician. The voice-over continued.

> Earlier this week Jones announced plans for an offshore luxury village with a twist. A research clinic for life extension of the residents is the main carrot. Although the price tag would be steep, Jones claims the first inhabitants could expect to live 150 years or longer.

The television screen now displayed three panels. The first panel showed an unflattering footage of Jones running to his car to evade reporters. A luxury resort filled with portly, middle-aged white men flirting with significantly younger women, was the subject of the second. The last panel showed a multitude of skinny and forlorn Asian children.

"Beautiful, just beautiful. They're on to the sucker," said Marcus, enjoying subliminal editorial comment of the program. He made a mental note to use the same techniques on his Web site.

> Although we don't agree with the philosophy of Dr. Marcus McQuillan and his Gaia Only Development movement, we share his concerns. Are we ready for two-tier humanity where the top 1 percent lives hundreds of years on island luxury while the poor roam the world outside scrounging for survival? For them life would be, as Thomas Hobbes noted, "nasty, brutish, and short.

"Tell it like it is Lou," said Marcus between bites of pizza and sips of chardonnay. Every night when he was alone, he watched CNN's *Moneyline* while he ate his dinner. He told friends he dined with Lou Dobbs regularly; few of them understood that he was speaking metaphorically. This was the first time Lou had mentioned his name.

> Will these clinics be legal? Are they morally the right thing to do? Authorities are looking at the proposal closely. Investors have already turned a thumbs down on Mr. Jones.

Marcus turned the volume down and sat back to enjoy the moment.

This was big, recognition in the cable world. And this was as well as the *Wall Street Journal* article of two days ago. The paper was still open on the table, page five; heading the page was a three-column article on Imagen-Pharmaglobe. The headline and subtitle of the article said it all

DISNEYLAND FOR GERIATRICS—IS IT LEGAL, OR IS J. J. JONES IN FANTASYLAND?

Marcus had read the article six times. He scanned the key sections again.

Imagen-Pharmaglobe announced yesterday a bold billion-dollar service venture of exclusive gated communities offering the latest in biotechnology and clinical trials to extend lives. J. J. Jones, chairperson of Imagen-Pharmaglobe, said the venture "will provide a unique opportunity to investors while clients have the chance live a century or two with the best that life has to offer. We want people focused on the long term.

Marcus skipped down half a column

A collective cold shoulder by investment strategists, scientists, and consumer watchdog groups is the early response to Mr. Jones. Stonewall Jorgenson, senior strategist of Merrill Lynch, said, "Both investors and potential clients should view this skeptically. It's the test of J. J. Jones as head of this new global behemoth. Unfortunately, it's got all the earmarks of a scam attack on aging baby boomers."
Informed sources claim that securities and drug regulators are considering a major preemptive strike. They want to educate investors and seniors to avoid becoming victims of life extension cons. Expectations are high that at least one Congressional Committee may call on Mr. Jones to testify."

Marcus zoomed to the last part of the article.

Consumer groups have been quick to respond. Dr. Marcus MacQuillan, leader of the Gaia Only Development organization, an environmental group resisting all forms of genetic engineering, challenged the venture.
"Imagen-Pharmaglobe has crossed the boundary of responsible science," exclaimed Dr. MacQuillan. "They've taken us back to the days of the snake oil pitchmen. What's worse is J. J. Jones has a two-planet vision. One of designer humans, rich, buffed, and decadent and the other of the great struggling masses, economic slaves to the ageless narcissism of the few. We will fight Jones on every front, legal, logical, and moral."

Marcus shook his head again and whispered, "Damnation."
They had spelled his name wrong. He had told the reporter "Mc" like McDonald's.

THIRTY-FOUR

*If you wish to succeed in life, make perseverance your bosom friend,
experience your wise counselor, caution your elder brother, and hope
your guardian genius.*

—Joseph Addison

Alex walked along Cumberland Avenue, buoyed by the late morning sun peeking
through brooding clouds, even though he was late for his lunch meeting. With
Victoria in the hospital, he had stepped into her shoes to look after her Imagen-Pharmaglobe files. Somehow this helped him feel closer to her. J. J. was still
irritable from Morrigan's mishap when the media stories burst out over the life
extension communities two days ago. J. J. called him hourly and finally arranged
a special meeting to discuss the problem.

Alex met J. J. and Pan at Sassafras, a four-star restaurant in the hub of Toronto's trendy Yorkville. A pleasing combo of taupe and tangerine minimalism,
featuring art deco pieces and flamingo style lighting, greeted him as he walked
through the door. The dining room's vaulted ceiling with its windows open to
the passing clouds, with the trees and plants that populated the dining area,
added to keep his spirits high. The maître d' led him to the table in the middle
section of the dining room, where J. J. and Pan were already seated.

Both gods got up to greet him, shook hands with token ceremony, and then
took their seats and ordered drinks. Alex checked out the menu.

"The place serves 'Cuisine de Soleil'?" he noted quizzically.

"Sun food in this place? Fat chance," said Pan. "Go for the calamari appetizer, the crème caramel desert, and finish with a cream-based latte. That's how you test a restaurant."

Alex nodded agreeably and had a look around at the other tables to see what was popular. His efforts were to no benefit. The serving plates had high edges with a built-in stand on a tilt. The servers placed the plate on the table in front of the patron who had ordered it, like a satellite dish homing in on a beacon. He returned to study the menu.

Soon enough the server took their orders and returned with their selections. Pan followed his own advice, while J. J. had a sirloin burger, and Alex went for the Shanghai noodles with shrimp. Now and then an attractive woman would walk past them on their way to the women's room. Pan would look up and take time to check her out. It reminded Alex of his university days when he and his friends would check out every young woman on the street.

"Isn't that Gwyneth Paltrow?" asked Pan over his menu, nodding his eyes at the table to his right.

"Gwyneth is blond. Maybe you're thinking of Nicole Kidman. Anyway, it's neither."

"Damn."

"But I'll keep my eyes open for you."

"Could you?"

J. J. intervened to bring them back to business. "I still can't believe Morrigan would strike out on her own like that."

"I told you so."

"What are you saying?"

"A day without killing, for her, is like a day without prayer for the Pope."

"And you're just a horny flute player who roams the woods."

"Aren't we sensitive today."

"Well, I thought she was more of a team player."

Alex had appreciated the time Morrigan had spent with Victoria in the hospital; she was always there when he couldn't be. J. J. was going a little too far, so he jumped in, "She is a team player; she was getting even for Victoria, whom she sees as an earthly role model."

"We want to get even. But that doesn't mean each of us goes out with our own agenda. Could ruin everything. She was about to do Schilling in when I walked into his office last week. Claimed he hadn't paid her for services delivered for getting rid of Neil Spenser. Schilling shrugs his shoulders, calls her a shill, and turns to me, laughing. Tells me he's disappointed in my recommendations, that Morrigan's a fraud."

"What happened?"

"I looked as stern as possible and asked her to join me in my office. Told Schilling I'd look after it, and he got this funny sneer on his face as we left. Back in my office, she tells me she had a deal with Schilling and wanted him to pay her. Some tangled logic about how she was trying to scare him. I agreed to pay her and told her to cool it until she received her next assignment. No more maverick work. Underlined how important it is that we don't resort to the old ways and draw attention to ourselves. And under no circumstances was she or anyone else to harm Schilling. Told her I had special plans. Anyway, she apologized and begged that I give her another chance. Told her he forgave her, but no repeats."

"Do you think Schilling suspects anything?

"Fortunately he thinks it's all a big scam. He didn't connect the crow outside his window on the day of the accident and the news report of the crow in front of Spenser's car."

"I don't think anyone would get the connection."

"Maybe not, but my point is, it's not worth risking everything to satisfy an emotional urge. Anyway, Argie came up with a red herring solution."

"Argie?"

"He's prepared a report linking Waite to Victoria's accident. It's all circumstantial evidence, of course."

Alex saw the ruse immediately. "We leak the information to the police in whatever form, and any good detective will take it from there, to look at Waite's involvement with Neil Spenser's accident as well."

"Good. I've also promised Morrigan that she can focus her efforts on James Waite when I give the word, but not a moment before."

"And?"

"And, she beamed a smile that made me feel sorry for Mr. Waite. I may never give her clearance."

Alex intervened, "Well, we're on a roll; let's go to the main event. What's up with the *Wall Street Journal* story?"

J. J.'s eyes turned cold. "We have problems."

"Wasn't Victoria to review the package before it went forward to the board, let alone to the public?"

"I wanted to wait."

"You mean you didn't announce it?"

"Sort of not."

"But the article quoted you."

"Once the article appeared and reporters started to call me, I had to cover. I didn't want to look as if I didn't have control of my own company. A few weeks ago, when I told Gerry I thought it was a good idea, it was still at the concept stage. I agreed to champion the venture with the board only after Gerry worked out the details. That was the last I heard of it until the *Wall Street Journal* called me. They told me more than what I had heard from Gerry. I assumed Victoria, or someone, had vetted the details."

"Some details. The media coverage is a disaster. And it's mostly focused on you."

"Doesn't look good does it?"

"It looks like the issue is out of control."

"Share prices are down 20 percent since the story broke. Congressional committees are sniffing around. I'm afraid they might call me as a witness just as a fishing expedition. Worse, I've had calls from key board members who normally support me, and they're unhappy. What should we do?"

Alex picked up on how J. J. had nicely switched it from an "I" problem to a "we" problem. But he was right, it was a "'we" problem. If J. J. went down, everything else collapsed as well. He paused for a long minute and then said, "I need to understand how we got here first. Could there be more fireworks? Is this just a bad case of communication or something more? I need as much background as you can give me, J. J. Whose idea was it? Why did you support it? Who's been working on it? Who might have leaked it? What would they gain?"

J. J. sat back, eyes still cold but now with a touch of sadness. As he glanced around the room, it was clear that he was blind to all except the inner replay of recent events. "OK, if you think it will help. Settle back."

Alex's phone rang. He took it out of his jacket pocket, flipped it open. and looked at the display. It was the hospital. Turning to his lunch partners, he said, "Excuse me."

J. J. nodded, "Go-ahead," and Pan sighed in exasperation, as Alex moved the phone close to his mouth.

THIRTY-FIVE

It is not things in themselves that trouble us, but our opinions of things.

—Epictetus

Lying in bed, on his back, sheets and blanket pulled up on his chest, Marcus yawned and cleared his throat; his waking voice belied his annoyance, "Sarah, let's try this again, Portland, Oregon, is on Pacific Daylight Time"

The room was still dark save for the red digital readout of his alarm clock and the tiny read lights on the phone receiver. He waited for her certain eureka moment.

"Right, I know that."

"Which means it's three hours behind Toronto on Eastern Daylight."

Sarah giggled. Sometimes that giggle was cute. Right now it was the emblem of ignorance, "Oh Markie, I always get it reversed," she said amid another giggle. "So I guess I woke you up because it's only 5:30 AM for you, not 11:30 AM."

The conversation went into free fall from there. He could not believe Sarah's tone. He had expected excitement from her or at least simple congratulations on all the media coverage he had received. Instead, she had wanted to know why he said all those mean accusations about Imagen-Pharmaglobe without checking with her first. Each comment from her seemed like one more sign of her losing her commitment to his cause and way of life.

"Markie, you need to meet J. J. He's not as bad as you say."

"What's happened to you?" replied Marcus. The disbelief of his tone had a sharp edge. He considered turning on the bedside light, then rejected the thought. The darkness made him feel as if he was outside his body, gave him room to think. "Do you realize what's at stake here?"

"He just wants to help people live longer. What's wrong with that?"

"Just take a good look around you, Sar," sighed Marcus. They had been through this a hundred times. "People crave money and power. They don't care about the cause and effect. They don't even care about traveling the stars or learning the secrets of the universe. They're driven by gut instincts. They just want to fuck like a bunch of rabbits, make money, and control others. That is ALL they care about."

"Well J. J. says that to create the perfect human being, or better yet, the perfect human hybrid, will take the use of intellect, knowledge, and wisdom and not natural instinct."

Marcus paused, reached for his ever-present water bottle on his bedside table and sipped some water. Feeling like a grade school teacher needing to repeat his basic message over and over, he continued. "Wake up, Sarah, big corporations won't use Jones's technology for such lofty goals. They will just magnify the evil that consumes most people already."

"He told me our destiny is to become 'gods' and populate the universe."

"Yeah, right, a universe filled with the gray goo of ageless morons is more like it; morons who fill their faces with Botox shots while getting their guts lipo-sucked. Look at his target market. The rich, the decadent. They don't deserve to spread their seed into the universe, until they realize what is truly important."

"Oh, Markie, maybe by living longer, people will be able to sort all of those things out. They won't feel so rushed."

"Sarah, greedy Sarah. Remember your commitment to the natural order of the world, the potential of people to live in harmony with their environment, with the universe, a universe where people celebrate death as a natural part of life, part of the cycle of renewal, knowing that at some level their energy is always present."

"Maybe, but I still don't see why life has to be so short, especially if we can do something about it."

"You don't get it, do you? You don't understand the need to stand on principle, Sar," said Marcus. He clicked the end button. Let her gestate on that thought for a while. It's time to raise the wager with Mr. J. J. Jones.

THIRTY-SIX

I have always believed helping your fellow man is profitable in every sense, personally and bottom line.

—Mario Puzo

Standing at his office window, Gerry searched the shifting colors of Lake Ontario for inspiration. As he turned his head, he caught the reflection in the window of Waite standing in his doorway. Since the mess-up with Victoria Malik, Waite was deferential, a little more cautious in his dealings with Gerry, waiting to be asked into his office rather than just walking in, as had been his practice. Maybe he had been too harsh in his treatment of Waite. Since the accident, he was less available to the man and curt when he was around. His early worries about a police investigation into the accident had waned, while the contact with the Marcus McQuillan guy was paying dividends. Turning slowly to face his faithful crony and would-be hit man, he smiled with an apologetic nod and said, "I have to hand it to you, James, all of this is working out way better than I expected."

"Thanks, Gerry," said Waite, stepping into the office. "By the way, Jones was on one of those *Good Morning America* shows this morning,"

"How'd it go?"

"Well, the man is as smooth as shit from a duck's ass."

"So he's recovering."

"Well, strangest thing, the charm just backfired. The interviewer was all over him."

"Good," said Gerry. He'd spoken with all the board members in the past three days. To a person, they had filled his ear with their concerns about J. J. striking out without board approval, the negative media, and the falling stock price. More comforting and reassuring was their flattery. Several had asked if he was prepared to step in as chairperson if they were to vote J. J. out. With this reverie, he smiled at Waite and continued, "I'm just one board meeting away from getting rid of him."

"Well, you know, I like the idea of living to 150. Do you think it could work?"

"Not the way you live."

"Well, I like the idea."

"You should. It could be good for your pension plan, if not you personally. Here's why. The fastest-growing slice of the United States population is age sixty-five years and older. At current rates, sixty-five-year-olds will outnumber teenagers by almost two to one in fewer than twenty years. Now here's where it gets good. Fifty percent or more of the baby boomer population will live one hundred years and beyond. Jones isn't out on too much of a limb in promising 150 years."

Waite looked at him, forehead furrowed in confusion.

"Take a look at the detailed business case," said Gerry. He hadn't shared the next steps with Waite, but once Jones was out of the way, he would repackage the venture so it would sell with the Wall Street analysts. The market potential was huge.

"The bottom line?"

For all of Waite's know-how about security and military tactics, he was short on business sense and vision. Gerry had often wondered about Waite's early years in the projects. It was unlikely his parents, poor and possibly illiterate, had any idea that they had named their son after Joseph Conrad's protagonist in *Nigger of the Narcissus*. Did Waite have any idea? No matter. Give him a bone to chew on, expand the possibilities of a limited mind.

"Anti-aging medicine is going to be big. Out of this world, big," said Gerry. J. J. Jones had unwittingly given him the key to his most treasured dreams. "It'll be the most intense social and economic issue of the twenty-first century, James. It'll redirect the trillion dollars plus a year of health care in radical new ways. Our way. Pharmaglobe will ride the wave. We'll be the new Microsoft."

"Right," said Waite, although the vacant look in his eyes belied his stated understanding, and Gerry moved back to immediate priorities.

"We're so close. We can't afford any screwups."

"Then I guess you want me to track this Alex Webster guy?"

"I want you to track him, and the rest of the Jones crew, find out about them. Find out what they're doing, and if it looks dangerous to us, make sure they don't succeed. No surprises. Got it?"

THIRTY-SEVEN

In the mountains there are thousand-year-old trees, but in the towns there are hardly any hundred-year-old people.

—Chinese Proverb

Victoria said, "Oh it's real, I spent some time checking it out after J. J. told me of his ideas for life extension."

It was midmorning, and they were in Victoria's hospital room, Alex felt that every time he saw Victoria now, there was something else to notice about her. First her hair, now her smile, dimples that he had never noticed before. She seemed alert and more relaxed having had a normal night's sleep and shower. They had spent the previous afternoon and evening renewing their interest in each other while they tried to piece together what had happened. Her doctors wanted to watch her for one more day before release.

"So this isn't new to you. Why hadn't you told me?"

"You wouldn't let me," said Victoria pressing the remote control unit of the hospital bed to raise the top half of it until she was propped up in a sitting position. Then she adjusted her pillows for added comfort. "Come here, sit on the bed by me while I fill you in. This is what I wanted to talk about the night of the accident, before you rejected my friendly advances."

Alex sat down beside her and instinctively started to stroke the calves of her legs beneath her silk pajamas. Leaning over, Victoria took his arm with one hand, while she ran her other hand along the inside of his thigh, giving him a playful squeeze. "This is so tempting," she said. Grinning, she squeezed again, winked and went on, "But we've got serious shoptalk to catch up on."

Resuming her sitting position, she began her briefing. "I've met with world renowned scientists on this life extension stuff. All fascinating people, particularly one guy, a Professor Aubrey de Grey at the Department of Genetics at Cambridge University. One of these guys with long hair, longer beard, and a deadpan English manner."

"Doesn't sound like the kind of guy who would have a hand in redesigning the human experience."

"Maybe not, but he runs something called the SENS project, which stands for Strategies for Engineered Negligible Senescence. Make sense of that?"

"Very punny. And no."

"Well, I don't claim to know the science, but he says the key is bioengineering. According to him, aging is a set of progressive changes—damage in body composition at the molecular and cellular level—caused as side effects of essential metabolic processes. Something like your car, with its rust buildup and breakdown of wiring parts. Traditional approaches to life extension are like rust inhibitors that try to slow the rusting. He says they won't work, however, because they need us to improve biological processes that we don't adequately understand. More importantly, they can only slow aging rather than reversing it."

"Why not just stave off disease like cancer and Alzheimer's?"

"Purely short-term geriatrics according to the professor, because it doesn't get to the root cause of the problem. It would be like fixing the rust spot and giving your car a new paint job. It's a losing battle because the continuing buildup of damage makes disease more and more inescapable. Think of your rusting car again."

"You keep picking on my car."

"Anything that'll help you get a new one."

"It's easy to be a critic. What's his approach?"

"De Grey favors genetic engineering that doesn't interfere with basic metabolism, but will repair the damage and postpone indefinitely the age at which trouble begins. Something like changing the chemical composition of steel so it doesn't oxidize. You can get Argie to brief you on the details. By the way, what's he up to?"

"On a tour with Angela Cooper to check out the security at the Imagen research labs. You're changing the subject. What's de Grey's bottom line?"

"Aging is curable."

"In whose lifetime?"

"This'll blow you away. At least it did me. He estimates that within one hundred years and possibly as soon as twenty-five years from now some newborns could have life expectancies of five thousand years."

"So the bad news is that we're born a generation too early. Hate to lose out on that one."

"Well, maybe, but let's to back to J. J. and his research labs. De Grey unwittingly gave me confidence in J. J.'s vision."

"I don't know about that. Richard Nixon declared war on cancer in 1970, wanted a NASA moon shot schedule, and ended with his second guerrilla war, one that still doesn't have an end in sight."

"You know this is different. I also think J. J. sees a possible link between life extension and reestablishing himself as a major god."

"I agree it's different. And has potential to fire his comeback. People have always looked to the gods to provide the unachievable. J. J. pitched that idea to me at lunch yesterday. Immortality is theoretical, beyond our ability to grasp. But a much longer life, like Adam, Noah, Abraham, and Moses in the Old Testament, who all lived hundreds of years, is something that most people could understand. That would be a beginning. But how to go about it? How to introduce it?"

"You get the idea. That's your job to figure out details. And J. J. has his godly ideas about strategy and tactics, not to move too fast, not wanting to attract his godly competitors. Who knows how Yahweh might respond? Might see him as a new Prometheus and go after him."

"And then there are the practicalities."

"I agree. Freedom 55 retirement probably doesn't work if you're going to live for another 4,945 years.

"Well at one level I'm beginning to understand how these gods operate. First Cupid with his chemistry of love and now this. Though, somehow, I like Morrigan's old-fashioned blood-and-guts routine. Anyway, what you've outlined is exciting and a good deal more credible than the material leaked to the media. That stuff's more like a new-age spa for the rich and famous—short on science and long on cosmetic fluff."

Alex got up from the bed and briefly considered the washed-out pastel green paint on the walls. Why was it that hospitals specialized in colors that had their lifeblood sucked out of them? He walked around to the visitor chair, sat down, and slid into a slumping position, hands in pockets, eyes on the floor. This was a favorite thinking position for him. He needed to sort through the information of the past twenty-four hours. Life was a guessing game, placing patterns on masses of information to make sense of the world. The greater the information, the greater the ways to look at it. Sitting up, he opened his eyes wide and said, "I have a scenario that brings all these stories together."

"Is it sensible?"

Alex paused. Did it matter? It's all a game of probabilities. Didn't need a theory that was true, so long as it helped predict what might happen next. He continued, "I don't know for sure, but if we act on it, it may help us save J. J. as chairperson."

"Go for it, Sherlock."

"We're midway through a daring gambit by Mr. Schilling."

"Boy, you're deep this morning, aren't you?"

"Just warming you up. Try this on. Schilling pitches the idea of the life extension communities to J. J. What he's thinking is to get J. J. to front a schlocky proposal that will drive share prices down, make J. J. look like a flaky entrepreneurial type unfit to be chair of a global enterprise. Pressure builds on J. J. to step down or be fired by the board of directors,"

"Why doesn't J. J. see this?"

"Because he thinks the life extension concept will work. His labs are close to clinical trials on several fronts. Pharmaglobe is the marketing vehicle. It fits right in with his original plan, and he thinks he's got Schilling finally on board. He agrees to lead it, and Gerry will put the package together. He's prudent and plans to have you review the package before it goes public, and Angela Cooper will review technical details."

"So that is why he was oblivious to Schilling's threat?"

"Exactly. He's covered. Then, I'm guessing Schilling begins to understand there is substance behind the various claims, in part because he is tracking you and Angela. As he puts more of the puzzle together, the more he sees you as a threat because you will vet the proposal for J. J. and will see through it. Angela, he doesn't have to get rid of as quickly, but she is still a threat."

"So Waite sets me up for a car accident."

"Yes, and when that failed, he rushed the leak of the schlocky version of the life extension communities to the media, hoping that you remained unconscious for as long as possible. And it worked, in fact almost too well. Some interest groups were all over it within hours. I don't understand that part. Anyway, now that you're back, my guess is that you're still at risk, as well as Angela."

"And probably yourself, given that you've been filling in for me. You're out of the closet so to speak."

"Could be. When does the Pharmaglobe board meet next?"

"Three weeks, and my guess is that Gerry Schilling is already lining up votes to remove J. J."

"Our first priority must be to shift momentum in the media. We need to spin J. J. in a positive light. We must persuade him to lay out the real proposal. And ideally do it with credibility, say, by appearing voluntarily before the FDA and a Congressional committee on trade.

"It's a long shot given the time frame. I'll get working on it right away with my Washington contacts."

"Meantime, I'll meet with J. J., Pan, and Argie to see what we can do avoid any more accidents."

PART FIVE
THE BEGINNING OF THE END ...
THE END OF THE BEGINNING

THIRTY-EIGHT

To see the world in a grain of sand, and heaven in a wild flower,
Hold infinity in the palm of your hands, and eternity in an hour.

—William Blake

Two days later Alex walked with Victoria through the academic elegance of King's College Circle, on the University of Toronto Campus. Overcast March skies presented a somber professorial tenor, wielding a cold, brisk wind to scold wayward students. Meeting at the corner of University and College, they went through the medical school building and into the Circle on their way to Hart House, where they planned to have lunch.

Alex ignored the stern gray architecture as he pondered the media images of the past two days. Protests against J. J. continued to climb. One of Imagen's Atlanta labs had been vandalized. Vandals had painted the words, "LIVE IN NATURE, DIE FOR NATURE" and, more ominously, "DIE, J. J. JONES, DIE," in large red letters on the walls of the building. Ironically, the letters were bleeding from excess paint. The image aggravated the chill of the day, driving it to his bones, and he slowed his pace to do up the top button on his coat.

Victoria said, "My Washington contacts will smooth the way for J. J. to appear before the FDA and one of the Congressional committees, a full meeting of the Senate committee on commerce, science, and transportation. There's much interest in what's happening. No one knows what the policy issues of life extension are. But most think it could be like the abortion or the stem cell debate."

Her animated voice focused him. "Does anyone support J. J.'s gated community idea?"

"Privately many senators and representatives of both parties do. They see life extension as putting tremendous demands on health care and Social Security, so a private-sector approach is appealing. If you can afford it, you can have it. Of course, they can't say this publicly."

Alex marveled at the minds of politicians. A major scientific breakthrough, the dream of humanity for thousands of years, and they focus on the impact of longer lives on Social Security and affordability. A few more days, and there would be policy papers on why living longer would boost the economy or kill it, enhance the moral character of humans or destroy it, be consistent with God's will or in defiance of it. And through it all politicians would thrust and parry with the media as master illusionists, using words to weave their way through each probing question to leave no doubt about the certainty of their uncertainty on the subject. Was this part of J. J.'s plan? It probably explained why he was so cautious. Finally he said, "So they'll support him in private and crucify him in public."

"Careful with the symbolism. There may be posturing by some of the left-leaning senators, but you know they all have ways of covering even their most critical comments."

"How soon can your friends arrange it?"

"Two weeks. A day after the board meeting."

"So is this good news or bad news?"

"Good news, because we want to get J. J. onstage to tell his story, not just react to somebody else's story. I hope it will at least buy a little time if the board will wait until after his appearance to take a vote on his future, if that's what they're thinking."

"Trust me. That's what they're thinking. I got that much from J. J. this morning. Anything else?"

"How about some enthusiasm here? It takes connections to make things like this happen."

Caught up in his own thoughts, he had failed to recognize Victoria's achievement. This may be their only chance to influence investors and public opinion in J. J.'s favor. Blushing with a rush of guilt, he stopped, performed a half bow, and apologized, "I know, I know, I'm impressed."

Victoria tapped his shoulder with her hand as a sign of forgiveness and said, "By the way, this Marcus McQuillan guy has emerged as a real media favorite in speaking against life extension." She lowered her voice to mimic his style, "If poets can find eternity in a grain of sand for free, why pay J. J. Jones to screw up your genes for a few extra years?"

"Yeah, right, a grain of sand," said Alex wistfully, wondering if the poets had it right. On the other hand, would poets have held that view if they had the choice of living forever? How much of such poetry was simply someone rationalizing their fate and accepting it? Besides, the average person didn't have much use for such poetics. Results counted, not ideas, not words. For several minutes they walked in silence, and as they arrived at their destination, Alex spoke again.

"Let me tell you about Marcus McQuillan, let me tell you about many things."

"Please do."

Alex stopped, as did Victoria. While she watched him, he turned and surveyed the path from the medical center where they had entered the Circle to the Hart House entrance. He felt foolish. and yet because of recent events he was suspicious of everyone who passed them. Students and professors outnumbered all other people by a significant margin and after several minutes of intense study, he felt secure.

Victoria, appraising him uneasily, said, "You seem so preoccupied. You keep glancing over your shoulder as if we're being followed. What's up? Tell me what's bugging you."

"Let's go inside—it's a long story."

∗   ∗   ∗   ∗

The Gallery Grill on the second floor of the east wing of Hart House overlooking the Great Hall, was a perfect Gothic setting for his tale. And the sight of the fire in the lounge area had relaxed Alex's mood. He had a gourmet hamburger with fries, and Victoria had the clubhouse sandwich.

Wiping his mouth with his napkin, he said, "We may need to expand our planning horizon."

"What do you mean?" said Victoria, sounding anxious at the implication.

"Sometimes I feel like we're the street cleaners, following the horses of the masters, cleaning up their messes."

Victoria laughed and said, "OK, what's changed? I thought you met with J. J. this morning to get things going our way."

"I did, but you know the story—one step forward, two steps back, maybe more, who knows?"

He told Victoria of his meeting with J. J. and Pan at J. J.'s office suite that morning. They had been easy to talk to, listened to his ideas about J. J. volunteering to meet with the FDA and Congressional committees. At first Pan had done most of the talking, and J. J. had been quiet. Not sulking, but different—like a little boy whose hand had been caught in the cookie jar. He hadn't said much of anything. Then at Pan's suggestion, they went to J. J.'s private boardroom, the one that was scanned daily for listening and watching devices. Although it had no windows, it had a bright, informal feeling with textured walls in warm Mediterranean colors and recessed lighting. A midmorning goodies buffet at the side of the room beckoned participants with oversized chocolate chip and oatmeal cookies, coffee, soft drinks, and bottled water. Although some might call it a bunker, Alex called it a retreat. It was quiet, pleasant, and he especially liked the chewiness of the oatmeal cookies. But he hadn't the chance to enjoy them the way he usually did.

Alex described the scene as he remembered it.

Pan asking Alex if he was in for a fight to the finish. He said, "Some things have come up that could make our task difficult."

J. J. slamming his fist on the table and making little lightning flashes from his fingertips, saying, "I didn't mean for things to work out this way. Can you believe it? This Marcus McQuillan guy and his Gaia Only Development. Do you think my grandmother's behind this guy?"

Pan saying, "Relax. It couldn't be. It's a red herring. Why would she bother? We haven't heard from her in years. And worrying about it will get us into more trouble, as you have already shown us. Maybe you better tell Alex the details."

J. J. sighing and apologizing to Alex before getting into details, saying the thought of Gaia meddling depressed him so much it led to another problem. "Yesterday I was feeling blue because of all this. Standing in my office, looking out my window, Sarah Orenstein, that intern woman, comes up behind me, blindfolds me with her hands, crushes her breasts into my back, her perfume filling my lungs. 'Guess who,' she says. I pretend I don't know and reach back, placing my hands on her hips, letting them travel further across her bottom."

Pan teasing J. J., "You mean her ass, you son of a gun. You should try meditation for stress relief."

Victoria interrupted. "Ha, do men mimic the gods or is it the other way around?"

"Depends on the man; depends on the god."

"I could write a book on men, their mothers, and a woman's body."

"Well, that could be our next project after you hear what happened next," said Alex, and he continued with his story.

J. J. looking stricken and saying, "Nothing happened, it was just play. Trust me. Suddenly my assistant is on the intercom saying Juno's on her way in. I panicked."

Pan laughing now, saying, "Sooner or later the great god, Pan, rules."

J. J. saying, "I turned Sarah into a long-hair Chihuahua just as Juno entered the room. Told her it was a gift. She loved it, much more than I expected. Took it to a lunch meeting with her. I managed to retrieve it later in the day. Saying it needed shots. Then I transformed it back into Sarah, who cursed me, threatened revenge, and then quickly ran out of my office."

Pan saying, "You should have left her as a dog."

J. J. saying, "A missing intern. Get real. The media would eat me, I'd be toast. On the other hand, an intern who she says she had been turned into a dog might not even make the *National Examiner*."

Pan saying, "She wouldn't be that stupid. She'll go for the throat and seek revenge in other ways. Anyway, J. J., you should be setting an example for the other gods."

J. J. saying, "Nag, nag, nag. I've always been kicked around for a little bit of sex. Philosophers, media. How many of them have been married to the same woman for thousands of years? And now I've got to find a real Chihuahua for Juno."

Pan saying, "It's not a moral matter but a practical one, at least until your comeback position is secured."

Victoria interrupted again with an amused smile on her face as she said, "He's blaming others? Our god sounds a little human. Good for Pan for going after him."

"Maybe, but it gets more interesting," said Alex, pausing for a moment to eat a French fry and then going on with his tale in headline form.

Argie entering the room, saying, "Guess what, Sarah's boyfriend is Marcus McQuillan, all on company phone records too." J. J. turning red, clenching his fists, heat emanating from his body as Argie went on, saying, "I've checked out all computer records, fund transfers, and credit cards and uncovered a link between James Waite and McQuillan. Waite is funding his activities. According to Sarah's VISA trail, she's gone to Portland to be with McQuillan."

J. J. grumbling as an electric arc formed over his head and the room's temperature becoming unbearable. Pan mumbling, "You've to focus on the endgame. You can't afford to blow it in the clutch again."

Victoria broke in again. "If this were a movie, the violins would now start doing the weird thing, and we would start to wonder if someone was going to get killed."

"I hope not. In fact, J. J. wants to avoid it. The bad news sobered him, cleared his mind on what needs to be done. The next seven days are key to saving his position. We developed a plan. He's asked me to join Argie in Atlanta to help Angela Cooper add extra security to Imagen's key research labs."

"Will you be gone long?"

"I hope it's just a couple of days. Meanwhile, I want you to work with Mercury getting J. J. ready for his Washington appearance."

"Let's hope they're ready for prime time. Anything else I should know about?"

"I'm not sure. J. J. knows time is working against him with the board. Oh, he'll also be talking to Dr. Apollo and Morrigan. And he wants all of us to get together when I get back."

Victoria nodded and said, "At least he's in action. What do you think of the Gaia angle?"

"I don't know. If J. J. has enlisted us, why wouldn't other gods be doing the same?"

"So what are we going to do about it?"

Alex looked at Victoria and then, after a long moment, said, "Nothing, at least not directly, and certainly not now. Let's focus on what we know and think we understand, which is keeping J. J. as head of Imagen-Pharmaglobe."

THIRTY-NINE

Jealousy is the jaundice of the soul.

—John Dryden

Marcus paced like the eccentric professor he was, back and forth, at the base of his bed. Dressed in boots, jeans, and a red cowboy shirt over a black T-shirt, he wore a scowl meant to intimidate Sarah, who was sitting on the bed's edge. Arriving unannounced at his door late last night, hair disheveled, and clothes crumpled, she had been angry, babbling about seeking his forgiveness. The red numbers of the bedside digital alarm clock said 4:00 AM. Her eyes were red from periodic bouts of tears and her increasing need for sleep. Like a CIA interrogator debriefing a double agent just returned from a terrorist cell, he wanted to test her story yet again, looking for a break point. As much as he loved Sarah, her story had undermined his confidence on many levels.

"OK, tell me again from the beginning," he said, his voice almost in a whisper.

"Not again. It embarrasses me."

"Think of what it's doing to me. How could you?"

"I didn't do anything."

"Tell me exactly."

"Well, I had snuck up behind him and put my hands over his eyes and whispered, 'Guess who?'"

"I don't believe it."

"And he had just started to touch me, when his assistant announced the arrival of his wife."

"Touched you where?"

"Who knows, because it was then that he turned me into a dog, a little Chihuahua, like the one Paris Hilton has."

"Were you doing drugs?"

"Honestly, I couldn't talk, only bark."

"Then?"

"Juno asks whether I'm a boy or a girl."

"And?"

"J. J. cradles me on my back in his arm, holds my legs apart and says, 'Check for yourself.'"

"Juno's bisexual?" Marcus's heartbeat increased.

"I told you, this isn't about sex, and I was a dog."

"Yeah, yeah."

"You don't believe me."

"I think he tricked you into kinky sex."

"Markie, if you don't believe me who will?"

"What happened next?"

"I turned over in his lap and bit his dick."

"Get serious."

"Then I urinated on him."

"Sar, this is disgusting, depraved," he said, as he turned away to hide his growing erection. He scrunched his eyes to look serious. "And then?"

"And then Juno says 'good girl,' comes over, and picks me up to cuddle me close to her face."

"Did she touch you?"

"She held my butt in one hand and stroked my back while telling me how adorable and cute I was."

"I told you she was bisexual."

"I licked her face, her neck. She wouldn't let my tongue touch her lips."

"My Sarah likes other women."

"Marcus, this wasn't sex. It was survival. I was afraid that J. J. might hurt me."

"You must promise me, Sar."

"Please Markie, I'll promise anything so long as you stand up for me and help me get revenge."

"You must promise me that if you ever do something like this again," said Marcus and then he stopped himself. His breathing quickened, and he felt hot and flushed. He wanted to open the window of his bedroom and scream into the night. He wanted to hit something. Most of all he wanted revenge. Revenge on J. J. Jones and Imagen-Pharmaglobe for abducting the love of his life.

FORTY

And we know that all things work together for the good.
—Romans 8:28, Webster's Bible Translation

"As you can see, we're prepared for anything," said Angela to Alex and Argie, while her head of security, a tall, solemn man, with a shaved bald head and a handlebar mustache, who had not smiled all morning, nodded agreeing. They were touring the Imagen headquarters located in suburban Atlanta, Georgia. Housing administrative offices, a training center, state-of-the-art research and development laboratories, a manufacturing floor, and an auditorium that held two hundred fifty people, the facility was composed of two ultramodern buildings of glass and steel with over two hundred thousand square feet.

Alex moved his head up and down as if to signal agreement, although he wasn't so sure. It seemed all systematic and rational, but he found certain irrationality mixed with rationality when dealing with madmen. The figure in black standing across the street from the Imagen complex when they arrived haunted him; no one else had noticed. Since arriving, they had spent all of Saturday morning going over every facet of security, from the physical protection around the complex and the guards, to the sign-in procedures. The head of security had even issued Alex and Argie bracelets that could only be removed by security staff. The bracelets sent signals to receivers in the ceilings or on walls.

"The receivers connect to a local network, send the data to servers that calculate location, and make the information available in various ways to our security staff," he had said. "If you are on Imagen's property, I will know where you are."

"So I can run, but I can't hide," said Alex.

"You got it, sport." The man was too clever, too proud of his work. When it came to preparation against terrorists of any sort, you needed humility and an open mind. What happened if he had a knife to cut the bracelet off? What if the power failed? And what a way to treat visitors and employees, although all the staff he spoke with loved their bracelets. Gave them a sense of belonging, a sense of safety. Their earnestness told him that he could never work in such an environment.

Angela spoke again, "Enough of this touring. Argie, you can finish your questions of my staff out here while Alex and I relax in my office. I want to catch up on the latest about Schilling and Waite."

She would have excelled in the military. A white blouse with buttons of silver complemented the severity of her black suit. The crease in her pants was as sharp as a knife. She walked like a soldier with chest out, shoulders back, stomach in. The low heels of her shoes clicked on the terrazzo floors. Smiling while she talked, her eyes took in everything around her. She had listened to each question that Argie and he had asked her, paused to consider her response, and then spoke in sentences that were models of logic and syntax. He understood why J. J. had hired her. She was bright, skillful, detailed, and loyal. She led the way into her office, holding the door for him, and then closing it, leaving Argie to consult with the head of security and his staff in the anteroom to her office.

The flash and the roar arrived at the same moment, throwing Alex across the room, filling his nose and mouth with cordite. The bitter residue remained in his respiratory system, and he tasted gunpowder with every breath. Both he and Angela had been knocked to the floor. Furniture was overturned, computers and papers scattered everywhere. He looked over to see Angela lying facedown by her overturned desk, but felt assured at some level when he heard her moans.

A second detonation punctuated his ears with a deafening roar, as if a thousand thunderstorms had struck at once. Then he lost consciousness. When he came to he saw the ceiling had caved in, He realized, too, that at some point he had put his hands over his head, as they were now bleeding. Blood also ran from cuts to his right cheek. Flying debris had torn his lower lip.

His mind raced.

Is Angela OK?

Where's Argie?

Is the building going to collapse?

We're on the fourth floor. Should we try to leave the building?

Will there be a third explosion?

He crawled over to Angela who was still on the floor.

"Are you hurt?"

"My leg."

He checked it in the dark haze of the room, feeling a thick shard of wood projecting from her thigh. He pulled it out like a cork from a bottle and gasped when the blood pulsed out from the wound. "A tourniquet. You need a tourniquet." His Boy Scout training clicked in as he pulled off his belt and secured it around her thigh above the ragged puncture in her leg.

"We've got to get out of here and get help for your leg."

"I'll try to hop along if you hold me up."

"Let's go for it," he said, taking her arm and lifting her up. Their time for escape was limited. The tourniquet had stopped the bleeding, but Angela would get gangrene if blood didn't circulate through her leg. If necessary, he would stop to loosen the tourniquet after twenty minutes if they weren't out of this holocaust and then reapply it.

They stumbled into the anteroom, and it opened into ruin. The partitions separating offices had collapsed. The body of the head of security staff slumped on the floor. A shard of glass ran through his back like a stylized bayonet. Argie was nowhere to be seen.

They struggled to the staircase, which was crowded with people. The hackneyed odor of hot metal filled his nose. Blood. The railing was slick with blood. He did not see anyone who was not bleeding; but there was no panic. People were moving as much out of caution as consideration, sharing the same thought that they would be better off outdoors. The dust and smoke limited visibility to fewer than three feet, so they relied on the steps and the railings to help them find their way out.

"I'm suffocating," cried Angela as they stumbled down the stairwell.

"Hang on. We'll make it," said Alex. It's times like this that people pray, visceral, instinctive prayer. To whom? Some higher force? Some inner strength? Are they one and the same, man as god, some inner force? He thought of the scene in the movie *Run Lola Run*, where Lola bets her future on the spin of a casino's roulette wheel. If she wins, her boyfriend lives, if she loses, he dies, and her life is over. An act of will rises in her to challenge fate and chart the future time. Taking in a deep breath, she wills the wheel to stop on her number by screaming like a banshee. Glass breaks, people stop their gambling and stare at her, while the wheel turns ever more slowly and the ball bounces with a carefree randomness until it falls into the slot of her number and stops.

Screaming was not his style, but charting his future was. Alex took a deep breath and pictured the path of escape out of building to the outside.

The trip down the rubble-strewn and dust-filled stairwell lasted an eternity. Reaching the shambles of what was once the downstairs lobby, he followed other survivors, many bloody and dazed, as they streamed out of the building.

"Let me help you," said the voice and a hand reached out to help.

"Please, my friend needs immediate medical care" Alex said, as new hands came to support Angela.

The helpers led them through the rubble to a clearing across the street, where they eased Angela into a sitting position. Alex turned to look back at the Imagen headquarters. The explosion had scalped the glass skin of the building, revealing a skeleton of iron, a postmodern vision of Dante's *City of Dis*, the place of unbelievers. The remaining offices and labs within the building now served as the burning tombs of heretics, who failed to believe in the god of a madman. Survivors provided a chorus of doleful sighs and cries of woe.

Two paramedics soon attended to Angela as she sat slouched on the curb across the street; stained with blood and hair that coiled into an ashen collection of serpents, she looked like one of the three furies.

"Are you OK?" asked one of the men who had helped them.

While another paramedic attended to his bleeding lip, Alex, looked over at the Imagen ruins, hoping to see Argie, and said, "My friend's missing."

The whole front of the building was rubble. In the visitor parking lot, the wrecks of several vehicles were ablaze. Charred corpses, black and shriveled, their hands outstretched in what looked like a last, futile prayer to ward off their death, were strewn about. A choking dust cloud hung over the site, uniting the living and the dead in its powdery shroud.

Two men approached. Alex recognized a familiar face. He saw the twitch. How could it be? Detective Cleve Morrison. His heart sank. He hoped that he wouldn't be recognized.

"Good evening, Sam Brown from the Atlanta Police Department," said the older man. "My partner's Cleve Morrison. You all right?"

"Thankful to be alive," said Alex.

Morrison studied Alex for a long moment and finally said, "You look familiar, don't I know you from somewhere?"

Alex decided to get it over with, better now than later, and said, "Alex Webster, detective. Couple of months ago, Savannah, Club One. What're you doing here?"

Morrison shook his head and whistled under his breath. "Let's just say our meeting that evening helped a transfer," came the curt reply. "My superiors thought it would be a good thing. But we don't want to go there. What brings you here? How'd you manage to be in that building when it blew up? A jealous husband after you and your friend Doctor Love?"

Although the question was way out of line, Alex chose to ignore it and recounted events as Morrison eyed him with a cool reserve. He told them of his work for Imagen-Pharmaglobe and the threats from the GOD group and Marcus McQuillan in particular. He also mentioned the figure dressed in black loitering in front of the building hours earlier. Morrison became more and more interested, as the enormity of the case grew before him, while Alex imagined a path to multiple redemptions for Morrison, J. J., and himself.

"Detectives, come here. Something strange." The request came from two rescuers, who were carrying a small hammock made of the shirt of one of the rescuers. Alex accompanied the detectives.

"Look at this," said the rescuer, a young man covered in a crust of sweat and ash. Lowering the sling to the ground, he leaned over, opened it up, and reached in, saying, "This might be the piece of equipment that set off the bombs. We thought at first it was the work of a shard of glass. But all these computer chips and wires changed our mind." Then, like the soldier showing the head of John the Baptist, he displayed a lifeless head with its two bulging eyes, staring at them unknowingly, wiring and circuitry dangling from the ripped neck. Nausea raced through his stomach and throat; Alex choked and turned away. It was Argie's head.

FORTY-ONE

Nowadays those are rewarded who make right appear wrong.

—Terence

Standing by the marble fireplace in the study of his Georgian home located in Toronto's Bridle Path area, Gerry stared into the flames, as if looking for a replay of the Atlanta explosion. Ten dead and scores injured. It was a small price. His only regret was that the dead did not include Alex Webster and Angela Carter. His philosophy was that you had to have a certain impassive scorn for the lives of everyday people, if it meant achieving a greater good for humanity. Never get seduced by the false arguments of noble means if it put your objectives at risk. And by historic standards, this explosion was nothing. That aside, he needed to quiz his playmaker to make sure he would take no blame. His numerous roles demanded credibility. First, as the primary empathizer to the families of the victims on behalf of Imagen-Pharmaglobe. Then as the protector to the shareholders concerned about their investment, as well as the bastion of corporate integrity to the public confused by the attack.

"Just perfect, better than expected," said Waite, who sat on the dark leather couch behind him. Gerry turned to study him; rarely had his second in command shown such enthusiasm, moving the rim of the small, tulip-shaped Riedel crystal stemware to his nose and sniffing the delicate caramel and fruit aromas of Gerry's best cognac. Undoubtedly he deserved it, having started the day in Atlanta, then flying back to Toronto to report firsthand to Gerry on results.

Indeed, Waite's smiling face had the look of caricature that overtakes people in later middle age when the color and tone of their skin starts yielding to time. Or was it the cognac?

"In what sense?" said Gerry, adjusting the photograph of his mother Hannah on the mantle of the fireplace, positioning it as if he wanted to shield her from the less-flattering details behind his emerging victory.

"First the setup. Great idea to frame McQuillan. Set him up in the Grand Hyatt in Atlanta's posh Buckland district. Luxury suite, champagne on ice. A young, large-breasted porn star arrived within fifteen minutes of his arrival. Poor bastard probably thought he'd died and gone to heaven."

"And while he played?"

"Arranged to have his double visibly active around the Imagen site before the explosion, drawing attention to himself, then jumping into a cab to get back to the Hyatt, garnering much attention on arrival. Poor dumbfuck Marcus. Within two hours of the explosion, police had issued a statement that he was a person of interest in the investigation."

"Has he been taken in for questioning?" asked Gerry. Prosecutors had become so gutless. Nobody was a suspect anymore, just a person of interest until the DA felt a reasonable confidence of victory in court.

"No, seemingly he disappeared," said Waite.

Gerry pictured the scene of McQuillan turning on the television in his room after hours of sex, only to see his picture on the screen as a wanted man. In panic he seeks escape, thus magnifying the appearance of guilt. That was one of the features he liked about Marcus McQuillan. Never thought his plans through. Real life wasn't *The Fugitive*. "What about the young woman?" he asked.

"Paid to disappear and forget the episode. And the icing on the cake, for me anyway, is we knocked out that security android, if anyone or anything was a threat to our secrecy that was it. Any reaction from the board members?"

"Five calls so far. They've had enough. Too much blood on their hands." Gerry had listened to the grief in their voices. He had said nothing, listening empathetically, repeating their words softly, and then he offered the point that their first duty was to shareholders in times of crisis. "They want Jones out, but his old supporters still want to do it in an honorable way, perhaps allowing him to stay on the board."

"Do we want that?"

"Don't worry. It won't happen. One of our other eggs has hatched—the intern."

"Sarah Orenstein?"

"She's prepared to sign a formal complaint of harassment against Jones," said Gerry. Some behavior is so wonderfully predictable, just set the pieces and players in place and wait for them to move to their own natural equilibrium. But he had to concede the timing was an unplanned bonus in this case. "Once the board hears the details of the affidavit, they will be less concerned about an honorable exit."

He briefed Waite on Sarah Orenstein. How she had come to his office yesterday, plainly distraught, eyes glaring, rambling that she wanted to file a sexual harassment charge against J. J. Jones.

Sarah saying, "He pinned me against the wall, and fondled my breasts while pressing his groin into me. He had an erection. I told him no, pushed him away, and ran out of his office."

"I told her it was proper that she had informed me. Promised her full support of the company's counseling and legal services if she chose to lodge a formal complaint."

"Do you believe her story?" asked Waite.

"Does it matter?" In fact, Gerry didn't believe her. Her story had been too neatly contrived to ring true. Details kept shifting as if to test his reaction. Something had happened with Jones that had provoked her, but not the story she was telling. It hardly mattered. With everything else, it would serve as the tipping point with the board. "It's appearances that count."

FORTY-TWO

This is the Scroll of Thoth. Herein are set down the magic words by which Isis raised Osiris from the dead. "Oh! Amon-Ra—Oh! God of Gods—
Death is but the doorway to new life—We live today—we shall live again—In many forms shall we return—Oh, mighty one."

—John L. Balderston

Alex winced as the twenty-something nurse injected a needle into the area above his upper lip. It was supposed to freeze the area, reduce the pain.

"Sorry," she said. "Lidocaine hurts for a few seconds with some people. You must be one of the unlucky ones."

"Right," said Alex. Doctors, dentists, nurses, hygienists. All the same. They were always sorry. Poke, jab, inject. "Oops, sorry. Did that hurt? Just a little more."

"It'll numb the torn area so the doctor can suture the tear. You'll be on your way in no time," she said, and then added with smile and a pat on his arm, "once you're home, rinse with lukewarm water or half-strength hydrogen peroxide after meals for one week. And no kissing."

He had ridden with Angela in the ambulance to the emergency department at the Atlanta Medical Center. On the way he had called J. J. and then relayed the results to Angela.

"Did you tell him about Argie?"

"Yes. He said he's glad it wasn't either one of us."

"That's it?" she said, mouth hanging open, her eyes wide in dismay.

"Well, he did ask if everything was all right. I said we'd manage," said Alex. The insensitivity of J. J. to their loss of Argie bothered him. Maybe endings didn't mean as much to immortals, but some sign of empathy would have been kind. Clenching his right hand around his left wrist, he squeezed as hard as he could to offset his sense of frustration. He regretted not telling J. J. that he felt devastated by Argie's destruction. Normally he preferred to deal with sensitive subjects face-to-face. And this wasn't the time to be petulant. Another complaint added to his list of issues he would someday discuss in private with J. J. Still, it should be obvious. Here they were putting their lives on the line, and J. J. had stayed focused on business. His prime concern was his own survival as chair of Imagen-Pharmaglobe. He had asked Alex to return quickly to attend the deposition of Sarah Orenstein scheduled for Monday morning in the Toronto head office.

"What's that about?" said Angela.

"A bogus sexual harassment charge. Don't ask for details." The Chihuahua episode, as Alex liked to call it, had been kept quiet, with details provided only to those that needed to know.

"But what about Marcus McQuillan?" said Angela.

"A red herring clearly. According to J. J., Waite set up today's explosion. Marcus was the fall guy."

"Then you should focus on Waite, not sit in on some stupid deposition," said Angela. Alex nodded sadly and paused for a long moment before replying that J. J. had promised Morrigan she could mete out retribution to James Waite.

"He's asked Morri du Morde to watch Waite."

"Don't you think that's a risky assignment for her?"

"She volunteered for it. As a favor to Victoria," dissembled Alex, wanting to change the subject. If J. J. was about to unleash divine powers on Waite, then the circumstances must be serious. "Besides, J. J. needs my help at head office. The board and Gerry Schilling are the big issues for him right now. After the deposition, he wants me to call Dr. Luther and Professor Laydback. He needs their support on the board, at least until his Senate appearance. But just in case they can't or won't support him, he wants me to brief them in detail on the governance clauses in the merger agreement between Pharmaglobe and Imagen."

"An unusual request. Any idea what he's up to?" said Angela

"No, but I promised I would do it. Told him he may need a miracle to save the day."

He wanted to track down Waite with Morrigan. However, he felt obliged to J. J., who had appointed Dr. Luther and Laydback to the Imagen-Pharmaglobe board of directors on Alex's advice. Their votes next week could end his career and his comeback. The thought alone produced stitches of guilt that motivated action.

Alex returned to the Westin Atlanta Airport after medical staff had treated Angela and assigned her to a private room in the hospital.

As he packed, his thoughts were of Argie and how well matched his humor had been to his own, how brave and generous and witty he had been. He was able to go from play to formal behavior, prudent at times, merry at others. Argie had become so much a part of Alex's waking hours that he had come to rely on his advice. He was quick in seeing the state of affairs, always obliging, always providing cool reason. He could be close in argument but never stubborn. Alex especially valued Argie's *lacks*: lack of envy, lack of lust, and lack of revenge. He didn't hate or even dislike; he didn't waste time meddling in the affairs of others, neither slandering strangers nor spiting foes.

Waves of loss rose and fell within Alex's chest. The experience was new. No one this close to him had ever died. What was the right act? Should he arrange for a memorial service? Argie was an android, a robot, simply an extraordinary machine. Why anthropomorphize him? He thought of his car. Yes, he would miss his car as well if it were stolen or destroyed. It occurred to him that if asked to name his top ten emotional ties, at least four of them would be inanimate objects: Argie, his car, his wallet, and his personal computer. Would he hold memorial services for all of them, observe the rituals of mourning?

After completing his checkout, he still had a few minutes to wait before the next shuttle to Hartsford International for the midnight flight to Toronto. He needed comfort. The familiar green and white of the Starbucks emblem on the other side of the hotel's lobby signaled him. The chalkboard announced, in green and blue pastels, the coffee of the day, Arabian Mocha Sanani.

"What's Sanani?" he asked the clerk, a young man dressed in a black shirt and black pants. His spiked hair was an unnatural black, and two long spiked labrets protruded halfway between his lower lip and the top of his chin. An effective way to avoid kissing anyone. Perhaps he had a jealous lover. Alex guessed at the selection criteria used by Starbucks for hiring their staff. "Is candidate under twenty-five years old? Looks good in black? Has prominent piercings or tattoos on display?"

"It's the coffee-growing region around San'a, the capital of Yemen. You know, the place Saddam Hussein invaded that started the first Gulf War."

"I think you mean Kuwait."

"No, I mean Yemen. I don't know of any coffee from Kuwait," said the young man. It clearly didn't occur to him that there was more than one way to be wrong. Sometimes it was best just to let sleeping dogs lie. So Alex nodded, and the young man continued, "This coffee rocks. Laden with flavors of deep port wine, juicy ripe blackberries, warm earthen spices, and arid cocoa. Not everybody can handle the intensity; it's perfect for the daring coffee connoisseur."

The last words arrived with a note of challenge. Or at least, that's the way it seemed. Alex wasn't going to back down to some punk kid wearing the veneer of expert knowledge, even if was only coffee.

"I'll try it. Give me a Grande. And I'm hungry. What do you recommend that I eat with it?" Alex wanted to throw the young man off. Food pairing with coffees was de rigueur urban wisdom for the young and sophisticated. Was the kid for real or a phony?

His reply was instantaneous. "I recommend a currant scone or a slice of spicy carrot cake. Either is a good match for the Sanani's wildness."

Alex was impressed. The kid stakes out his area of knowledge and rides it proudly. "Carrot cake wins."

"Good choice, one of my favorites," said the young man. Yeah, right. As a final test of his coffee server, Alex asked the question he asked of every Starbucks clerk. And one that had never been answered.

"Who's the girl in the middle of the logo?" Not expecting an answer, he fumbled in his pocket for his cell phone. He wanted to try Victoria again.

"Isis, the Great Mother of creation to the ancient Egyptians," came the quick reply. "She is the power of nature in all her glory, the creative power of the universe, causing physical form from the womb of the unmanifest."

Alex released the phone. Not bad. The kid doesn't know Kuwait from Yemen, but he knows coffee and goddesses. How deep can he go?

"So do people ever complain that she doesn't have any clothes on?"

"Only the shallow and insecure. Besides, she's not naked you know," said the young man. He took a cup and pointed to the logo, and continued, "Look, her hair falls over her breasts in six wavy lines. Very stylish actually. And she's wearing a crown with a five-pointed star. You know what that means?"

"I give up," The discussion had passed the merely amusing stage. Heading into uncharted territory, Alex recalled his lawyer's advice, to never ask a question for which he did not know the answer.

"It's positive. The upper point represents Spirit, having dominion over the four elements. And those chevrons that she's pushing at?" Alex nodded. The young man continued, "Those are fish being pushed away, the end of the age of Pisces. A global age of destructive values. Can you see it?"

"Well," said Alex, opting for a noncommittal nod of his head as he studied the logo anew. How does someone who doesn't know geography and geopolitics start lecturing on affairs of the world? And the Starbucks girl was no Miss Chiquita Banana. For Alex, the brown-skinned beauty, with a teasing smile and gold-looped earrings, held more allure that this alleged Egyptian goddess. Her blue dress adorned with yellow ruffled sleeves and hems beat the wavy hair over the breasts act. In a low whisper he sang, "I'm Chiquita Banana, and I've come to say I offer good nutrition for you every day."

"What you say, man?"

"I guess I never looked at her closely enough," Alex said.

"Few do. Hey, it's symbolic. She's emerging from the darkness of the late Piscean era where most of us are still hovering."

"And you believe this?"

"In their hearts doesn't everybody?" said the young man. Aah, bliss of the true believer, thought Alex. So clear is the vision that they think everyone can see the same light. Deciding that further discussion was futile, Alex took out his wallet, counted out exact change, and placed it on the counter. "Thanks."

"Uh huh. Y'all have a good evening," said the young man. Alex took a last brief look at him and walked away. One final irritation. "Uh huh," the lazy half groan standing-in for "You're welcome." A step back in civilization. It was unworthy of analysis. At least right now. Comfort was his goal. Focus on the trivial, the mundane.

In less than a minute, he was seated in a corner table, savoring his first bite of carrot cake. The idea of the divine feminine lingered as the sugar raced to his brain. Did it suggest a new age of spirituality? Or rather people's expectations of one? Is J. J.'s problem Yahweh or something bigger? J. J. frets about Gaia's actions, although he hasn't heard from her in thousands of years. Marcus McQuillan uses her as his imaginary muse. But how imaginary? And now the Starbucks girl. So many signs pointing in the same direction. Was there a message in all of this? He'd bounce it off Victoria.

"Hey man, here's the McQuillan story on TV," said the young man interrupting his thoughts and turning up the volume on the television on the coffee kiosk. The gravelly voice of a news reporter recounted the story of the explosion. The man must gargle razor blades every morning to preserve that grating voice. The smoldering Imagen research building, framed by flashing red lights of ambulances and police cars, filled the screen. Mr. Gravel Throat said that informed sources saw nothing but trouble for J. J. Jones.

> While police continue their search for Marcus McQuillan as a person of interest, today's attack raises the stakes for Mr. Jones in his appearance before the Senate committee two weeks from now. If he lasts that long. Informed sources suggest the board of Imagen-Pharmaglobe might ask Jones to step down as early as next week.

The voice grated, irritated, annoyed. As did the message. This was so unfair.

"Please turn the volume down," someone said.

The voice was familiar. Very familiar. The very sound lifted his spirits. And then they fell again, as visions of Argie's severed head rolled through his neuronal synapses. But still, he was curious. Trying to appear natural, he slowly turned his head in the direction of the voice. His eyes made immediate contact with … Argie. Was he hallucinating?

Argie walked toward him, arms open, big smile on his face.

"You're alive!" screamed Alex, jumping up to hug his favorite android. "But how? How can you be destroyed and together? Your head was severed from your body. And your body was blown to bits."

"I'm too valuable to be destroyed," said Argie with a touch of his usual arrogance. "My memories are crucial intellectual property. They're continuously backed up in real time at the Imagen Robotics Lab in central Atlanta."

"But your body,"

"Is also backed up by a clone, which automatically activates whenever the active version of me goes dead."

"And J. J. knows?"

"Of course, he designed me. He accessed my memory banks to view the explosion firsthand. I guess you could say I've had an out-of-body experience"

"That's a clever way to put it," said Alex as he pondered metaphysics of android existence. Memory and body are separate. But what about mind and memory?

"And fortunately, my clone was close by. I wanted to get back to you as soon as possible. We've got to get back to Toronto."

"Why wasn't I told about this?"

"You know now."

"But I could have had a heart attack seeing you in pieces."

"Sentimental but unrealistic, given your age, health, and psychological profile."

"Unreal. So you're immortal as long as there are backups?" said Alex. He felt a twinge of envy at Argie's privileged way of being.

"Depends on how you define life and immortality."

Argie had a point. Be careful about greener grass. "But what if I had been blown up?" said Alex.

"Now that could be a problem. But you didn't, and we need to get back to Toronto."

Alex thought about the Monday morning deposition and smiled. The return of the Three Amigos. Their first outing together since Club One in Savannah.

As they walked out to the shuttle bus, he turned to Argie and said, "By the way, what do you know about the Starbucks girl?"

FORTY-THREE

God will tear you limb from limb,
Sweep you up and throw you out,
Pull you up by the roots
From the land of life.

—The Message, the Bible in Contemporary Language

The hot water of the shower pulsed over Waite's head and shoulders and splashed onto the sandy white porcelain tiles. He took pleasure in the natural earthy smell of his African black soap from Ghana as he scrubbed the deceit and lies of the past few months from his very being. Soapy rivulets merged with unsullied droplets of water into a shallow pool at his feet before escaping down the drain. Steam smothered the glass door of the shower stall before escaping into the bathroom, where it searched for other surfaces to deface with condensation, the mirrors, the chrome brass faucets, and the granite top of the vanity.

In his bedroom, Morrigan du Morde was preparing for him. At least he hoped she was. He tried to imagine her stepping from the guest bathroom, drying herself with an oversized towel, and shaking the remaining water from her blond hair. The easy melodies of Norah Jones, emanating from the speakers of his Bose surround sound system, would be soothing her. Surely, fate had chosen her as his just reward.

Lingering under the hot water massage, he retraced the events of the week so far. Gerry had called him into the office yesterday afternoon, saying, "We're home free. In fewer than 48 hours, J. J. Jones will be history." Gerry had walked over to the wine refrigerator, opened it, and taken out a bottle of champagne, a 1992 Palmes D'Or. After uncorking it with some flair, he had poured two glasses, handing one to him, saying, "A toast to my man, James Waite. Only the best for my best."

It was the best bubbly Waite had ever tasted. After a few sips, he was able to identify a faint port taste to it. Gerry had continued with his story, saying, "Jones didn't even show up to hear the deposition of Sarah, can you believe it? Just sent that Alex Webster and his talking robot. I thought it got knocked off in Atlanta."

Waite had raised his eyebrows, and the drink in his hand wobbled ever so slightly. The robot had been destroyed, no doubt about that. He had seen photographs. Jones must have had a backup. However, why? Gerry noticed his quizzical look and said. "Hey, don't sweat it. Jones probably has a dozen of them. Anyway, it was them and a person named Cupido, some sort of consultant. Doesn't matter what, because he did not say anything. Just stared at Sarah and then at me throughout the whole session. Maybe they were trying to psyche Sarah. Court reporter got it all down. Our lawyers have reviewed the transcripts. The case is airtight." Gerry had topped up their glasses again. "Here's to us and the future of Pharmaglobe. Long lives to us all."

Laughing at his own jokes, Gerry luxuriated in his victory, not so much vindictive as vindicated, as if he had finally proven something to someone. Waite had felt uncomfortable with Gerry. It was out of character for him to be so relaxed and carefree. He preferred the more distant reserve of his boss, whom he understood, than the easy familiarity he was now witnessing. Fortunately, the moment was brief. Gerry had reached into his suit pocket, producing an envelope that he handed to Waite. "Here's a special bonus." Gerry's words had faded as Waite ripped it open and scanned the key words. "Forgiveness of one million dollar loan for penthouse apartment. Bonus of one million dollars."

This was the reward for loyalty, for competence, and most importantly, for moral ambiguity. The model had worked for him since he was four years old. "What matters in life is helping your team get over the goal line" had been his father's mantra, while his mother's had been "Ya dance with those what brung ya." Those two guidelines had governed his life, first the military and now Pharmaglobe. Don't worry about why the two sides are fighting, just remember whose side you are on and do your job. He did his job well, and he was always loyal. Gerry had bubbled on saying, "After we finish with Jones on Wednesday, why don't you take a few weeks off? You've earned it." Waite had not argued. Just said, "Thanks."

Preoccupied and pleased with himself while returning to his office, he literally had walked into Morrigan du Morde. Startled more than embarrassed, he had given her a crisp apology. "Sorry, Morri."

"If you want a date, James, you should just ask, not run me over," she had replied. Her feisty, quick wit both taunted and tantalized him. That and her arrogant attitude toward him, sometimes teasing him, sometimes ignoring him. That attracted him, made her a challenge, a prize to be won. Who did she think she was? Too young for any serious experience. Barely out of her twenties, she acted as sidekick to Victoria Malik and in recent weeks had been spending more and more time working with the senior executives on some project. Exposure to senior executives and corporate chiefs was an occupational hazard for young consultants, making them feel disproportionately important. Now, in the last week, she had started flirting with him. At least that is how he interpreted it. You could never be too careful these days, especially given that they had set up Jones. Although Morrigan was younger than most of the women he dated, he had been in the mood for celebration, so he had invited her to dinner that evening to explore her availability. Not only had she accepted, but she had also hinted that it could be an evening that both of them could remember for a long time. Perhaps his lucky streak would continue.

She had worn a crinkled silk ombré dress with beaded single shoulder strap, side shirring, and asymmetrical hem. Open-toe leather sling backs with a two-inch heel brought her face-to-face with him. The white gold of her double citrine drop earrings resonated with the candlelight of their table. Her perfume, although delicate, added layers of meaning to her every smile. Her elegance and allure had distracted him so much that he could not think his way through the menu. In fact, she had ordered for both of them, amused at his tormented befuddlement. When their server left, she turned to him.

"Tell me a secret you've never told anyone, and I'll tell you one of mine," she said, looking at him with a smile that mixed innocence with enticement.

In another setting, he may have been embarrassed, but he took the comment as an invitation. He wanted to share something that showed how much he thought of her, without revealing too much of himself. Moreover, he wanted to find out more about her. After a long pause, he started.

"Did you know that Gerry Schilling has fallen head over heels for the intern, Sarah Orenstein?"

"Get out. Is this a tale out of school?" She had said, eyes wide in mock surprise.

He lowered his voice, "They spent last night together."

"No way. Are you ratting on the boss?"

Waite smiled. Everyone loves malicious gossip. "Yes and no. There is nothing wrong about it, as such. Ironic that Gerry gets involved with the woman that will end J. J.'s career."

"And unbecoming. I thought Mr. Schilling was married."

"His wife was paralyzed by a stroke years ago."

"Still, what if she sues for divorce?"

"Impossible. She's hardly human now, depends on 24/7 nursing and the best care that money can buy."

"But why does a man of your talents stay with him?" asked Morri.

Waite had sipped his wine. This game of secrets was not too bad. Almost fun. Dish a little dirt on his boss. Tarnish Gerry's image maybe, but not in a way to hurt him.

"Got to hang your hat somewhere."

"So you trust in big money."

"Don't we all?"

"And you make your living from catastrophe?"

Did her words have an edge? What does she know? She was probably teasing.

"No need to be nasty. Anyway, that is my secret. Your turn."

"You're good James. A secret with no revelation about yourself."

Her smile was faint, enigmatic. He had known a few people with this smile. They had a look that suggested they knew something that you did not. Nevertheless, it was all appearance in his experience. The trick was not to fall for it. She could be planning her grocery shopping. Returning her smile, eyes locked on hers, he raised his cocktail glass, saying, "I'm sure you're up to the challenge."

"OK, a little secret about the near future." She paused a moment. The woman had a natural sense of dramatic flair. He liked that. She continued, "I promise you an evening that you could never imagine." Her dark eyelashes blinked in slow motion. The pupils of her eyes opened so wide the ice blue of her irises disappeared into the depths of the universe. What he thought was a sparkle, could well have been a shooting star. He had read somewhere that a woman's irises open to full when in love. Was she in love with him? At least infatuated? Alternatively, lust? On the other hand, was it the same old interracial curiosity that he had faced with other Caucasian women? No, he did not sense that interest with Morrigan du Morde. Beyond their silly game of secrets, she had seemed genuinely interested in him as a person, asking him questions about his childhood, his parents. What did he do in his spare time? Or did he even have spare time working for someone like Gerry? Was corporate security and espionage different from war? If he could live his life again, would he make the same choices? Clearly, she was interested in him. In addition, he was interested in her, although he had done all the talking tonight. No problem. He had read the backgrounder on her, prepared by his staff. She seemed like a clone of Victoria Malik. Same schools, same profession, same firm. Well, he guessed that was the way the world worked for women, same as for men, networks, whether old boys, or old girls.

"James, are you going to keep me waiting forever?" came Morri's voice from his bedroom. He detected a hint of impatience. They were always impatient. Fun for an evening, but always too demanding for anything more, at least as far as he was concerned. Brief recreational encounters suited his style, his strength, and his interests.

Entering, he found the room gently lit with a lush red glow, courtesy of a diaphanous red scarf, which she had hung over his bedside lamp. Where had that come from? Between the bed and him, holding a glass of wine, stood Morri, wearing a smile, a string of pearls, and nothing else.

Demure but sexual, assertive but vulnerable, her contradiction excited him. And enlarged his need, now obvious in ways that he felt confident would please her.

"My, my, look who's happy to see me," said Morrigan as she stepped toward him and offered him her wine. Was she taunting him? He needed to take control, gain his natural mastery. As he took her glass, she surprised him again by taking hold of him in her hand. "Not bad," she said and led him to the bed.

"Lie down on your back James," she whispered. "You have no idea how long I've been planning this moment." His mind raced in anticipation. She was confident, in control. He liked that. He finished the wine, put down the glass, and lay on the bed as directed.

"You are such a magnificent man. So strong, so big, so worthy of special treatment," said Morrigan, as she turned off the light and reached for him. He would have preferred to watch, be both participant and a voyeur of his own pleasures. Then again, who was he to complain? Into the mystique of the night, he surrendered, forgetting the phantoms of the last few months. Plotting with Gerry had energized him, until the attempt to kill Victoria Malik. Why should anyone die for the sake of feuding corporate titans? The deaths in Atlanta preyed on his heart. He needed to redeem his integrity, his sense of right and wrong. After tonight, after his vacation, he would set out in a new direction.

The room transformed into a dark chasm of expectation. His sense of remorse evaporated in the fervor of more primal wishes. The heat of Morrigan was near.

He immersed himself in the bouquet of rich soaps, expensive perfume, and natural pheromones that announced her overwhelming presence.

At last, a familiar pleasure engulfed him as he surrendered to the void. This was nice, really nice. He might even ask her out again. Norah Jones sang softly in the background.

Without warning the music stopped; smoothness gave way to abrasion. Something was scratching, scraping like wet sandpaper. Morri's fragrant bouquet gave way to a bitterly acrid odor. Reaching down to her head with his free hand, his fingers became entangled in what felt like the frayed end of oily rope used by dockworkers to secure the load. What had happened to her silken hair?

Raising his head and shoulders, he groped for the bedside lamp, found the switch, and turned on the light. Looking down at his groin area, he saw a wiry, withered crone of unspeakable filth. The stench of decay escaped from her pores. A green mucus dribbled from the sides of her mouth, dripping onto his lower stomach, pelvis, and upper thighs. Cold, steel gray eyes looked up at him and through him. Then she lowered her head to continue her assault.

The scene had the look and feel of a Wes Craven horror flick. Freddie Krueger as a cross-dresser. He hoped he was imagining the sight before him. He breathed in slowly, deeply. To limited effect. The stink strangled him. Hardwired for reflex action, his reptilian brain kicked into survival gear. Shutting his eyes to the horror was his next defense. Fight or flight? His heart pounded in readiness. Fear begat indecision. Indecision made him quiet for an instant. An instant that went on and on while her sandpaper tongue scraped with a growing urgency.

"Good lordy woman, that hurts," shrieked Waite, as he lurched and opened his eyes. She stopped and lifted her head. Glancing down he saw that she had drawn blood. She smirked without mercy. Leaning back, she parted her legs widely to his view. Flaking scabs sheathed her inner thighs. Her matted pubic hair transformed into hundreds of tiny, black, coiled forms slithering in an oozing gray slime. Malodorous fumes of putrid decomposition filled his nose. Nausea rose as increased salivation streamed from the side of his mouth. What possibly was going on? Had she slipped something into his drink?

Leaning toward him, she grinned a wicked grin, revealing what few teeth she had. "Here, maggot mortal, come rub the ditches of my groin. Beat these swarming worms of my essence."

Again, he closed his eyes; however, he could not shut out the smothering, fetid smell. His abdominal muscles contracted, propelling his stomach contents into his esophagus. Out of control, he surrendered to his own retching. When his upper esophageal sphincter finally relaxed, his vomitus spewed out of his mouth and down his chest. Then his lower sphincter gave way, and his bladder released its flow. Another everlasting moment passed. Even while sitting and soaking in his own night soil, covered in his own regurgitation, he experienced a sense of clarity. "Break loose, get away, escape," screamed an inner voice. Somehow, he had to flee from this corroded, corrupted version of Mad Madam Mim before he retched again. If dreaming, he needed to wake up. However, this was no dream. Dreams do not reek. Drugged. Obviously, someone had drugged him. Morri?

No more thinking.

Action needed.

Kamikaze time.

His arms and legs jerked out in a frantic effort. If he could not leave as a person, perhaps one of his limbs could escape and return with help. With an instinctive push for survival, he grabbed her head and thrust her away.

"Big man bet on the wrong horse," she scowled in contempt.

Free for the moment, he leaped from the bed and ran for the door as a laugh from hell pursued.

FORTY-FOUR

Luck is in the sovereign power of all things, but especially in war. By moving small weights in the balance it produces great vicissitudes

—Julius Caesar

Cold hands and a tightly wound tension accompanied Alex as he walked into the boardroom of Imagen-Pharmaglobe. This was the morning of final decisions. Because he had skipped breakfast, his regular Verona Grande from Starbucks had not lifted him. Instead he had a sinking feeling as it sloshed around in his stomach. Walls of dark oak panels with Jacobean pilasters chilled him further. Floors flush in deep purple carpeting silenced his footsteps. Portraits of past CEOs and chairs of Pharmaglobe looked down on him in judgment. The boardroom table could accommodate thirty people with microphones for both teleconferencing and voice reinforcement. Along the perimeter walls, chairs and desks also had microphones for observers and support staff. The absence of windows choked him, while the artificial blue recessed lighting of the room sapped him of his life-blood with a vampire's adeptness. The faint strains of Clerambault's Grand Jeu for Organ overlay the stillness of this secular sanctuary. The great game indeed. Probably a personal selection by Schilling. Involuntarily, he lowered his chin in obedience to the unseen divinity that rested atop this corporate hierarchy.

Six people sat around the table, and he nodded to those that he recognized, Dr. Luther, Professor Laydback, and Angela Cooper. Angela had flown in from Atlanta this morning. The crutches that leaned on the table beside her were testimony to the drama of the last week. The other three were board members favorable to Gerry. This committee would decide J. J.'s fate. The only absent member was Gerry Schilling.

Dr. Luther got up from her chair and walked around to greet Alex by extending a welcoming hand and a warm smile. It helped to put him a little more at ease. "I've arranged for you to sit beside me to advise me in my role as chair."

Alex sank into the plush leather of the chair next to Dr. Luther. It was an Eames, named after Charles and Ray Eames, who had designed executive chairs for the Time-Life Building in New York City in the early 1960s. That's why some people still called them Time-Life chairs.

In 1972, chess grand master Bobby Fischer specifically requested the Eames executive chair while he competed in the World Chess Championship in Reykjavik, Iceland. He said he could concentrate well in the chair. When opponent Boris Spassky saw it, he refused to play until he got one, too. Alex hoped the chair would help him concentrate.

Recalling this bit of trivia further eased Alex's tension. Nevertheless, time sat heavily on his shoulders as they waited. Each minute added a greater burden. Negative meditation. "Wherever you are, there are you, full of peace," his friend's yogi had told him. Well, for every rule, there is an exception. Here he was, and all that he was full of was the sense that his metabolic rate was running at twice it normal rate. Dr. Luther sensed his continuing unease.

"It doesn't look good, Alex," she said in a whisper. "The committee is evenly split. Schilling has the deciding vote. Just as you noted. I'm sorry things had to turn out this way."

Professor Laydback was on the other side of the table. He looked at Alex, then away with a sheepish shrug. It was that same look of embarrassment that a powerless person adopts when someone calls on them for help.

Schilling entered the room followed by two of his lieutenants, Larry Kirkpatrick, head of finance, strategy, and communications, and Ann Horowitz, head of legal and general affairs. "Ha," thought Alex, "the two people he needs to handle the details of a severance package." Schilling spoke briefly to them and then pointed to the observer seats along the wall, motioning where they could sit. Walking to the board table, he glanced at Alex with raised eyebrows. Alex realized how special his own status was, being able to sit next to Dr. Luther.

As Schilling was about to sit down, J. J. entered with Juno at his side. He was ready for battle. It wasn't just the pin-striped Brooks Brothers suit. No, the telling detail was the black tie with the gold-flecked lightning bolt artistically painted on it. Juno mimicked J. J.'s business style in a tailored black suit with fine pink and blue pinstripes. A white shirt with French cuffs showing pearl-mounted cuff links completed the outfit. A scarf instead of a tie covered the buttoned shirt. She smiled, nodding at each of the players as she took a seat near Gerry's supporters.

*   *   *   *

Gerry spoke first. "Good morning, J. J.. I guess this jig is up."
"Jig?"
"This dance, this *pas de deux* between you and me. It's over. The board wants you out. Your gated communities for geriatrics is just too much too soon for them—although I hope to salvage some of it. Like most entrepreneurs, J. J., you're a great visionary."

"Well, as Caesar said when he crossed the Rubicon, 'Let the dice fly high,'" said J. J., tossing his arm forward as if throwing a pair of dice onto the table. Gerry didn't waste any more time or energy in small talk. He took his seat at the head of the table and nodded to J. J., who sat down at the other end. This was the moment of final combat. When wolf meets gray wolf, there shall be no talk of dogs. Who had written that? Rupert Brooks? Kipling? Whoever. The words described this moment. Two enemies, surrounded by dogs. Whining, subordinate dogs.

"Dr. Luther," he said and nodded in her direction. It was a command. He had briefed her earlier about the agenda and purpose. He wanted no time wasted. The mere mention of her name was signal enough for her to start the meeting.

Dr. Luther straightened in her chair. She sat midway along the table. Strange. Gerry could never understand why she didn't take the head of the table, given that she was chair. Too deferential for his liking. He had only agreed to her appointment as an early concession to Jones. She looked around the room, fixing eye contact with all participants the way a nervous student might. Taking a deep breath and clearing her throat, she started. "Yes, thank you, Gerry. We are now a full quorum for this meeting of the Human Resources and Ethics Committee of the Imagen-Pharmaglobe Board of Directors. We have only one agenda item. Mr. Schilling has agreed to lead us through it."

"Thank you, Lilith. I have a sense of great regret in bringing this item to the board. However, at the end of the day, we are all here to serve the interests of the shareholders. Our role is to decide what will best increase their share value. In the highly political and media-sensitive world in which we live, events that would have been insignificant ten or twenty years ago can threaten a company's survival. I need not remind you of Enron and WorldCom, among others." He knew it was unctuous bullshit, but he had to start with the groveling sincerity of the syco-phant, the CEO as servant of the shareholder.

Speaking quickly, Gerry closed, "So, Madam Chair, Mr. Jones has become the lightning rod attracting the thunderbolts of protest against Imagen-Pharmaglobe. The survival of the company takes precedent, and therefore I am recommending that Mr. Jones step down." Gerry paused for a moment. If logic alone governed decisions, he had said enough. But logic is rarely enough, so he moved to his coup de grace. Pausing briefly, he then went on.

"But the need for Mr. Jones to step down does not stop there, as the board well knows. I am referring, of course, to the conduct of Mr. Jones with Sarah Orenstein, an employee of Imagen-Pharmaglobe. An allegation so serious has emerged that it alone would justify the board firing Mr. Jones. Because all mem-bers of the board have copies of the young intern's deposition, I will not repeat the sordid details." Gerry paused a little longer this time so people's imaginations could play with the flora and fauna of inappropriate contact between J. J. and Sarah. Then he finished.

"Despite these facts, several board members asked me to prepare a favorable severance package, which I am tabling. If accepted, then the expectation is that J. J. will resign, to save the board the embarrassment of firing him."

He paused again, looked up from his notes and straight at J. J., and then resumed in a more personal tone, "I'm really sorry it has to end like this, J. J., but for a company like Imagen-Pharmaglobe, you're just a little ahead of your time. I want to be fair about this. If you bow out gracefully, well, nice guy that I am, I think you'll find this a very generous package under the circumstances."

Gerry stopped and sat back, steepling his fingers while he allowed his words to sink in. An awkward silence suppressed all but the nervous breathing of several board members, as Larry Kirkpatrick and Ann Horowitz got up from their seats on the sidelines and handed out copies.

Once everyone had a copy, Dr. Luther said, "Thank you, Mr. Schilling. Mr. Jones, do you wish to say anything?"

"Madam Chairperson, I simply ask for a fifteen-minute break for Mr. Webster to review the severance package, on my behalf. During that time, I beg the com-mittee's indulgence, while I step outside to gather my thoughts."

"A reasonable request. Mr. Schilling?" said Dr. Luther, who then turned to Gerry.

"Sure," said he with a brisk nod. It came out "Suurrre." His inner Gerry smirked. "I'm way ahead of you, Billy Bob."

J. J. spoke again, "I must leave the room, but before I do, I have one question, Gerry."

"Yes?"

"Is the package one that you would accept if our roles were reversed?"

Schilling stared at J. J. for a long minute. The question brought back memories of one of Susan's favorite mantras. "Write a social contract as if you didn't know where you would end." The Veil of Ignorance principle of fairness developed by the philosopher John Rawls. The rationalist's version of the Golden Rule, "Do unto others as you would have them do unto you." One didn't have to act out of goodness, just rational self-interest, according to Rawls. Of course, Rawls had never been a CEO. This was not a meeting of philosophers. "Study the *Art of War* by Sun Tzu if you want to do business" had been his reply to her. "The clever combatant imposes his will on the enemy, but does not allow the enemy's will to be imposed on him." He bit his tongue before replying.

"Does it matter?"

"In one sense, no, but it would mean that I didn't have to read the fine print if I knew you could accept it."

"It always pays to read the fine print."

"I'll keep that in mind. Now please excuse me. I'll be back within a few minutes."

"Make it a very few minutes, J. J.. Time is shorter than you think." The words were ominous, the tone stony, the eyes decided.

The door closed behind J. J., and silence drove out conversation in the same way that darkness drives out light.

Gerry studied the index finger of his left hand while he waited. The last two nights with Sarah Orenstein had recharged him. Made him a man again. Not only was he getting rid of J. J., but he was now starting to enjoy the lifestyle of his antagonist. Maybe they could share notes. He hadn't had this much sex since his early days with Susan. Just as his daydream took flight, his executive assistant, Laura, interrupted his daydream with a tap on his forearm and a phone in her hand. Her usually serious expression was today one of mortification. Well, she always was a glass half-empty person. He cupped his ear as she leaned over and whispered into it, "It's Toronto General Hospital." Her fingers chilled him as he took the phone from her hand.

With growing disbelief, he turned in his seat to face the wall as he listened to the message recited by a nurse whom he did not know and probably would never meet. She spoke quickly, and he responded with brief comments of neutral acknowledgment. "I see." "I understand." But he not see; he did not understand.

The information was utterly bizarre. Could it be a hoax? Waite had been found outside his condo complex, naked, bleeding, talking about an old, ugly crone who was trying to castrate him. And that was only the beginning. Waite was now heavily sedated in an attempt to bring his paranoid ranting under control. What had happened to the man? No time right now; he would follow up later.

"Yes, of course we will cover all treatments," he said, and then added, "please keep us informed of any major changes in his condition." His heart thumped briefly before he asserted control. Years of experience gave him some small comfort. The others at the table saw only a cool, confident executive. Experience also told him there was no good news or bad news, only information. What he did with it made it good or bad. If someone dies, it may be bad for an insurance company but good for a funeral home. He was not a superstitious man nor did he have faith that God intervened on a day-to-day basis in the affairs of men. Neither did he hold to any philosophical or psychological doctrines of humanism as many of his educated contemporaries did. But he did believe in the secret workings of fortune. He felt himself and all human achievement dependent on the rule of this power. Although not a modest man in estimating his own genius, he did admit that he had had a remarkable amount of luck in his life. He had escaped poverty by marrying wealth, he had achieved his corporate empire dreams because of the timely stroke of his wife, Susan, and now he would gain control of the world's largest pharmaceutical with the resignation of J. J. Jones. No amount of wisdom could have foreseen his life's path. Sure, a religious person might see the hand of God in history. Certainly many American sports heroes felt the hand of God tipping a pass into their hands for the winning touchdown or helping a basketball through the hoops in the last second of play.

Gerry, however, belonged to those who believe in luck or chance. Daring and winning throughout his life had merely strengthened his belief. He could act with the confidence that fortune favored him. If he were superstitious, he would analyze Waite's condition in every which way. But to do so would make him no better than the ancients, who, before launching a major initiative, inspected the sacrificial entrails of a bull, a ram, and a pig. No, he was a man of intelligence, a man of good fortune. Whatever happened to Waite would in some way work to Gerry's advantage. It always had.

Gerry looked around the table for someone intelligent, someone who might meet his standards, someone CEO ready. He came up empty. No surprise. A string of zeros, Luther, Laydback, Cooper, and Webster. Useless. Sheep wanting to be shepherds. Once he was rid of Jones, he'd get rid of these squatters as well and send them packing for good.

FORTY-FIVE

Man's greatest good fortune is to chase and defeat his enemy, seize his total possessions, leave his married women weeping and wailing, ride his gelding and use the bodies of his women as a nightshirt and support.

—Genghis Khan

Alex leafed through the package with no idea of what J. J. expected him to do. He recalled the apocryphal story of the great hockey player, Eddie Shack, whose coach had benched him before a big game. Finally, minutes left before the end of the match, his team losing eight to nothing, his coach decided to send him in. Shack grabbed his stick and got ready to go on the ice at the next break in play. When the whistle came, the coach motioned Shack to go. Just before he jumped over the boards and onto the ice, Shack turned to him and said, "What do you want me to do, coach? Tie it or win it?"

The package provided no clues, no loopholes, and no magic lantern to show the way out of this darkness. It included a summary of views from investment analysts showing that Imagen-Pharmaglobe stock could rise by up to 25 percent if J. J. were to step down. A move worth billions of dollars. Scanning the document for headlines on the severance package raised his concern for J. J, and indirectly for himself. Immediate resignation. Schilling would have final approval of the public statement. No-competition clause. Full patent rights of all Imagen research. If J. J. left quietly, Pharmaglobe would not aim for legal action to compensate the company for loss in shareholder wealth because of scandal.

Dollars. He looked for a dollar figure. He did not want J. J. to be insulted. Just as he was examining the last page, the door to the boardroom opened, disrupting his train of thought. Afraid it was J. J. returning, he kept his head down. Without a clear-cut answer, just duck. Pretend to be deep in thought. The voice of a stranger took his ears by surprise. "Good morning, Gerry. I hope I'm not too late for the vote?"

Alex looked up. A mature woman of quiet elegance and dignified style stood in the doorway. Her presence demanded the attention of all as she surveyed the room, in the end resting her eyes on Gerry.

No one spoke.

Dr. Luther leaned over to Alex and whispered, "I don't know who she is, but I'd die for her Vera Wang." It was a rich black wool suit with black satin lapels and front flap pockets. An ivory cashmere sweater under the blazer completed the look.

A convulsive choking issued from the front of the room. It was Gerry. In mere seconds, his color had paled, and his eyes expressed disbelief. Something else showed in his widening eyes. Was it anger? Or was it fear?

"Whatever are you doing here?" The words shot out of his mouth as if intended to shove the woman out of the doorway.

"Why shouldn't I be here? I am the majority shareholder of Imagen-Pharmaglobe."

Schilling did not flinch, did not move, and did not speak. Dr. Luther grabbed Alex by the arm. "My God, it's Susan Schilling." Alex studied the woman more closely. He had only seen the pictures of the young Susan Schilling in Gerry's office. The woman standing in the doorway was at least twenty years older. But yes, he could see the young Susan with the oval shape of her face, the high, prominent cheekbones, and the blue eyes. Eyes with personality, with depth, and with power. The great actor Giancarlo Giannini once said he spent an hour and a half every day doing eye exercises to communicate his feelings intentionally on camera. Susan Schilling had such eyes. All eyes now focused on Gerry. Looking at him, through him, examining him, as if searching for someone who was no longer there.

Gerry's face reddened, his neck muscles visibly pulsed. He spit out his words, "You're sick. You shouldn't be here. You can't be here."

She held her look on him, her eyes narrowing as if to focus more clearly on the present moment.

"I am here. Fortune smiled on me when you agreed to merge with J. J. Jones. For that, and only that, do I thank you," she said.

Gerry's eyes bulged in panic at the now predatory gaze of Susan.

"Get out. Get out. You're an invalid, and you are interrupting an important meeting," said Gerry. His hands gripped the arms of his chair as he raised himself up as if preparing to lunge at her.

Cued by this exchange, Alex nudged Dr. Luther, who immediately converted from deferential voyeur into assertive leader. Slamming her copy of the report on the table and clearing her throat, she said, "With all respect, Mr. Schilling, Mrs. Schilling seems healthy and able, and she has every right to be here. Indeed, let me remind you that your membership on this board was as proxy for Mrs. Schilling. Now that she is here, your presence is no longer needed."

"Claptrap, academic nonsense. I'm CEO. I'll have you off the board by the end of the day."

"Not so fast, Mr. Schilling." Heads turned to Laydback, who had come to life, arms in the air. "Dr. Luther, for all of her academic overheads, is quite right. In fact, I personally reviewed the terms of the merger agreement in preparation for this meeting."

Two men in darks suit came into the room and stood on either side of Gerry. Alex thought they might just pick him up and carry him out of the room.

Susan Schilling spoke again. "Your time as CEO is over, Gerry. These two gentlemen will escort you to the door. Company lawyers will provide you with details of your severance. Under no circumstances are you to return to the offices of Imagen-Pharmaglobe."

Gerry looked up at the leviathans on either side of him, first left and then right. He matched their forced smiles as he shoved back his chair and stood. He glowered at Susan.

"This isn't over. Not by a long shot."

"Oh, it's over, Gerry. Trust me. I'm suing for divorce."

The two Goliaths in suits now moved closer to Gerry, standing on either side of him, each taking hold of one of his forearms. His face red, his lips pulled back, Gerry yanked himself from their grip with an exaggerated show of bravado. "I can escort myself. I don't need help."

He stood still for a moment as waves of anger emanated from his body and washed over all within the room. Then, with a surly frown, he walked quickly from the room.

Silence again followed. However, this time it was the silence of relief. Susan Schilling sat down in the chair formerly occupied by her husband.

The relief was short-lived as Professor Laydback spoke, "Well, Ms. Schilling, welcome to the board. I'm happy that you support J. J. However, it is essential that we vote on the issue before us for proper record keeping."

"Whatever are you talking about, professor?" said Susan

"The two issues about J. J. Jones, our leader. First, the company's shares have fallen dramatically in the last month due, in large part, to his vision for this company."

Susan Schilling's response was quick and crisp, "Two points, Mr. Laydback. First, I have a sworn affidavit by James Waite that my soon-to-be former husband orchestrated most of the media problems of the past two months. J. J. is without blame."

Another man in a black suit stepped forward and gave out a copy of the affidavit to everyone at the table.

After he had studied the document, Laydback said, "This is tragic."

"Yes, it is," said Susan.

"But part of the misfortune is that it doesn't help J. J.," said the professor, dogged in pursuit of his point. "Perceptions are everything. His reputation is tarnished. He's damaged goods."

Susan Schilling looked at the professor with a mix of dismay. At length, she spoke. "Tell me, Professor Laydback," she said with the tone of a trial lawyer who has cornered a hostile witness. "Tell me true. Is holding out hope to those who are ill bad business? If it weren't for J. J. and Dr. Apollo, I'd be a helpless invalid." She paused again, like an experienced stage actor who knows the eloquence of a considered break in speech. "So, on that count alone, he has my vote."

Laydback quickly chimed in, "And mine as well. I was simply pointing out that people still might not accept J. J. In fact, it could well send Imagen-Pharmaglobe shares into a downward spiral." He then paused while he took off his reading glasses and leaned forward across the table toward her and said, "Besides, we also have the not insignificant issue of sexual harassment brought forward by Ms. Orenstein. J. J.'s alleged behavior, if true, is simply not acceptable."

"Ridiculous charges. The mad ravings of a scorned woman," said Susan, waving her hand dismissively.

"We have her deposition," said Laydback.

"Not worth the paper it's written on. In fact, Ms. Orenstein withdrew it less than an hour ago," said Susan. She turned and nodded to another man in a black suit who stepped forward to deliver a thin folder to each participant at the table. Laydback put his reading glasses on as he opened his folder. Alex opened his copy. It contained a single sheet, bearing a statement signed by Sarah: "I regret any harm and grief that I may have caused to Mr. Jones and his wife because of my false statement."

Laydback placed the paper on the table in front of him, bowing his head respectfully. Susan moved in for her own coup de grace in this duel with the persistent professor. Alex had mixed feelings. He wanted to move on with a more important issue, like the Senate hearings, now that Schilling was gone. That said, he admired the professor for following due process rather than just jumping on the bandwagon. Nonetheless, it was painful to watch as Susan Schilling chopped him into little pieces.

"Fish or cut bait, professor. You are J. J.'s appointment to the board along with Dr. Luther. He expects your support and has a right to it unless there is incontrovertible evidence that he has not met his duties. Am I clear?"

"Well, my duties are to the shareholders."

"I am the largest shareholder in Imagen-Pharmaglobe."

"I see your point. Well spoken. We owe J. J. an apology. Case closed."

EPILOGUE

▼

What we call the beginning is often the end.
And to make an end is to make a beginning.
The end is where we start from.

—T. S. Eliot

Hilton Head in June. Emergence of summer season. Vacation living. The ocean breezes of early evening boogied over the beach and through the open windows of the great room in Alex's townhouse. The curtains billowed in response like a diaphanous membrane, yielding with grace to an unseen visitor. The vanillalike scent of dried hay, courtesy of the curled, dried leaves of sweetgrass that Victoria had gathered earlier in the day, ran in retreat. Alex and Victoria sensed this invisible intruder from their respective plush red leather chairs.

"All's well that ends well, according to some old English bard," said Victoria. Alex had been reading the latest issue of *Newsweek*. On the cover was a photograph of J. J. standing with Susan Schilling on the grounds of the U.S. Capitol in Washington. The backdrop was a perfect blue sky. The photographer must have been lying on the ground to capture the shot that made J. J. look, well, godly, appearing from on high. He held Susan's hand in the air with one hand and reached out with the other to a crowd of media and admirers. In the background was the Capitol dome, whose design, like the rest of Capitol designs, had been inspired by the architecture of ancient Greece and Rome. "Ironic and fitting," thought Alex. The *mise-en-scène*, by chance or design, evoked the ideals that guided America's founders as they framed their new republic. The beaming smiles of J. J. and Susan left no doubt of their ebullient mood, while the cover story headline summed up the frame of the media's collective mind: "The Modern Miracle Worker. What Next for J. J. Jones?"

"So it seems. These two look like they could conquer the world," said Alex, holding up the cover. The media had swooned over the return of Susan Schilling, her miraculous recovery and support of J. J. and his program, and J. J.'s appearance before the Senate subcommittee, which had transformed from a lynching committee to an enthusiastic hearing of support.

"Maybe they will. Just one question, though. Why did Sarah withdraw her deposition? It was very brave to be sure, but also very humiliating. I couldn't have done it."

"Perhaps you've never really been in love."

"What do you mean?"

"Recall, she was head over heals in love with Gerry, found him irresistible, felt she couldn't live without him, courtesy of Cupid. J. J. had briefed Susan with details, without mentioning Cupid. To help out, Susan said she would divorce Schilling right away if Sarah would recant."

"So Ms. Schilling is no one's fool?"

"You got it."

"Oh, by the way, Angela Cooper called."

"And?"

"She's redecorating her CEO's office. She wants no hint of Gerry Schilling around now that she's head of Imagen-Pharmaglobe."

"J. J. wanted her to take a month off before taking over, just as he did for us."

"I know, but this is much too exciting for her,"

"You might say a fairy-tale ending," said Alex.

"Well, I don't know about that. Isn't the handsome prince supposed to carry the beautiful princess into the sunset of everlasting happiness?"

Alex smiled, put down his magazine, and reached out for her.

"Perhaps it is a new beginning for us."

A familiar voice from the doorway of the balcony interrupted. "Anyone for a walk on the beach?"

The spell of the moment snapped under the weight of those words. Victoria spoke first. "And remind me again why Argie is renting the place next door?"

"J. J. wants us to be secure. Something about keeping us safe until our next assignment. Excuse me while I go suggest he take a long walk by himself."

Several minutes later, when Alex returned to the great room, he found Victoria standing in the French doorway to the master bedroom. She was wearing a silk bathrobe and, from all appearances, nothing else. The backlighting from the bedroom created a discreet contour of her form. She had one hand on her slightly cocked hip, in her other hand she held a small blue bottle.

"A friend suggested you might consider giving a girl a romantic massage with this perfumed oil."

"Friend?" blushed Alex, momentarily confused.

"Yes," replied Victoria. "He even suggested that you may want to play Mark Antony to my Cleopatra."

Alex blushed an even deeper red, as he recalled Stan, the alligator god, and the oath of love. Perhaps it hadn't been a dream. In which case, his dream was about to come true. Now he couldn't help but smile.

"Didn't things end badly for those two?"

"Things might end badly for you if you don't get over here this minute."

*   *   *   *

On a deserted stretch of sandy beach less than a mile from Alex and Victoria sat Marcus McQuillan. Face to the horizon, body motionless, his eyes drank in the seamless union of the ocean and the night sky. Gone were his black Levis, his black turtlenecks, and his jet-black hair. He wore an orange bathing suit and a lime T-shirt. He had dyed his hair purple and yellow. Not that anyone could see him now.

Night breezes fanned over him. The light of the moon passed through the filter of clouds that floated by like untethered hot-air balloons. Shades of dark brown, black, and gray played across the sand, water, and sky. The emptiness chilled him. No sign of life.

Was this the way it was at the beginning?

This is how it probably looked before Gaia.

Empty, vast, uncaring.

Waiting for a spark to set life in motion.

Where was she? Where was the muse who knew all? It wasn't supposed to end like this. Sarah running off with that deposed corporate pig, Gerry Schilling, to some island. That damned gay cop, Cleve Morrison, hunting him. Didn't he read the papers? He'd been cleared. But he was still a person of interest. A life in refuge, a life of quiet despair. Had all of his efforts been for naught? He knew who to blame. It was the fault of J. J. Jones. And his people, Alex Webster and Victoria Malik.

Jumping up, he shouted sorrowfully at the night sky, "A sign, I need a sign."

For a moment an unbearable darkness followed. Silence surrounded him. He was alone in the universe.

Then, out of nowhere came a flash, an explosion of light, as a shooting star ignited the sky.

978-0-595-42316-3
0-595-42316-7

THE Big Sheep MIX-UP

By Tisha Hamilton

Illustrated by Pam Tanzey

MODERN CURRICULUM PRESS

Pearson Learning Group

Computer colorizations by Lucie Maragni

Cover and book design by Lisa Ann Arcuri

ISBN 0-7652-1368-0
Printed in the United States of America
    10   07

Modern
Curriculum
Press
Pearson Learning Group

1-800-321-3106
www.pearsonlearning.com

CONTENTS

To my favorite reader, Will—
you are the best!

Down on the Farm

Everyone knew about the town of Woolhaven. People traveled to Woolhaven from far away. They wanted to buy the beautiful sweaters that were made there.

The sweaters came from three farms outside the town. Each farm raised sheep. The farmers made sweaters from their sheep's wool.

The farms were all the same except for one thing. White sheep lived on one farm. Black sheep lived on another farm. Brown sheep lived on the third farm.

Ten white sheep lived on White Sheep Farm. They ate crabgrass all day.

Snowy was the oldest sheep on White Sheep Farm. Whatever Snowy thought, all the other sheep thought so, too.

"Our wool makes the best sweaters because our wool is the softest," said Snowy. The other sheep nodded their heads.

Ten black sheep lived on Black Sheep Farm. They ate long, thin grass all day.

Midnight was the oldest sheep on Black Sheep Farm. Whatever Midnight thought, all the other sheep thought so, too.

"Our wool makes the best sweaters because our wool is the warmest," said Midnight. The other sheep nodded their heads.

Ten brown sheep lived on Brown Sheep
Farm. They ate tasty hay all day.

Fudge was the oldest sheep on Brown
Sheep Farm. Whatever Fudge thought, all the
other sheep thought so, too.

"Our wool makes the best sweaters
because our wool is the prettiest," said
Fudge. The other sheep nodded their heads.

People agreed with all three flocks of sheep. Everyone loved the white sweaters that were as soft as a kitten's fur. Everyone loved the black sweaters that were as warm as a summer day. Everyone loved the brown sweaters that were as pretty as a child's big brown eyes.

The white and black and brown sweaters all sold as soon as they were made. Everyone had to have one of each color. Then one day, something terrible happened.

CHAPTER 2

Baa Baa Bad News

People stopped buying the white sweaters. No one bought any more black sweaters. No one wanted even one more brown sweater.

The farmers started to worry. The sheep started to worry, too.

"No more eating crunchy crabgrass," said Snowy. "It must be making our soft white wool scratchy. We are the best. We are going to stay the best. This means working harder to find soft grass to eat."

So the white sheep stopped eating crunchy crabgrass. Still, the white sweaters did not sell.

"We can't eat any more long, thin grass down by the pond," said Midnight. "It must be making our wool thin. So our sweaters aren't as warm as they used to be. We are the best. We are going to stay the best. This means giving up our long, thin grass."

So the black sheep stopped eating long, thin grass from the pond. Still, the black sweaters did not sell.

"No more eating tasty, dry hay," said
Fudge. "It must be making our pretty brown
wool look dull and ugly. We are the best. We
are going to stay the best. This means giving
up our tasty hay."

So the brown sheep stopped eating dry hay.
Still, no one wanted to buy the brown sweaters.

18

The sheep on all three farms were feeling grumpy. They were working very hard to make the best wool they could. It hurt their feelings that no one wanted their sweaters anymore. Then they heard more bad news.

Sheep for Sale

One day, Midnight heard the Flacks talking. The Flacks owned Black Sheep Farm.

"If the sweaters don't sell, we must sell the sheep," said Mr. Flack.

"Oh! That will be terrible," cried Mrs. Flack. "The black sheep have been here since my grandparents owned the farm."

"I don't like selling the sheep any more
than you do," said Mr. Flack. "What else can
we do?"

"Oh, I will miss them," cried Mrs. Flack.
"I guess the sheep won't be upset."

"Won't be upset?" Midnight said to
himself. "Of course we will be upset. We
don't want to be sold and move far away.
What can we do?"

21

Meanwhile, Fudge had heard almost the same thing over at Brown Sheep Farm.

"What are we going to do?" Fudge said to herself. "We don't want to be moved far away." Fudge thought and thought.

At last, Fudge called the flock of brown
sheep together. "We must have a talk with
the other sheep," she said.

The brown sheep were shocked. They
never spoke to the other flocks.

"But, Fudge," said the littlest sheep, "we are the best. We don't need those other sheep." The other sheep nodded their heads.

"Maybe we haven't needed each other in the past. Now we must work together to help all the sheep," Fudge said.

"We never talk to the other sheep," the little sheep spoke up again. "I don't know what to say to a black sheep or a white sheep."

"That's silly," said Fudge firmly. "Sheep are sheep. There is no reason we can't talk to the other sheep." Fudge looked the little sheep straight in the eye and said, "I will do all the talking."

The brown sheep agreed. If Fudge wanted
to talk to the other sheep, then all the brown
sheep wanted to talk, too.

The brown sheep walked to the fence at
the far end of their field. They were
surprised to find the black sheep and the
white sheep already standing near the fence.

CHAPTER 4

The Sheep
Make a Plan

The sheep talked all morning. It was hard at first for the three flocks to work together. After a while, they began to feel like a team.

"It's much more fun when we work together," said Midnight.

The sheep kept thinking and talking. At last, they had a plan.

"It's a good plan," said Snowy. "We need to show these farmers what to do."

Snowy, Midnight, and Fudge opened the fence gates with their noses.

"Follow me!" said Snowy to the white sheep. The white sheep followed Snowy into the black sheep's field.

"Follow me!" said Fudge. Then the brown sheep followed Fudge into the black sheep's field.

The sheep mixed themselves up. There were black sheep, white sheep, and brown sheep in each flock. They had a lot of fun and made a lot of noise.

"Baa! Baa! Baaaaah!" they all cried.

"Oh, dear," cried Mrs. Flack. "What is that noise?"

"It sounds as if there is something wrong with our black sheep," shouted Mr. Flack.

"It's not just our black sheep," yelled Will Flack. "All the sheep have gone crazy!"

"Look!" cried Sue Flack. "Brown sheep and white sheep are mixed up with our black sheep."

Mrs. Flack picked up the telephone and called the Brite family. They were the owners of White Sheep Farm.

"Your white sheep are over here at our farm," Mrs. Flack said to Mr. Brite. "They are making a terrible noise." The Brites said they would be right over.

Then Mr. Flack called the Crowns. They owned Brown Sheep Farm.

"Your brown sheep are all mixed up with our black sheep," said Mr. Flack to Mrs. Crown. The Crowns said they would be right over.

All the farmers looked at their mixed-up sheep. "What are we going to do?" they asked.

CHAPTER 5

Mixed-Up Sheep

The Flacks and the Crowns and the Brites worked all day. They tried to keep all the black sheep in one place. They tried to keep all the white sheep in one place. They tried to keep all the brown sheep in one place.

At last, they got all the sheep in the right places. Then the Crowns and the Brites tried to take their sheep home.

Mr. Crown opened the gate to Brown Sheep Farm, but the brown sheep turned around. Some of them trotted to White Sheep Farm. Some went to Black Sheep Farm.

Mr. Brite opened the gate to White Sheep Farm, but the white sheep turned around. Some of them trotted to Black Sheep Farm. Some went to Brown Sheep Farm. Again, the black, white, and brown sheep were mixed up on all three farms.

"Oh, no!" cried Mr. and Mrs. Crown. "We must get all our brown sheep back home."

"This is terrible!" cried Mr. and Mrs. Brite. "We can't let our white sheep stay at the other farms."

"Well, let's try again," said Mr. Flack. All day long the families sorted the sheep. All day long the sheep mixed themselves up again.

"I don't know how we will ever get these sheep sorted out," sighed Mrs. Brite.

"I've never seen anything like it," said Mr. Crown.

"Look," yelled Will Flack. "The sheep look like squares!"

"These sheep look like dots," said Mrs. Brite, pointing to the sheep at her farm.

"These sheep look like stripes," said Mr.
Crown, pointing to the sheep at his farm.

Everyone started to laugh.

"I can't believe we didn't think of this
sooner," said Mrs. Brite.

"I can't believe it took them this long to see what we were doing," said Snowy.

"People just don't learn as fast as sheep do," said Midnight.

"They need sheep to help them out," said Fudge.

A Great Idea

The sheep had thought of a way to make a new kind of sweater. They showed the farmers how to make this new kind of sweater. It wasn't all white. It wasn't all black. It wasn't all brown.

White Sheep Farm made beautiful
sweaters with white, black, and brown stripes.
Brown Sheep Farm made beautiful
sweaters with white, black, and brown dots.
Black Sheep Farm made beautiful sweaters
with white, black, and brown squares.

Again, people came from everywhere to buy the sweaters. The people were happy with their new sweaters. The farmers were happy that they didn't have to sell their sheep. The sheep were happy, too. Now they all had many new friends. Now no one flock was better. They were all the best.

crunchy [KRUN chee] chewable, crispy

flock [FLAHK] group of sheep

grumpy [GRUM pee] feeling angry or sad

shocked [SHAHKT] very surprised, shaken up

sorted [SOR tud] separated into groups of things that are the same

surprise [sur PRYZE] something that happens without warning or unexpectedly

terrible [TER ih bul] very bad

trotted [TRAH tud] ran slowly